Adolphe Jullien, Florence Percival Hall

Richard Wagner

His life and works

Adolphe Jullien, Florence Percival Hall

Richard Wagner
His life and works

ISBN/EAN: 9783337386122

Printed in Europe, USA, Canada, Australia, Japan

Cover: Foto ©Raphael Reischuk / pixelio.de

More available books at **www.hansebooks.com**

ADOLPHE JULLIEN

RICHARD WAGNER

Ibis Life and Works

TRANSLATED FROM THE FRENCH BY
FLORENCE PERCIVAL HALL

WITH AN INTRODUCTION BY B. J. LANG

Illustrated

WITH FOURTEEN PHOTOTYPES FROM ORIGINAL DRAWINGS
BY M. FANTIN-LATOUR
FIFTEEN PORTRAITS OF RICHARD WAGNER]

AND ONE HUNDRED AND THIRTEEN TEXT-CUTS; SCENES FROM
HIS OPERAS; VIEWS OF THEATRES, AUTOGRAPHS AND
NUMEROUS CARICATURES

VOLUME ONE

BOSTON
J. B. MILLET COMPANY
1892

TO MY FRIEND

FANTIN·LATOUR

TABLE OF CONTENTS.

WAGNER COMPOSING.

The Illustrated Sporting and Dramatic News, — London, June 9, 1877.

LIST OF ILLUSTRATIONS

I.

FULL PAGE PLATES,

Reproduced from Originals by M. Fantin-Latour.

xv

II.

ILLUSTRATIONS IN THE TEXT.

WAGNER IN THE FIRE OF COMPOSITION.
Kikeriki, Vienna, Nov. 13, 1876.

INTRODUCTION TO THE AMERICAN EDITION.

N view of the fact that almost the whole of our English Wagneriana has come from Germany, this French biography is of uncommon interest. The standpoint from which Jullien writes is absolutely new — his history of the Paris *Tannhäuser* episode in Wagner's life being of itself a matter of very great interest, coming as it does from a Parisian who was one of the participants. The illustrations are authentic and of great value. While a collection of Wagner caricatures would make a large volume by itself, the examples here given are eminently well chosen and throw a fantastic and suggestive light over the admirably written picture of this wonderful man's life.

It seems to be peculiarly fitting that a translation into English of Jullien's Life of Richard Wagner should come to publication in the United States. Nothing pleased Wagner more than the knowledge that his works were becoming well known in this country. His interest in America led him to turn his thoughts in this direction as a possible refuge in the period of his life when adversity followed him like a shadow.

In later years, when both fame and wealth were abundantly his, he sent to the United States a proposition full of practical detail, having for its end the removal of himself and his family to this country, where he purposed devoting the remainder of his life to the composition of new works and their dedication to this country exclusively. However remarkable such a proposition may seem, the fact that it was made in downright earnest is none the less interesting to Americans.

This superb volume has many features that would have warmly commended it to Wagner; in turn, these same characteristics must make it right welcome to the English reading world. That this work will be keenly appreciated by our American public would seem inevitable : a public that has been unfailing in its enthusiastic devotion to " the master."

                                                B. J. LANG.

Boston, Mass., April, 1892.

PREFACE.

T has been nearly four years since Richard Wagner was suddenly stricken down. Does his death date back far enough to enable us to put ourselves in a position to judge the man in all impartiality? Has the hour at last arrived to accord to this great genius the full measure of justice which his most savage detractors promised him after his death, but which, it seems, they would still like to defer until after their own? Apparently, for the great mass of French auditors, no longer occupying themselves with the paltry spites of writers in love with their own prose, or moved by petty commercial interests, have openly made reparation to Richard Wagner for the injuries that were heaped upon him during his life, and the French public, taken as a whole, has shown itself much more generous, much more just, than certain jealous, fanatical and rancorous individuals. One may say to-day that Wagner, even in France, has won his rightful place; the dissenting voices are now very few. Formerly, to defend him was to make one's self conspicuous; now, to disparage him has that effect.

This rehabilitation was not fully and strikingly produced until after the master's death had quieted all susceptibilities; but for some time before, it was easy to foresee, from certain *indications, that the mind of fortune was going to shift, and the numerous writers who always contrive to put themselves in accord with the momentary preferences of the public, cunningly planned their conversion in time to laud to the skies a man, an artist, upon whom they had for many years inflicted the most cruel outrages. The public,* en masse, *makes no such calculations; it changes front in a day, and is disturbed very little by having its judgments of yesterday flung in its face. It simply denies them without hesitation, and with the best faith in the world. But it is quite otherwise with those who wield the pen, and it is no small matter for them to seem consistent with themselves while giving their astonished readers a complete change of opinion.*

This reaction in favor of a genius too long misunderstood has necessarily given rise to hosts of books, articles and pamphlets, each more laudatory than the last, on the subject of Richard Wagner. Excess of blame has been instantly succeeded by exaggeration of eulogium, and the blindness of hatred has given way, in more than one case, to the blindness of fetichism. What a deluge of critical, historical, anecdotic, apologetic, dithyrambic articles or studies on Richard Wagner since the time of the appearance of Tannhäuser *at Paris! And yet where can people find the circumstantiated information which they are always desirous to possess about a man of genius, and which they have a right to demand of any serious work, outside the current chronicle? Nowhere, if they be restricted to writings published in the French language; for Gasperini's interesting article, aside from the fact that it stops with* Tristan and Isolde, *is rather meagre in its proportions, and not very dependable as to its historical facts. And how many French writers have since then pretended to enlighten us on the subject, who have served us up, one after another, the same rhetorical developments, seasoned with a grain of poetry, a suspicion of the æsthetic!   To-day, philosophy is the fashion, and one can lay no claim to understanding Wagner, if he believe that the master's works were made merely to be performed.   By no means!   Writers comment on them until they render them unintelligible, and then they are satisfied.*

It is so much easier and more expeditious to let the pen run at random in regard to a man or his work, without having heard the work nor studied the man, than to make careful researches into the circumstances of an artist's life which have accompanied the production of his works, and to keep always to the just point of criticism and eulogium, shunning alike laudatory, dithyrambic hyperbole, and spiteful, injurious censure. As to analyses of lyric productions, there are more of them than we want, it seems to me.   But it is far less easy to find a work in which the life and the productions of a bold innovator are described and studied from beginning to end ; where one may follow at the same time the life of the man and the career of the artist, from the day of his birth to that of his death.

Not only does there exist no work of this kind in our own tongue, but, even in foreign languages, one does not know where to find a single one which will satisfy the conditions of independence and impartiality necessary in order to make the work of interest and value.   Indeed, the German biogra-phies conforming to this general plan are conceived in such a spirit of admiration and carried out in such a laudatory style that one detects on every page the direct influence and the per-manent stamp of the master or of his representatives.   Each author, in taking up his pen, has laid aside his own personality, and has put himself, in a manner, at the disposal of the artist whose life he has undertaken to write; thus not only do his estimates lose all weight, but the simplest material facts are presented in such a fashion that one instinctively distrusts them, and accepts them only after minute verification. On every page one feels the presence of a partial hand, and such books, it seems to me, do not contribute to the master's glory; on the contrary they injure him, and render him disagreeable by their exaggeration of praise and abuse of flattery.

The best way, with such a genius, is to give an account of his life, and judge his actions and his works as if he had been dead fifty or sixty years, not loading him with extravagant encomiums which make him seem ridiculous in the eyes of sensible people; in a word, to write a book of history, and not a book of combat or of prejudice. Wagner, at the height of glory which he has attained, has no need for people to break their lances for him; he is well able to achieve his own victory, through the power of his genius and of his works. Enough, then, of books of combat. Enough of books of prejudice; we will have no more of them. For it would be showing a singularly narrow mind to rekindle old extinct quarrels, by republishing, for the sake of tormenting the critics, all their former judgments, so recently repudiated. And then what would be the object of it?

Surely, nothing would be easier for me than to make myself disagreeable to the writers who formerly led the attack against Richard Wagner, and I would be amply fitted out for this little war. It is not a rare thing at present to see people devotedly treasure up articles which are published about the master whom they admire; but this is a recent fashion, and has developed only since Wagner's death. Let one look back but a few years, and he will find no trace of a collection of this kind. This is still more true of ten, fifteen, twenty years ago; at that time how singular such an idea would have seemed, and how entirely without interest would have been such a research! There are only two of us, I believe, who have been for a long time past collecting everything printed about Richard Wagner, whenever a new work called forth opinion, or a quarrel over him was surging in the musical world.

We were acting as simple collectors in undertaking this tedious task, and we had no suspicion of what usefulness, what value, such a collection of articles would acquire in after years. To-day, whether it be a question of the representation of Rienzi at Paris, or the appearance of the Nibelungen at Bayreuth, on which we have scrupulously gathered in the least scraps from the French journals and a quantity of important articles from all the countries of Europe and of the New World; whether it be a question of the tumult raised at the Popular Concerts when M. Pasdeloup had the Siegfried funeral march performed, or of the conflict provoked quite recently by the announcement of Lohengrin at the Opera-Comique, — one may find, immediately, not only all the articles great and small from the professional critics, but the smallest jests, the slightest witticism which escaped from the pen of the chroniclers in merry mood, who remember them no longer, and who would scarcely laugh, to-day, if one were to amuse himself by recalling them to their minds.

What a rich arsenal to draw from if it had been in my project to wound with their own arms those who fought the

*hardest against Richard Wagner! But I am totally averse
to giving to my book a character of retaliation. I prefer to observe a strict impartiality between Richard Wagner and his
former detractors, and not to make use of the material in my
possession for the purpose of entertaining the gallery at their
expense; it would be doing them altogether too much honor,
thus to give them a new lease of life under shelter of the great
name of Wagner. Silence, then, in regard to those who took
part in last year's polemics, and a truce to personalities. Let
us aim first of all to have a book of history, as exact and complete as it is possible to make it, where formality shall be
avoided, where verified anecdote shall have a place, where
praise and criticism shall speak a language accessible to all;
such a book, in short, as an independent admirer of the master
ought to write.*

*It is to my mind an indispensable condition to a correct
estimate of an artist like Wagner, to enjoy an absolute independence, and to be under no obligation, however small, which
calls for a settlement. The man has lived, the work is immor-
tal; there are all the elements necessary in order to judge him.
But one may gather, besides, much detailed information from
those who have been intimate with him, and to avail myself of
such information, I have spared no effort. I have been careful,
however, not to solicit the least scrap of information from those
who would demand, in exchange, that I submit the entire work
to their approval. An admirer of Wagner I certainly believe
myself to be, and since I began to write — nearly twenty years
ago — I have never ceased to defend him energetically, at the
risk of drawing upon myself bantering attacks from the very
writers who accuse me now of being too moderate and cautious;*

but it is one thing to pen a militant article of criticism which is almost immediately forgotten, and another thing to write a volume of history on which the author claims that one may safely depend.

I am impelled, therefore, to write a work that is entirely impartial, not only towards Richard Wagner, but also towards those who, for one reason or another, have held him up to public ridicule and abuse. It belongs to the historian to discern the truth or the falsehood in such attacks, their origin or their hidden end, and afterwards, with a full cognizance of the facts, to pronounce between the artist and his enemies. This task is indispensable in the case of such a man as Richard Wagner; but it is a very delicate one, as may well be believed, and all the more difficult as nothing of the kind is to be found in all the biographical writings devoted to the master. With all the French or German writers, and even with Mr. Dannreuther, whose English article on Richard Wagner is one of the best, there is a want of calm scrutiny and of moderate judgment. There is no middle ground; it is all one way or all the other; either Wagner is a wretch or he is a martyr. But the absolute is not of this world, and in order to arrive at the relative truth concerning Richard Wagner and those who attacked him, it is not enough to scatter eloquence and high-sounding words; it is necessary to examine the question closely on every side, without bias, and, as far as possible, without illusion.

In order that such a work may put in its proper light the genius to whom it attempts to render a just homage, the products of the pencil must be given the important place due them as proofs of the opposition which the master encountered in all countries, and the energy he was obliged to expend in order to overcome the numerous obstacles which defied his progress. Nothing shows so well as the caricature, which instantly attracts the eye, what a change has taken place in public opinion on the subject of Richard Wagner. The caricature, therefore, ought to be a valuable adjunct to the written text, and as no composer, not even Rossini nor Berlioz, has been a greater inspiration to the humor of his contemporaries, it was only a question of choosing from among the numberless caricatures of Germany, France and England, being careful to avoid those that were too gross or in the slightest degree injurious to persons still living.

I regard the caricature in the light of a historic document, aside from the more or less venomous thrusts which it directs against its subject. Besides, the caricature has become, in our century, one of the forms of celebrity, a striking proof of fame, and Wagner, who knew the fact, should not have viewed with an indifferent eye this deluge of facetious sketches inspired by himself and his works : in catching the attention of innumerable people who would never have had the time nor the taste to read an article, they did more to spread his name and fame than hundreds of writings could have done. In no instance has he protested against the parody, written or drawn, and if ever a satirical sketcher had believed it his duty to ask permission to burlesque him, he probably would not have replied like our great Lamartine, that one ought not to authorize anybody to caricature the face of man, the only creature made in the image of God.

To this series of caricatures I have added a series of scenes from the operas, and another of portraits. For the first, I

have made it a point to give at least one engraving contem-
poraneous with the original performances, in order to preserve
to each piece the stamp of the times; for the second, my aim
has been to collect the rarest portraits, and those to which the
name of the artist and the date of the painting gave a particu-
lar importance, such as those of Herkomer and Renoir.   It

RICHARD WAGNER, ABOUT 1840.
His first portrait, drawn by Ernest Kietz, at Paris.

has not been easy to arrange in exact order this long series of
portraits.   For some of them I have the precise date; for in-
stance, those which were made in Paris, or London, and the one
showing Wagner at the age of forty, about which Messrs.
Breitkopf and Härtel kindly informed me.   For the others it
has been impossible to get any exact information, even from

those who, it would seem, ought to know the most about Richard Wagner; their replies have been vague, or manifestly
erroneous. So that I have been obliged, in inserting these
doubtful portraits between those whose dates I knew, to be
guided by modifications in the physiognomy and the changes
in the style of the clothing. I dare to entertain a slight hope
that I have established an exact relative order for all the portraits inserted in the text, but I cannot guarantee it.

At the last moment I have received Wagner's first portrait,
by Kietz, which I have been vainly seeking in all directions,
and which I deem myself fortunate to be able to make figure in
the preface. This portrait was made at Paris, in 1840 or
1841, by Ernest Kietz, a young Dresden artist who was
studying painting at the studio of Delaroche, and whom Wagner had the good fortune to meet at Paris during his first
stay among us. Here we have Wagner at twenty-seven or
twenty-eight years of age. The portrait which I have given
on page 51, supposing it to be the first, and perhaps that of
Kietz, was made two or three years later, and gives us Richard Wagner at about thirty; the date indicated is therefore
correct. It seems that Kietz, author of Wagner's first portrait, after having spent the best part of his life in Paris,
from 1830 to 1870, has now gone back to his native city. It
was his brother, the sculptor Gustave Kietz, who made at
Bayreuth, in 1873, the two white marble busts which adorn
the lower hall of Wahnfried.

In preparing this work, I have been obliged for illustrations as well as for the text, to have recourse to a great number of people with a view of obtaining from them useful information, and I am happy to say that, almost without excep-

tion, I have encountered only obliging attention and good will.
For the caricature part, which has such a great importance in
my eyes, I am much indebted to M. John Grand-Carteret,
author of the excellent History of the Caricature, in Germany,
Austria and Switzerland ; and M. Emerich Kastner, the great
Wagnerian collector of Vienna, has also given me very valuable
assistance. In general, all the managers of caricature papers
and satirical publications have shown the greatest kindness
and courtesy, — those of Charivari and Triboulet in France ;
the German editors of Kikeriki and Floh, at Vienna ; MM.
Braun and Schneider, of the Fliegende Blätter, at Munich ;
M. Heck, of Vienna, for the caricatures of Gualtier, Gaul,
etc., etc. M. A. Hofmann, proprietor of the Kladderadatsch of
Berlin, put at my disposal the whole humorous pamphlet,
Schulze and Müller Nibelungen Ring, in which the amusing
sketches are drawn by the principal artist of that celebrated
sheet, M. W. Scholz. Punsch, of Munich, has also been a very
useful sheet to consult for the period of Wagner's residence in
that city ; but here I address my thanks to a journal which
has disappeared, an author who is dead, for the year 1875
witnessed the simultaneous demise of this satirical paper and
its artist editor, Martin Schleich.

To return to France, it gives me great pleasure to thank
M. Charles Nuitter for his customary kindness in opening to
me the Archives of the Opera ; and my friend George Charpentier, who possessed the originals of certain drawings, like
the portrait of Renoir ; also MM. Charavay brothers, who
have served me with an important portrait, and particularly
those of my friends whose Wagnerian libraries, still better
supplied than my own with articles, engravings or original

documents, were quite at my disposal. I have been careful always to indicate very exactly — when I could find it — the origin of the portraits, caricatures and other illustrations which it has seemed to me good to reproduce; and in the same way, I have successively noted in the course of the narrative all the works which have been of the slightest use to me in making my book. It would have been ungracious to pass over in silence the different French books which have treated of this rare genius, and rather than neglect a single one, it has pleased me to name them all, without undertaking here to criticise or to discriminate between their greater or less value; that, however, is evident.

Such as it is, with its inevitable imperfections, I submit this work to the enlightened admirers of Richard Wagner, begging them to excuse the defects which may have escaped me. It is for this class especially that the book has been written; but for all that, it would not displease me to interest those people of good faith for whom the Wagnerian work is still a closed letter, and to play for them the modest rôle — or immodest, as one prefers — which Goethe assigns to translators: "They are," says he, "zealous agents who extol to us the irresistible charms of a half-veiled beauty; they produce in our hearts an ardent longing to know the original."

And now that I have said all, a short fanfare as at Bayreuth; let the curtain part, and let the master himself, before the representation of his own life — the agitated life of a hero of the art, — come to intercede with the public in behalf of his new historian!

INTRODUCTION.

T is now just ten years since, at the moment that the *Trilogy* was first performed at Bayreuth, the Figaro published a certain article to which it would be well to lend attention.

The lapse of ten years has in no wise diminished the force of this defence of a man accused of faults which he was not the only one to commit, but with which he alone was charged. So it seems to the author that he could not better commence this extensive work on Richard Wagner than by reproducing here without alteration, this short study to which there has never been any response save by empty declamations. But the facts are clear, and the texts are there; and no oratory, however eloquent, will hold against such irreproachable testimony.

Let us suppose, then, that we are still in the month of August, 1876.

The musical festivals which are soon to be held at Bayreuth, and which, whether triumph or failure, will remain one of the most audacious artistic attempts that has ever been seen, hold to-day the attention of all musical Europe fixed on this little town of Bavaria, and make once more a hero of this Richard Wagner, so much admired by some, so much abhorred by others, and so scoffed at by the indifferent and idle throng.

Would it not be fitting to examine in all justice, without indulging in prejudice one way or the other, the grievances so often formulated against this composer, by those who carry this purely musical question into the noisy world of politics, without recalling the fact that others have written and have done still worse by us, and have nevertheless been admired and praised by all France? The question of genius or of talent is not for discussion here, and all dissertation would be idle in the face of decisive facts. We will therefore abstain from judging or even examining the theories and the creations of the German innovator, however great the charm which a careful examination would offer us.

Indeed, the artistic nature of Richard Wagner is so complex, his musical genius reveals such a vigor, and exercises such a charm, that in default of a profound knowledge of his works, people have recourse to the strangest comparisons for judging him, whether favorably or otherwise. This same year (1886), almost on the same day, a German composer likened him to Napoleon III. while a French journalist compared him to Bismarck; and both of them, the musician and the litterateur, the German and the Frenchman, believed that they had summed up Richard Wagner in this single comparison.

Let us preserve, at least as a matter of curiosity, these two portraits which so decidedly contradict each other.

Ferdinand Hiller, director of the Cologne Conservatory, and intimate friend of Mendelssohn — this ancient friendship explains his active hatred for Wagner, — wrote to the Deutsche Rundschau:

"In many respects Wagner resembles Napoleon III. Like him, he always had faith in his work, notwithstanding the most adverse circumstances. All the means which could

help him towards the goal of his aspirations, he has employed with a constancy and an energy which no musician
has possessed before him to the same degree. Another point
of resemblance between him and Napoleon, is that he was
able to indissolubly bind his partisans to the success of his
cause, while with regard to those whose self-seeking would
tend to overshadow him, he managed to turn all their efforts
to his own advantage. It is thus that he has arrived at a
supreme power. As a climax to his brilliant career, the exposition at Bayreuth will follow in 1876 the Universal Exposition
of Napoleon in 1867. Will Wagner also have a Sedan? It
is difficult to believe; in the first place, until now, there has
been no announcement in the musical world of the advent of
a Bismarck or a Moltke. In the second place victories in the
arts are not so quickly won as in the field.

" But his cause will end nevertheless by being vanquished,
for it rests on false principles, like the power, formerly un-
questioned, of Napoleon III."

On the other hand, what says the *XIXe Siècle?*

" Richard Wagner is will, energy, and perseverance incarnate; like all who cling persistently to the pursuit of a
fixed idea, he has long been regarded as a maniac. To-day,
Bismarck and he, these two men whose characters, if not
geniuses, have so many points of resemblance, are the idols
of Germany. The élite of the French-hating and music-mad
Germans is prostrate at their feet. Bismarck and Wagner
have given proof in their two very different spheres of action,
of the same absolute and systematic spirit, of the same passionate tenacity, of the same impetuousity of temperament,
of the same absence of scruples in their choice of means to
an end. The unity which the diplomat has accomplished
through tact or by vital force in politics, the artist has endeavored to realize in his art."

Of these two parallels the second is perhaps less forced

than the first, but it proves nothing more, either for or against the author of *Tristan and Isolde.*

Animosity was more than ever redoubled against Richard Wagner when it was learned by chance that he had written against France, in the spring of 1871, a political comedy attack entitled *A Capitulation.* On this subject it would have been advisable not to cry too loudly, and thus call attention to our protracted ignorance. People interested in criticism and musical matters had known for a long time that of which the public was yet ignorant, and in order that the public should be enlightened, it was necessary that a tourist-writer should travel into the " pays des milliards," and there make this unexpected discovery.

This tardiness of information and this fashion of becoming possessed of facts five years after they happen, are scarcely to our credit. Either this hostile publication had a paramount importance, and we should have recognized it from the first, or else it was a matter of no particular consequence, in which case it had been wise to make less noise about it. To attach so much importance to a parody quite inoffensive in its extravagance was to make all the more conspicuous our lack of foresight and knowledge.

It is also held a crime on the part of Richard Wagner that he should have composed in 1871 a triumphal march for the coronation of the German emperor. Assuredly, it would have been better, if he, who had lived several years in France, had abstained from doing this. But is it not the privilege of all musicians to celebrate the military triumphs of their country, and do they not always expect an unquestionable success? Furthermore, would the French do well to blame a German composer for having celebrated a German conquest when they have been so loud in their praises of Félicien David and Gounod for singing the future victories of France, and have never blamed the Italian Spontini for celebrating in official cantatas the oppressor of his country, and even dedicating to him upon his order a grand opera like *Fernando Cortez?*

Weber acted otherwise, and better than Spontini, he who made himself the Tyrtæus of the Germans during the campaign of 1813; who put to music the most violent war songs against our invading flag and against a conqueror justly abhorred. But Weber went in this sense farther than Wagner; he composed not only his cantata of victory *Combat and Triumph*, after the battle of Waterloo, — as Wagner did for the crowning of the Emperor, — he had already, in the very height of the war, launched against us those patriotic songs which kindled the ardor of the combatants.

And for all that, who would dream to-day of banishing Weber from France, of denying his genius, because he was our bitter and victorious enemy? Nobody dreamed of it when twelve years after this explosion of hatred, he passed through Paris on his way to London to direct his Oberon. French society received him with a flattering eagerness, and desired to remember but one thing, that it ought to honor genius, wherever found and whence it might come.

Richard Wagner, then, has done less against France than has Weber. But, it is said, he has not only composed a march of triumph; he has also done an injury to a vanquished people in order to avenge his offended self-love for the repulse which that people had formerly given to his *Tannhäuser*.

But another German composer has also wronged, also injured us, in return for our kind reception and our bravos. And this composer enjoys to-day the most unalloyed glory, both as a man and a musician, even in France, where everybody is ignorant of what he thought of us. The revelation which we are about to make will perhaps detract a little from the ideal image of the tender Mozart, but however greatly it may surprise his devoted admirers, it will not touch his genius nor his work. It will prove however, that one can as well detest and injure France with the gentle nature of a Mozart, as with the rancorous spirit of a Wagner.

And to begin with, in what did Mozart, whom they have wished to make a model of all the virtues, differ from the rest of mankind? Had he truly that inflexible integrity, that honesty which would shun even the thought of evasion or of subterfuge; he who, after having sold his *Symphonie Concertante* and two overtures to Legros, director of the Concert Spirituel, remarked quite innocently, " He believes himself to be the sole possessor, but that is not so, for I have it still fresh in my head, and I will write it out from memory as soon as I get home." The act does more credit to his memory than to his delicacy.

Was he of a nature so amiable, and did he preserve an invariable recognition of the services rendered him; this young man who presumed to cast reflections and calumnies on Grimm, who had been his most devoted protector at the time of his first visit to Paris with his parents? The enthusiasm of Grimm was considerably chilled, it is true, when he saw Mozart return, a presumptuous boy of twenty-two, gifted with a prodigious vanity and entirely lacking the qualities of tact and amiability which are necessary in order to succeed in Paris; but he had still accorded him a constant friendship, if not a very efficacious protection.

And even had he not done so. nothing warranted Mozart in making this denunciation so full of anger and harshness; at least the recollection of past favors should have prevented him from speaking of Grimm in these rude terms: " The greatest benefit which he has accorded me, consists of fifteen louis d'or which he loaned me in small sums during the illness of my mother. Is he afraid of losing them? If he has any doubt on this subject he truly deserves to be kicked, for that would be showing suspicion with regard to my honesty (the only offense which can put me in a rage) and my talent."

Had he, finally, that profound respect for his family, or even a mind so delicate, he who would terminate thus a letter to a respectable parent :

"I wish you, *mon cher oncle*, good health, and 1,000 *compliments à ma cousine. Je suis, de tout mon cœur*, Monsieur, *votre invariable cochon*,

"W. A. Mozartin."[1]

They have jeered and still jeer at Wagner for his uncouth wit, and "ses plaisanteries d'éléphant." They are too often sufficiently heavy, but they are less rude than the above, and moreover do not address themselves to an aged man.

This short digression on the character and humor of Mozart does not concern us Frenchmen, it is true, and will simply weaken the ideal which people have been pleased to form of him,—of this young man so timid, chaste and respectful, who was nothing less than all that. But, here is what touches us more, and what will surprise our readers, for the biographers and translators of Mozart have carefully passed over it, to this day.

Several of his letters written from Paris, contain marks of contempt, and insults to our intelligence, as for instance his letter of July 9th, 1778. After having spoken of his ballet of the Petits Riens, of which, he says, he has only composed six pieces out of the twelve, the rest being, according to him, only an arrangement of "*miserable French airs*," he goes on to say: "The Capellmeister Bach will soon be here, and I think he is coming with a view to writing an opera. *These French people are, and always will be asses. They are incapable of producing anything, and they are forced to depend on foreigners*." The compliment is worth its price, especially coming from a young man, whose pride was wounded at not finding the French people more worshipful of him.

---

[1] The words here in italics are in French in the original, Mozart readily resorting to the French language for little pleasantries of this kind.

Nearly a month later, Mozart wrote to his father under date of July 31st : "There is no middle course, I must either write a grand opera, or write none at all. If I compose only a small one, my profit will be insignificant, for in this country all is taxed, without reckoning that if the opera has not the good fortune to please these *boobies of Frenchmen*, that is the end of it ; I should have no more orders, I should derive little from it, and my reputation would suffer. But if I compose a grand opera I will get better returns, I will be in my special element, and I will have greater chance of success because a great work offers more opportunities for gaining applause. I assure you I will not hesitate a moment if I obtain an order for a work. The devil has forged this language, it is true, and I understand too well the difficulties it has presented to all composers : but notwithstanding all, I feel myself in a position to conquer them, as well as they.

" On the contrary, when I fancy—and that happens often —that my opera will go well, then I feel myself on fire, my whole being vibrates, and I long to teach the French people to know the Germans, to esteem and to fear them. Why is it that the French can never make an opera ? Why must they always look to foreigners ? The greatest obstacle for me, would arise from the singers. But my resolution is taken ; I will not seek a quarrel, only, if I am driven to a corner I must defend myself. I wish to avoid a duel, *for I have no taste for fighting with dwarfs*."

Mozart, who had this pecuniary question very much at heart, refers to it again in his letter of September 11, the same in which he disposes so well of his protector Grimm. " I have not wished to reject flatly the proposition of Noverre, because that might have caused them to think that I lacked confidence in myself. In truth my conditions were not acceptable, but I knew it in advance, for such is not the custom here. Here is how those things work; you probably

know it already. The opera finished, they rehearse it. If it
does not suit the taste of these puppies of Frenchmen, they
do not give it, and the composer has his trouble for his
pains. On the other hand, if it is judged good they put it
on the stage, and if it succeeds, the gain is in proportion to
the success. You see how it is; one can never count on
anything."

Asses, dwarfs, boobies, puppies; we are only puzzled to
choose between the epithets with which Mozart has favored
us; surely, he has treated us scarcely better than will be done
later on by the author of *Lohengrin*.

And yet there is between them this difference, that Richard
Wagner will abuse us as a foreigner, after having returned to
his own country; after one of his principle works, good or
bad, shall have been hissed by us, without understanding a
note of it, whereas Mozart slung these amenities at us in his
letters written from Paris even, when society was receiving
him with a marked kindness, notwithstanding his unpleasant
humor and his pride; when his ballet of the " Petits Riens "
was obtaining success at the Opera, and two symphonies had
made his name famous at the Concert Spirituel. An essential difference, and which is not, it seems to us, to the advantage of Mozart.

But all this is nothing, and in the hatred which he has
vowed to Paris, Mozart goes on to treat French society, its
customs and morals, in a fashion which quite defies excuse or
extenuation. These passages, it must be repeated, have been
patriotically omitted by the French critics or historians of
Mozart, who did not wish to awaken the public from its blind
confidence in the singer of Donna Anna, nor to disfigure the
beautiful ideal which it had formed of the heart and mind of
the sweet Wolfgang.

Mozart, who could be kind-hearted, but who was of an incredible lightness, commenced in this brisk fashion, his letter

of the 18th of July, the second that he wrote after his mother's death, which occurred only a fortnight before. " I hope that you have received my two preceding letters. We will not speak further of that which formed the subject of them, it is done, we can change nothing." And after this stoical passage, he adds, in speaking of a visit paid by him to the celebrated singer Raff, who was then at Paris ; " When I had finished playing, — and Raff during the whole time had never ceased to applaud me very vigorously and very sincerely — I exchanged some words with Ritter. I remarked among other things, how little I enjoyed my sojourn in Paris, even setting music aside, for, as I said to him, I do not find a single relief, a single support, a single agreeable or honest relation with the world, particularly with the women, who for the most part are ——, and the rare exceptions are not well-bred. Ritter could not do otherwise than agree with me." From the women, let us pass to the young men. Two days after, Mozart, learning that a captain by the name of Hopfgarten had been killed in a skirmish between the Prussian troops and those of Archduke Maximilian, wrote to his father : " Could it by chance be the brave baron Hopfgarten, whom we met at Paris, with M. de Bosé ? That would be sad, but it were far better that he should meet a glorious death, than to die in his — bed of a disgraceful malady, like most of the young men of Paris. Impossible to talk with a man here who has not been three or four times, or who is not still favored with some gallantry of this sort. From the cradle children are infected with it ; but I am telling you nothing new, and you have known all this much longer than I have. Believe me, however, if I add that contagion has done much to increase it."

Although he has been hissed by us as strongly as Mozart has been applauded, Wagner has never permitted himself, on the whole, to make accusations so objectionable against the so-called infamy of French society. He has been reproached, not without reason, for crying down afterwards the Parisian amateurs, from whom he had demanded glory, and who had received him with jeers, but Mozart himself, the pure Mozart, what was he doing in the midst of a people whom he judged so corrupt, both in soul and body?

As a composer, Richard Wagner has shown himself less hostile to France than did Weber; as a man he has wronged us less than did Mozart, and yet, we heap upon him all the abuses which are spared his two compatriots. Besides the fact that these revengeful excommunications have no force when they do not strike at all the guilty ones, they are sure to be only temporary, and to be quite effaced in the course of a few years, if not months. Were it not that the self-love of the French, wounded that their judgment has not been made a law in other countries, continues to oppose the failure of *Tannhäuser* at Paris to the brilliant triumphs of *Tannhäuser* and *Lohengrin* on so many of the other stages in the world, it would not be long ere Wagner would be received back into our favor, free to reward us afterwards with compliments after the manner of Mozart.

But what matters it, after all? Posterity cares neither for the writings nor the thoughts of a man, nor even for the man himself, when it is a question of judging his works, and therein it gives proof of wisdom and impartiality. It will forget, then, the injuries of Wagner, as quickly as it has forgotten those of his predecessors. And if the author of *Lohengrin* and of *Tristan* possess true musical genius, his wrongs will, in the end, hurt us no more than the graver wrongs of Weber and Mozart have done.

RICHARD WAGNER

CHAPTER I

THE YOUTH AND FIRST ATTEMPTS OF RICHARD WAGNER. — THE
FAIRIES AND THE NOVICE OF PALERMO. — SOJOURNS AT MAGDE-
BURG, KÖNIGSBERG, AND RIGA

ICHARD WAGNER was born at Leipsic,
on the 22d of May, 1813, in an old house
called "The House of the Red and White
Lion," No. 88 Hause Bruhl.[1]

He was the ninth and last child of
a family in humble circumstances. His
grandfather was a simple custom-house
officer at Leipsic, and his father held the
modest position of clerk of police. The latter had a good
knowledge of languages, particularly the French, which was the
cause of his being chosen by Marshal Davoust to organize
the police of the city during the occupation by the French
army. He had a very keen taste for poetry and the theatre.
He even took pleasure in playing at comedy, and on one
occasion he and some of his friends produced, at a certain
salon of Leipsic, *Die Mitschuldigen* of Goethe.

After the desperate battles of the 18th and 19th of Octo-

[1] This was the great commercial street of Leipsic, in the centre of the city. On
May 22, 1873, the sixtieth anniversary of the birth of the master, a commemorative
tablet was placed on the old house, which to-day threatens demolition, and which
must soon disappear, notwithstanding the worthy project formed by some admirers, to purchase and repair the building. The architects of the city have pronounced such restoration useless and impracticable.

ber, 1813, which took place under the walls of the city, and which delivered Germany from the hated yoke of Napoleon, there broke out in Leipsic a deadly fever, caused by the enormous number of dead, sick and wounded, accumulated in and around the city; and this epidemic carried away the clerk, Frederic Wagner, on Nov. 22, six months after the day when Richard was born. The latter had, therefore, an innate liking for the theatre. Nor was he the only one of the family to inherit the tastes of his father, for his sister Rosalie acquired a real fame as tragedienne; while his elder brother Albert, actor and singer at Wurzburg, at Dresden, and afterwards manager of a theatre at Berlin, had two daughters who became singers, and one of whom shed a lustre over the name of Johanna Wagner, worthy of comparison with Schroeder-Devrient.

The mother of Richard Wagner retired to Eiselben, where she lived for two years in a state bordering on indigence, depending for support on a small government pension. About this time she married a friend of her former husband, the comedian Ludwig Geyer, and came with all her family to reside at Dresden, where Geyer held a good rank in the royal troupe. After having had a prolonged success at Leipsic, this Geyer, who was not only a comedian of merit, but had also tried his hand at the dramatist's profession, and cultivated painting with some degree of talent, gave token at once of a decided affection for the child Richard. Unhappily he died when the boy was only seven years old.

Nevertheless, Wagner always remembered his second father. He spoke of him with an affectionate respect; he guarded lovingly his portrait by the side of that of his mother, and was much touched when at Bayreuth, on the celebration of his sixtieth anniversary, they organized in the family the representation of one of the little pieces by Geyer, " The Massacre of the Infants of Bethlehem."

The very evening before his death, Geyer had asked little Richard to play him two airs from *Der Freischütz*, which had been taught him on the piano. As the child did not acquit himself badly, he murmured in a feeble voice to his wife, "Do you think he might have a taste for music?" And the next morning, when he was dead, his wife, in recalling to the children how many proofs he had given them of a warm paternal affection, said to Richard, "He would like to have made something of you." The child always remembered these words and tried from his heart to realize them.

Nobody at that time would have dreamed of making a musician of Richard Wagner, — his second father would have wished to make a painter of him, had he not decidedly rebelled at the plan; and when he was nine years old, his mother, assisted by a brother of her second husband, placed him at the school of the Cross, in order that he might make a serious study of the classics. He was then a headstrong and fantastic child, at once impetuous and self-willed, and would fly into a passion at nothing.

"I have grown up," said he, "outside of all authority, and with no guides except life, art, and myself." And he was one of those to whom such independence is quite necessary. He gave himself up especially to the study of Greek, and became the favorite pupil of Prof. Sillig. He also had a great liking for mythology and ancient history, but he had little taste for the piano, instruction on which he received from his professor of Latin.

The technique of the instrument bored him, and he amused himself by playing from memory instead of studying, so that one day the Professor gave up, and said that nothing could ever be made of the boy. And, in fact, Wagner could never learn to play the piano properly.

His professor gone, he continued to repeat from memory, with extravagant fingering, two overtures, which then constituted his entire musical repertoire, — that of the *Magic Flute*, and, above all, that of *Der Freischütz* which he had just heard at the theatre, and which made on his mind its first deep musical impression. Moreover, he would play these two pieces for himself only; and as he was incapable of correctly executing a scale, he conceived thenceforth an instinctive aversion for all that was mere virtuosity. But the childish admiration which he had for Weber was so great that he would run to the window as soon as the hour approached when the composer was wont to pass the house on his way to the theatre. Eagerly he watched him, with a sort of religious terror, and jealously preserved his image in the depths of his heart.

Weber, who exercised from the first such an influence on a child of nine years, was then leader of the orchestra at the Dresden theatre, where, since 1817, he had been fighting for German music, and against the Italian school; having the whole court against him, and only succeeding in having *Der Freischütz* performed in the theatre which he directed, a year after its brilliant success at Berlin.

Weber, so it appears, was fond of coming in and chatting with the charming and intelligent Madame Geyer, whose sweet manners and playful disposition had a special charm for artists; but he was never in any way the instructor of Wagner. Indeed he died at London when Richard was only thirteen years old and was giving no attention to music; but he had awakened his musical instinct, as Wagner was pleased to recognize. In his *Letter on Music*, in 1860, Wagner writes : —

"Notwithstanding a serious scientific education, I have lived from my earliest youth in close relations with the theatre. This part of my life fell in the last years of Carl Maria von Weber. He personally directed at that time the execution of the operas in Dresden, the city where I lived. I received from this master my first musical impressions. His melodies filled me with enthusiasm. His character and his nature exercised a veritable fascination over me; and his death in a foreign country filled my childish heart with desolation."

BIRTHPLACE OF RICHARD WAGNER.

The small savings amassed by Geyer had been quickly absorbed, and his widow found herself again in straightened circumstances. At that time, three of her children had turned towards the theatre, and her daughter Rosalie, in particular, had concluded a fine engagement as "leading lady" at the Stadt Theatre of Leipsic. In 1827, Madame

Geyer decided to go and live near her. She removed to
Leipsic with her young children, and Richard was made to
enter Nicolai College. But he was admitted to the *tertia*
only, notwithstanding he had already commenced his *seconda*
at Dresden, where he passed for a good student *in litteris*,
having translated with taste, after class-hours, the first twelve
books of the Odyssey, and having had the honor to carry off
the prize in a poetical contest, the theme being the death of
one of his comrades. His piece had even been printed, after
a good deal of the pathos had been cut out. He had then
taken it into his little head to be a poet, and so put himself
to the study of Shakespeare, in order that he might be able
to read in the original text. As he had an exceptional facility
for German verse, he had undertaken a metrical translation
of the monologue of Romeo. Then he had constructed
tragedies in imitation of the antique, after the manner of
those of Apel, and another, inspired by Hamlet and King
Lear, where more than forty individuals died, one after
another, so that he was obliged to resuscitate some of them
in order to furnish a denouement.

The humiliation which he experienced at finding himself
classed in the *tertia* in Leipsic had the effect of disgusting
him with the classic studies, and turning his attention towards
music.

That very year Beethoven died, and the hearing of his
symphonies at the concerts of the Gewandhaus, under the
direction of the celebrated Matthaei, made on him a most
profound impression.

"One evening," says the hero of his story ("A Pilgrimage
to Beethoven"), "having listened to one of Beethoven's symphonies, I had an attack of fever; I fell ill, and on recovering,
I became a musician." Thus goes the story, but history bears
some analogy to this account. In his *Letter on Music* he
writes more seriously:

"The death of Beethoven closely followed that of Weber. That was the first time I had heard him spoken of, and it was then that I became acquainted with his music, attracted, if I may say so, by the news of his death. These serious impressions developed in me an inclination more and more ardent for music. It was only later, however, when my studies had made me familiar with the classic age, and had inspired some poetical efforts, that I came to study music more earnestly."

His project in cultivating music was to set his famous tragedy of the forty-two victims to a score similar to that of *Egmont*, which he had just heard. He imagined that a week's study of harmony would enable him to compose such a work, and he buried himself in Logier's *Treatise on Harmony*, which he had bought of an itinerant bookseller. But it was in vain, he did not succeed in mastering it.

Then he resolved to announce his new vocation to his family as soon as he should have actually composed something, — a sonata, an air, a quartette. At first they combatted the idea, as a mere passing fancy on the part of one who could not even play the piano; but they finally gave him a master, Gottlieb Müller, afterwards organist at Altenburg. The poor master had a hard time with his pupil, who was infatuated with Hoffman, and whose brain became so turned with so many whimsical inventions, that he dreamed in broad daylight, and saw fundamental notes appear to him, and thirds and fifths with which he held mysterious conversation.[1] At last the master of harmony, not wishing to lose his own head, gave up his pupil in despair, declaring, like the professor of the piano, "Nothing can ever be made of that boy."

This prediction, twice repeated, in no wise troubled the

---

[1] These stories, however, were not lost, for *The Brothers of Serapion* contains an account of the poetical tourney at Wartburg, and some germs of *The Meistersinger* are found in another story by Hoffman, *Master Martin, the Cooper of Nuremburg.*

dreamer, who bravely wrote an overture, and carried it to
Dorn, leader of the orchestra at the Royal Theatre, with
whom his sister Rosalie had put him in communication.
Dorn accepted the overture, and rehearsed it, in spite of the
laughter of the Matthaei orchestra. Furthermore, he kept
it on the program, and had it performed between the acts
of a piece. The public, quite unaccustomed to that style of
composition, could distinguish nothing but the roll of kettledrums, which persistently returned every four measures, to
the very end, — so that the piece was known after a single
hearing under the name of "The Overture of the Kettledrums."

"This overture," wrote Wagner, "was the culminating
point of my absurdities. For facilitating the study of it, I
had conceived the idea of writing the score in three colors
of ink : red for the stringed instruments, black for the reed,
and green for the brass. The composition was so complicated, that the Ninth Symphony of Beethoven seemed beside
it as one of Pleyel's sonatas."

The reaction of the Revolution, which overturned in
France the throne of Charles X., made itself felt over all
Europe, and particularly in Saxony, where the king saw him-
self forced to grant to his subjects a constitution.

"With one bound, I became a revolutionist," wrote Wagner, "and arrived at the conclusion that every man with any
aspiration should occupy himself exclusively with politics. I
was never so happy as when in the company of political
writers. I also undertook an overture on a political theme.
It was under these circumstances that I quitted college to
enter the university, not however, to devote myself to the
study of any one of the Faculties (for I still intended to
follow music), but to take up a course of esthetics and
philosophy. I profited as little as possible by this occasion
to instruct me ; on the other hand I abandoned myself to all

the follies of the student's life, and that, to speak the truth, with so much recklessness, and so little restraint, that I very soon became disgusted."[1] And this revolutionist and man of the world was only seventeen years old.

When Wagner had sown his wild oats, he realized that it was time to devote himself to the regular study and pursuit of music. He had previously left the Nicolai school, for the Thomas School, where his philological studies had not progressed much more smoothly. In 1830, he entered the University of Leipsic, as a student in philosophy and esthetics. He had the good fortune to meet there an excellent professor in the person of Theodore Weinlig, *precentor* at the Thomas Church. This admirable musician seemed to gain immediately the confidence of the youth, and put him on the right path. And Wagner always recognized the fact, for even to the end of his life he was accustomed to say to his friends, "Weinlig had no special method, but he was clear-headed and practical. Indeed you cannot *teach* composition : you may show how music gradually came to be what it is, and thus guide a young man's judgment; but this is historical criticism and cannot directly result in practice. All you can do is to point to some working example, some particular piece, set a task in that direction, and correct the pupil's work. This is what Weinlig did with me. But the true lesson consisted in his patient and careful inspection of what had been written. With infinite kindness he put his finger on some defective bit and explained the why and wherefore of the alterations he thought desirable. I readily saw what he was aiming at, and soon managed to please him. He dismissed me, saying, 'You have learnt to stand on your own legs.'"[2]

---

[1] Autobiography, translated by M. Camille Benoit, in his Souvenirs of R. Wagner. One vol. 18mo. Charpentier, 1884.

[2] Personal conversation with M. Dannreuther, given by him in Grove's Musical Dictionary, article *Wagner*.

It was Weinlig, and not Weber, as has been too often repeated, who said one day to Wagner, "It is probable you will never have to write a fugue, but you must know how to write one. By that means, you will acquire independence, and all the rest will be easy." He worked with so much ardor under Weinlig's direction, that the latter dismissed him in about six months. Thanks to him, Wagner had learned to profoundly admire Mozart; but Beethoven with his symphonies, particularly the Ninth, was always his idol. After this period of study, he composed a number of pieces; first a polonaise and a sonata for the piano, which had the honor of being published by the well-known house of Breitkopf & Härtel; then a concert overture with a fugue, and above all a symphony in four parts, which he himself declared to be inspired by Beethoven, and certain pieces by Mozart.

Dorn, in writing later to the *New Musical Gazette* of Schumann, has noted in an amusing passage this enthusiasm of Wagner for Beethoven. "I doubt," said he, "if ever a young musician has lived in closer intimacy with Beethoven than did Wagner at the age of seventeen. He had copied by hand the overtures and the grand instrumental compositions of the master. He slept with the quartettes under his pillow, he sung the *lieder*, and whistled the concertos, for his talent as a pianist had never been brilliant. In short, he was possessed of a 'Teutonic fury,' which, joined to a good education and a rare activity of mind, promised to bear rich harvests."[1]

During the summer of 1832, Wagner accomplished a double artistic pilgrimage. He went first to visit the

---

[1] During the year 1830, he made for the piano a transcription of Beethoven's Ninth Symphony, which he offered, by letter of Oct. 6th, to the house of Schott; and in 1831, feeling sure that he could do work of that kind, he wrote a very modest letter to a musical bureau (Peters), in which he offered his services in the capacity of corrector and arranger of proof. That is the trade which he afterwards followed in Paris.

musical city *par excellence*, the one where Mozart and Beethoven had lived, but he was terribly disappointed to hear
at Vienna only refrains from *Zampa*, and potpourris on
Zampa.

He took himself quickly away and went to Prague, where
Mozart had found success and happiness. He had fondly
hoped to find at Vienna an opportunity to hear his symphony
rehearsed, and had furnished himself with scores of his symphony and his overture. He was more happy at Prague,
where he became acquainted with Dionys Weber, who
directed the Conservatory, and who procured for him the
pleasure of hearing his symphony on the orchestra. This
little success had induced Wagner to try some theatrical
music. At Prague, he had even written a frightfully dramatic
poem, entitled *The Nuptials*. And soon after his return
to Leipsic, he had written the first part, a septette, which his
master Weinlig approved. But his sister Rosalie having
found the libretto detestible, he destroyed the whole thing,
and awaited another occasion to attempt an opera. In the
meantime he had given his overture and his symphony to
the directors of the concerts of the Gewandhaus, and the
president of the Committee, the Aulic Counsellor, Frederic
Rochlitz, had written for an interview with him. "But you
are a very young man," he cried, on seeing him enter. "I
expected to see a man of some years, judging from the experience of the composer." He then proposed to have his symphony tried by a new society, the Euterpe, on Christmas Day,
1832, and this trial scarcely satisfied the author. But he
chanced to be praised in the *Journal du Monde Elégant*, by
Heinrich Laube, a writer of some standing, and a fortnight
later, on the 8th of Jan., 1833, his symphony had the honor to
be performed at the Gewandhaus under the direction of
Auguste Pohlentz. His overture also was played there at a
concert on the 30th of April. These two productions were

received fairly well, and gave Wagner a standing at Leipsic, all thanks to the support of Heinrich Laube, an excellent, but hare-brained fellow, who exercised much influence over this musician of twenty years.

This symphony was really his first work, and Laube's article was the first that had been written about him.[1]

Wagner had gayly recounted these reminiscences, when, fifty years later, being at Venice with his family, the idea occurred to him to celebrate the fiftieth anniversary of his debut as composer by having performed for the benefit of his wife and father-in-law "this youthful production, — superannuated," he added laughing. The execution, entrusted to the professors and students of the San Marcello Lyceum, took place on the Christmas of 1882, to celebrate thus the birthday of Madame Wagner, and provoked on the part of the author some retrospective remarks on himself.

He recognized the fact that this symphony proceeded indirectly from Beethoven; that the andante, in particular, would never have seen the light without the andante of the symphony in C major and the allegretto of the symphony in A. Then he continues thus: "If the work bore the mark of Richard Wagner, it would be found at most in that unbounded confidence, which at that period prevented him from doubting anything.

"This confidence in myself I drew not alone from my skill as a contrapuntist, a quality which, in course of time, was called in question more than any other by a court musician at Munich (Strauss), but from the great advantage which I had

---

[1] History of a symphony in the Souvenirs of Richard Wagner. In 1834-35, in a visit to Leipsic, he had prayed Mendelssohn — then leader of the orchestra at the concerts of the Gewandhaus — if not to read, at least to preserve this symphony, and Mendelssohn never spoke of it to him again.

This work would have been lost, had not the separate pieces been found one fine day in an old valise, which had been forgotten by Wagner, when he left Dresden, in 1849.

over Beethoven. While pausing at the point of view of the second symphony, I was already quite familiar with the Heroic, with those in C minor and A major, all works of which the master had no idea, or at least a very vague idea, when he wrote his second symphony." Thus he modestly explains the flattering exclamation of Rochlitz. Meanwhile he constantly visited the theatre, and looked about him for a poem to put to music; refusing one on Kosciuszko, the hero of the Polish Revolution, which was offered to him by his friend, Heinrich Laube. His brother Albert, who had a good tenor voice, was then actor, singer, and manager of the theatre at Würzburg. Richard went to spend a year with him, and willingly accepted the place of leader of the chorus, at ten florins a month. The experience of his brother in theatrical matters was of great service to him. The Musical Society performed several of his pieces, and as his post was not confining, he found time to compose his first grand opera. This opera of *The Fairies* was taken from a fable by Gozzi, entitled *The Serpent Woman*. It is a story of a fairy who is in love with a mortal, and wishes for his sake to renounce immortality; but it is necessary that her lover should have confidence in her, however cruel she may show herself to him. He is unequal to the test, and the fairy is changed into a toad in the story of Gozzi, into a statue in the opera of Wagner. In order to recover her, and to regain his happiness, the lover brings himself, in the fable, to kiss the unclean animal. In the opera, he recalls her to life by the ardor and beauty of his songs.

Thus, even at this period, Wagner's mind was haunted with the eternal myth of Psyche, which later on was to furnish him the subject of *Lohengrin*. In both these dramas, indeed, absolute confidence, resting not upon facts, but upon inward persuasion, is presented as a necessary condition of love. As for the music, it reflected, according to his own declaration, the triple influence of Beethoven, of Weber and of Marschner.

They had tried several fragments of it in the family, at Würzburg, in 1834, and it seemed to the author that there were many good points about it, and that the finale of the second act was especially destined to produce a fine effect; but he was not able to put it to the test. On his return to Dresden, he had proposed the work to the Director Ringelhardt, who had accepted it. The *Journal* of his friend Laube had announced that immediately after *Le Bal Masqué*, by Auber, would be played the first opera of a young composer called Richard Wagner; but when *Le Bal Masqué* had finished its run, the director, with no thought for *The Fairies*, mounted Bellini's *I Capuletti e Montecchi*.

If Wagner was never able to bring out this opera at Leipsic or anywhere else, it was because the public at that time had ears for foreign music only,—for French and Italian operas, to the great detriment of German productions. Wagner himself was much taken with *La Muette de Portici*, and was delighted with *I Capuletti e Montecchi*, less on account of the music, it is true, than because of the pathetic and superb playing of Madame Schroeder-Devrient, who came to sing at Dresden in the spring of 1834. He saw then for the first time that incomparable artist, who came to exercise so great an influence over him, and to suggest to him that intimate union of the music with the drama, to which he afterwards directed all his efforts. He always said that the example of Devrient had been his constant ideal, and each time that he conceived a role he had her before his eyes. The impression which she produced on the young admirer of Beethoven, notwithstanding the poverty of Bellini's music, was most profound. But when, in course of time, they represented *La Muette* at Leipsic, Wagner was quite surprised to see that the striking scenery and rapid action of this opera produced a great effect and held the public breathless without the aid of an exceptional artist like Schroeder-Devrient. That made him reflect: certainly the heroic music of Beethoven was the ideal ever present before his eyes; but was it possible for him to write something similar for the theatre? On the contrary, could he not draw inspiration from Auber and Bellini at one and the same time, and by combining their different merits, would he not arrive more quickly at the immediate and tangible success which he sought? What would be necessary to accomplish this? First to imagine an animated scene of action, then to write music easy to sing and of a nature to catch the public ear. He set himself quickly to work. He was twenty years old, had the happiest possible disposition, and was overflowing with exuberant vitality.

So breaking off from the abstract mysticism of his early youth, it was of material beauty and of woman that he undertook to sing in his second opera, *The Love-Veto*, which he conceived during a holiday sojourn at Töplitz, in Bohemia. He had borrowed the subject of this piece from Shakespeare's *Measure for Measure*, but he had totally changed the character of it, aiming only to scoff at hypocritical Puritanism, and to glorify sensual love. This piece, of a sufficiently lively and daring intrigue, in which are given full play all the juvenile passions that fermented in this youth of twenty, has the peculiarity that it forms an absolute antithesis to the preceding subject treated by Wagner; and these two operas, *The Fairies* and *The Love-Veto*, fixed the two poles between which his genius was to be evolved. As he himself has noted, the tendencies of these two dramas, so opposed to each other, will be merged in *Tannhäuser*. He means by that, the idea of sacrifice and of renouncement which triumphs in the *Flying Dutchman*, in *Lohengrin*, in *Parsifal* and the indomitable appetite for physical enjoyment which prevails in the *Walkyrie* and in *Tristan*.

During the autumn of 1834, Richard Wagner, in order to provide the necessities of life, accepted the place of director of music at the Magdeburg theatre. He commenced now to live by his art, and his new vocation pleased him very much for a while; the world behind the scenes and the jovial company of the actors, and especially the actresses, were not displeasing to one of his age and temperament. For the rest he performed his duties as well as could be desired, and during the year or more which he spent at Magdeburg, he became an excellent leader, and did his best to promote the prosperity of the theatre. For example, the director having decided to mount Auber's *Lestocq,* which opera Wagner always thought charming, the latter gave himself much trouble to render the work a success. He reinforced by several chorus singers taken from the army, the Russian battalion which comes to sustain the revolt; and thanks to this unusual number of singers he obtained an immense effect of sound, which for a few evenings, at least, attracted crowds to the theatre, — and then that was all.

Wagner continued to compose in the midst of his duties and distractions of all sorts. He had performed, under his direction, his overture to *The Fairies,* and one other which he had written in 1835 on a drama by Apel, *Christopher Columbus.* He composed at random a piece to celebrate New Year's Day of 1835, by simply using the theme of the andante from his unique symphony, and tacking on some songs from a fantastic farce entitled *The Spirit of the Mountain,* and the favor with which such productions were received confirmed him in the idea that there was no need of being conscientious and painstaking in order to insure success. How many of our composers in the best circumstances think the same thing to-day, and will never change their aim.

He thus finished setting to music the *Love-Veto,* having always in mind Auber as his model, and Schroeder-Devrient for the principal role. He had at first hoped to have this opera accepted by the leader at Leipsic, in recompense for his

treatment of *The Fairies*, but the application had been in vain,
and he was thrown back upon Magdeburg. The theatre of
this city was then directed by a man named Bethmann, who
was always on the verge of bankruptcy, notwithstanding a
small subsidy furnished by the court of Saxony, and who had
the habit of disappearing on pay-days. The troupe was in the
most precarious situation in the spring of 1836, and already
the actors were taking leave, to try their fortunes elsewhere.
Some of them, however, consented to remain, out of regard for
Wagner, and the latter made superhuman efforts to forestall
the failure. He was justly entitled to a benefit performance, to reimburse him for the expenses of a trip which
he had made the preceding year to gather in recruits for the
chorus ; but the director having borne the expense of staging
the piece, it was agreed that he should take the receipts
from the first performance, and that Wagner should have those
from the second. There were only twelve days before the close
of the season. It was nothing but rehearsals at the theatre, and
rehearsals at the artists' houses. The whole city was in a
flutter, and meanwhile nobody knew his part and everything
went at cross purposes. At the general rehearsal things
progressed pretty well, thanks to Wagner, who conducted,
gesticulated, sung and shouted for the whole company. But
at the performance (March 29, 1836), which had attracted an
immense crowd and brought large returns to the director,
absolute confusion reigned, and it was quite impossible to
make anything out of it. This was so much the worse for
the musician, who believed he had written a good work, and so
much the better for the poet, whose piece would probably have
been seized by the commissary of police, had he been able to
comprehend the details. As it was, only the title had appeared to
this functionary too free, considering that the piece was to be
played during holy week, and he had authorized the performance only on condition that the title should be changed to

The Novice of Palermo, and on the repeated assurance from
Wagner that the subject had been borrowed from a very
serious drama of Shakespeare.   Oh, the trickery of authors!
Oh, the simplicity of censors!

The second performance of *The Novice of Palermo* was
to close the season, and Wagner, whose turn it was to pocket
the receipts, had put the prices up very high.   What was
his surprise and consternation to find, a few minutes before
the rising of the curtain, that there were only three people in
the room, — his proprietors, husband and wife, and a Polish Jew
in gala costume.   At the same time, to make matters worse,
the husband of the prima donna was belaboring the first
tenor, and then his own wife, behind the scenes ; this resulted
in the whole troupe taking sides, and engaging in a rough
and tumble fight, which rendered them all quite unable to
appear before the public.   The curtain rose, and the manager
solemnly announced to the three spectators that, owing to
unforeseen difficulties, the performance could not take place.

In the humorous account which Wagner has given of this
failure, and of the previous experiences of *The Novice of
Palermo*, he shows that these misfortunes did not in the least
shake his confidence in making a start.   Besides, he was not
criticised over harshly.   The Magdeburg *Journal*, while deploring the haste brought to bear on the rehearsals, and the final
result, — a hurried execution, where the actors did not even
know their parts — judged that if the composer were to have
his opera performed in a more important city, and under more
favorable circumstances, he would stand good chance of success.   "There are many good qualities in it," said the writer.
"What pleases me is that it vibrates ; it is true music, and true
melody, such as one would wish to find oftener in the work
of our composers."   In reality, Wagner had come so much
under the influence of French and Italian musicians, especially
Auber and Bellini, that very little of the German influence

was left, and it was that, no doubt, which caused him to be so well received in his own country.

About this time, Richard Wagner, relying on the approbation given to his opera, resolved to make another attempt to get *The Novice of Palermo* played at Leipsic. He remembered with satisfaction that the director of the theatre at this city (the same Ringelhardt) had a young daughter; and in order the better to persuade him, he asked the director to reflect what an immense advantage it would be for his daughter to make her debut in the pretty role of a young girl in this new opera. Unhappily the director was not so easily duped as the commissary at Magdeburg, and after going through the piece, he severely replied to the author: "I do not know whether or not the magistrate of Leipsic would authorize the performance of a work like that, and I doubt it very much, through respect for his authority; but in any case, understand, sir, that a person like my daughter would not figure in it." Wagner beat a retreat before this touchy parent, and presented his work next at Berlin, not at the Royal Opera, but at the more modest Residenz-Theatre, where he was pleasantly received, without obtaining anything. It was on this short visit to Berlin that he saw Spontini for the first time, directing a performance of *Fernando Cortez*. He was much struck by the effect which the old master obtained by bringing out the rhythm very strong, and making the evolutions on the stage to correspond with a mathematical precision. But more than all, the score of *Fernando Cortez* produced on him a deep impression, which was still very vivid when, two years later, he undertook the composition of *Rienzi*.

Now *The Novice of Palermo* was tossed about from right to left, and Wagner, who had left nothing but debts behind him at Magdeburg, solicited a place with his old friend Dorn, now precentor and director of religious music in the little Rus-

sian town of Riga.[1]   But Wagner was not the only one to be
provided for.   He requested employment for his fiancée also,
the pretty comedienne, Wilhelmina Planer, with whom he
had fallen in love at Magdeburg.   They had been betrothed
for a long time, but he had not married her, for want of
money.   In the meantime, as she was engaged in the capacity
of leading lady at Königsberg, he followed her to that little
town, with the intention of becoming leader of the orchestra,
and there he organized some concerts at the theatre.   At
last he obtained the desired position, and on November 24,
1836, he married Minna Planer.   "I was in love," he wrote
later, in a letter to his friends.   "I married through obstinacy,
and rendered unhappy myself and another, tormented by the
weariness of a domestic life for which I had not the bare
necessities.   It was thus that I fell into poverty, the effects
of which kill so many thousands."   He stayed only a year
at Königsberg, a prey to a thousand anxieties, unhappy, a
torment to himself and to others, writing meanwhile but two
overtures, one on *Rule Britannia*, and another entitled
Polonia.   Then he went to Riga, where Dorn had been able
to obtain a place for his wife at the theatre, another for his
sister-in-law, Theresa Planer, and for Wagner himself the
position of first director of music.   At first he was delighted
with a post so much more profitable than those which he had
hitherto occupied.   He gave ten concerts, in which he had
performed, not without success, his overture on *Christopher
Columbus*, and that on *Rule Britannia*.   He also wrote
several airs, and chose *Norma* to be performed at his benefit,
on Dec. 11, 1837.[2]

---

[1] He will utilize later a religious melody from *The Novice of Palermo* to express
in Tannhäuser the respect and awe of the Pilgrims, admitted to the presence of the
holy father.   It is the melody which the wind and stringed instruments repeat alternately in the introduction to the third act.

[2] His admiration for Bellini reached its highest point in giving vent to his

Then all at once he took a dislike to his duties, at the same time that he felt awaken within him the first scruples of his artist's conscience. In writing his previous works, as he said himself, he had not shown himself scrupulous in the choice of means employed to bear away success. But one day, while engaged in composing the score of an opera comique in two acts, *The Happy Family of Bears*, after a tale from *The Arabian Nights*, he paused in disgust, re-read his pieces, and perceived that he was again fairly on his way to the composition of music à la Adam. He laid aside his work, feeling deeply hurt at the discovery. From that day, he despised the position of leader of an orchestra in a provincial town, facing a public unqualified to judge any new work, because it never heard anything except works with a reputation already made ; and therefore, in order to guard against a weakness which might drive him to use means of execution close at hand, he decided to undertake a work of proportions too vast to admit of its being mounted in a small theatre. And since it was from Paris that all the operas came, which were then applauded in Germany, he turned his eyes towards Paris, and longed to go there and start afresh.

From the time that he was at Königsberg, and, poor and miserable, saw dance before his eyes the three hundred thousand francs which Meyerbeer was said to have gained from *The Huguenots*, he had been possessed with a mad desire

feelings in an article published in the *Spectator* of Riga, Dec., 1837. " The song, the song, and still the song, O Germans. The song is the language by which mankind should communicate one with another, and one will not understand you if this language is not made and kept as arbitrary as any other cultivated language should be. That which is bad in Bellini, each one of your village schoolmasters will do it better. If Bellini had served his apprenticeship with a German village schoolmaster, he would probably have learned it better, but he would have unlearned the art of song." Read the entire article translated in the *Wagnerian Review* of Paris (Feb., 1886). One may recall in this connection the keen *boutade* of Rossini, who said to Bellini himself, " It is very fortunate, *Vincenzo caro*, that you do not know music, for if you knew it, you would make it very badly."

to try his fortunes at Paris. He had just fancied that he had found a good subject for an opera in a novel by Heinrich König, *La Grande Fiancée*. He had immediately outlined the plot, and sent it to Scribe, hoping that the latter would not be too much occupied to write the poem, and obtain an acceptance at the opera. Naturally, he never heard a word on the subject from Scribe; so, when, in reading Bulwer's *Rienzi*, he believed that he had discovered therein a subject preferable to the preceding one, he took good care not to repeat his blunder. He undertook to make the whole thing himself, poem, score and all.[1]

It was during the summer of 1838 that he commenced to write the poem of *Rienzi;* and he put into it so much the more ardor, from the wild desire which he had to be freed as by a lightning stroke, from the evils of a precarious existence. On returning to Riga, he took lodgings in a lonely place outside the ramparts, in order to break away more completely from the paltriness of the theatrical life, and devote himself more thoroughly to the composition of his opera. By a happy coincidence, he was at that time teaching his opera troupe Mehul's *Joseph*, which, he says, elevated his thoughts, and aided him in correcting some past blunders. It was not that in undertaking *Rienzi* he had dreamed in the least of departing from the usual forms of the opera, but in writing the poem he had endeavored to make it less commonplace than the ordinary libretto; and as for the music, he wished to compose a great work, strong, noble, — in a word, the exact

---

[1] Later on, when he was chapel-master at Dresden, with Reissiger, as the latter attributed the non-success of his music to the fact that his librettos had been poor, Wagner offered to rhyme for him his old plot of *La Grande Fiancée*. But Reissiger feeling some hesitation about setting to music a poem which Richard Wagner had renounced, it was finally inherited by Kittl, director of the Prague Conservatory; and his opera was represented at Prague on the 19th of Feb., 1848, under the title of *Bianca e Giuseppe, or The French at Nice*. It had some success, for it was put on again in 1868 and 1870, and they played it at Frankfort in 1873.

opposite of what he had hitherto done. He himself has very well expressed the singular state in which he then found himself; how the grand opera was like a glass through which he looked at everything, and outside of which he perceived nothing clearly. In all the different parts of the opera, it was, to be sure, his subject which guided him primarily; but that subject he determined, unconsciously, according to the only form which then floated before his eyes, that of the grand opera.

Full of ardor for his work, he composed without ceasing during the whole winter, so that by the spring of 1839 he had finished the first two acts of *Rienzi*. But at that moment the engagement which he had at the theatre at Riga expired; and as he was completely disgusted with running about from town to town in the quality of orchestral leader, and as, moreover, the poet Karl de Holtei was going to give up the direction of the theatre to a simple tenor, he did not hesitate. He got together a little money, returned to Königsberg, where he made a mighty effort to pay his debts, then induced his wife to depart with him for Paris, where he knew absolutely nobody. It was the unknown, but the unknown which might in a short time be fortune and glory — with *Rienzi*.

THE SLEEP OF BRUNEHILD.
From the Schultze & Müller Nibelungen-Ring, 1881.

CHAPTER II

NSTEAD of taking the overland route, and probably for economy's sake, Wagner embarked with his wife and dog, a magnificent Newfoundland, on a vessel sailing between Pillau and London. The voyage, which lasted for more than four weeks, and was fraught with peril, remained always in his memory. Three times, off the coast of Norway, the vessel encountered a frightful tempest, which forced the captain to take refuge in the nearest port.

This passage through the narrows by the Norwegian coast made a very vivid impression on his imagination, and it was in the midst of the raging elements that he heard the sailors sing with terror that legend of *The Flying Dutchman*, which took so strong a hold upon him. Wagner spent eight days in London doing nothing but roam about the city. He was much interested by his visit to Parliament, but not once did he step inside a theatre. Then he crossed the channel.

Once landed at Boulogne, he learned that Meyerbeer was spending a season there for the sea-bathing, and he lingered about the place for a whole month, in order to make the acquaintance of the celebrated composer, and to gain some assistance from him. Meyerbeer received his compatriot very kindly. He examined the two completed acts of *Rienzi*, declared himself pleased with them, and asked the young

24

author if he had the wherewithal to live comfortably while he was trying his fortune in Paris. On receiving a negative reply, he gravely shook his head; nevertheless, he promised Wagner to aid him as much as it might lie in his power, but he frankly warned him that in a case of that kind, letters could scarcely be of much avail, whereas personal persistence, day after day, could not fail to have its effect. Having said this, he gave him some letters of recommendation to Anténor Jolly, director of the Renaissance, which at that time produced both dramas and opera-comique; to Léon Pillet, director of the Opera, the editor Schlesinger, and Habeneck. In fact, all that Wagner was able to accomplish in Paris, he owed to these gentlemen, and indirectly to Meyerbeer. "Do you know what makes me mistrustful of this young man?" said Heinrich Heine. "It is because Meyerbeer recommends him." And this shaft, as cutting for the protégé as for the protector, is all he has ever let fall with regard to Richard Wagner.

Wagner arrived at Paris in the month of September, 1839, and took a furnished apartment in the rue de la Tonnellerie, near the Halles, in a quarter little haunted by artists, but where he could live very cheaply. He commenced immediately his round of visits in Paris. Everywhere he saw the doors open to him, thanks to the patronage of Meyerbeer, and each evening he returned to his lodgings, delighted with the reception which he had met on every hand, and sure of immediate success. Then the admirable stage arrangements at the Opera increased his desire to see *Rienzi* very soon performed there. He did not for an instant doubt his success, and he did not believe it could be long in coming. So he hastened to finish this work, at the price of daily privations. He saw everything equally rose-colored on the part of the Renaissance, where the director, out of regard for Meyerbeer, had agreed to accept his unfortunate *Novice of Palermo*, so quickly dispatched in an evening at Magdeburg.

Dumersan, the vaudevilliste, had been charged with translating the poem, and had performed his task so well, that these new verses appeared to Wagner to adapt themselves better to his music than those which he had written himself. Finally the young musician believed himself so sure of success, with an opera well suited to the French taste, upon a subject a little light, that he did not hesitate to leave his old quarters at the Halles, and establish himself at No. 25 rue du Helder, in the heart of elegant and artistic Paris. Schlesinger, on his side, had not been backward in helping the protégé of Meyerbeer. He obtained a promise from Habeneck that the Société des Concerts du Conservatoire would try an overture, which his young friend, desiring to put the whole drama to music, had undertaken to compose for Goethe's *Faust;* and Wagner, highly pleased with the good news, worked away at it with joy and enthusiasm.

Wagner had lived in Paris only six months, — for all this happened during the early part of 1840, — and he already felt sure of having an opera played at the Renaissance, and an overture performed at the Conservatoire, while awaiting *Rienzi.* All at once the scene changed. He had finished his overture in the month of February, they tried it on the last of March, and the editor Schlesinger hastened to insert in the *Gazette Musicale*, the following little notice: "An overture by a young German composer of very remarkable talent, M. Wagner, has just been rehearsed by the orchestra of the Conservatoire, and has won unanimous applause. We hope to hear it immediately, and we will render an account of it." The truth was, that the performers had declared this overture "a long enigma," and had decided not to play it. There remained *The Novice of Palermo*, the performance of which was looked for from day to day. One morning, towards the middle of April, Anténor Jolly assembled all his artists and employés, and announced to them that he was at the end of his resources, and that notwithstanding the recent success of *The Chaste Susanna*, he found himself under the necessity of closing the theatre.

It is impossible to say exactly what the overture to *Faust* was worth at that time, since Wagner completely changed it, after having finished the *Rheingold*, but it is very difficult to believe that it was inferior to those of *Rienzi*, or *The Flying Dutchman*, which are contemporaneous; and when one reflects that the society executed at about the same time an overture to *Jeanne d'Arc*, by Moschelés, it seems that it might have shown itself more hospitable towards Richard Wagner. The latter, quite discomfited, laid aside his overture, which was performed after a fashion at Dresden, in 1844, and he never thought any more about completing his musical *Faust*. It is strictly true that if we have only an overture in place of a complete score of *Faust*, we are indebted for this loss to the gold-laced musicians of the Conservatoire in 1840.[1]

One other attempt still remained to miscarry. Paris was then occupying herself with the affairs of Poland, and a grand performance for the benefit of the Poles out of work, had been organized at the theatre of the Renaissance, through the labors of Princess Czartoryska, who had recruited soloists and chorus singers from the fashionable world, and at whose house they had rehearsed all winter. The celebration was fixed for

[1] Wagner altered this overture at Zurich in 1865. As an inscription, he has put the following lines from Goethe's drama: "The God who inhabits my soul can stir it unto its very depths, but he who reigns without me can awaken no response in my breast. Thus existence is a burden to me, I long for death, and life is odious to me." In its final form, this overture, bearing a strong impress of sorrow and passion, is a creation of the first rank, a work which stands by itself. It is not treated, indeed, in long crescendo, like the magnificent overtures of *The Flying Dutchman*, of *Tannhäuser* and *The Meistersinger*. It is of a conception not more admirable, but more free, which permits him to follow closely all the phases of the drama, and to interpret them with a striking truthfulness. A masterpiece, in a word, only comparable to the overture to *Faust*, which Schumann wrote in 1853.

Friday, the 3d of March, and they were to represent a Duc de Guise, who was no other than the Henry III and his court, by Dumas, arranged as an opera by a noble amateur, and set to music by the young Flotow. The principal interpreter was quite a young girl, called Anna de la Grange, who was to render her name famous. Wagner, recalling the overture of *Polonia* which he had composed, and which he had vainly proposed to the *Concerts Valentino*, carried it bravely to the leader of the orchestra at the theatre, a man named Duvinage, and the latter promised to look at it; but nothing could be done for a poor devil of a musician in the midst of this busy and fashionable world, and his overture was not even discussed.[1]

Wagner saw vanish in an instant all his various chances for success. Moreover, he had exhausted his resources while laboring to become famous, and had been obliged to buy on credit all the furniture necessary to fill his new lodgings. But

[1] Wagner quitted Paris without reclaiming this overture; what was his surprise on learning, forty years later, that it was in the hands of M. Pasdeloup. One of his friends at Paris undertook to trace the matter back, and after a minute and careful research, he succeeded in getting at the facts. Behold through what a series of adventures *Polonia* was obliged to pass. Duvinage had kept the unclaimed overture for nearly twenty years, until one fine day, M. Henri Litolff, who gave piano lessons to his daughter (now Mme. Theodore Dubois), begged him for the overture, and Duvinage gave it to him. Litolff, no doubt with the best intentions, sent it immediately to M. Arban, who wished to play it at some Casino concerts, and the latter, in order to try it, had ordered the copyist of the Italian theatre, to separate it into several parts. Then Arban, as well as the copyist, had totally forgotten it, so that it got mixed in with a mass of old papers of Ventadour; and the editor Choudens, having bought all this music in the lump, after the failure of the director of *Escudier* (April, 1879), was quite surprised to discover a manuscript by Wagner among the sheets of unclassified music. He spoke of this overture to M. Pasdeloup, who borrowed it, never played it, and in his turn, put it in the rubbish pile, when it was reclaimed from him, in Wagner's name, first by the person who made all these researches, then by M. Nuitter. It was thus that, in 1881, Wagner regained possession of a work lost since 1841, and that he arranged to have it performed that year to celebrate his wife's birthday. He thanked his friends in Paris very warmly for the pains which they had taken in the matter.

before paying for his furniture it was necessary that he should earn means of support for himself and wife. There was no longer any dog to care for: he had been stolen before they moved to rue du Helder.

The editor Schlesinger was still his providence. He ordered several articles of him for his journal, the *Revue et Gazette Musicale*, of which the first, "On German Music," appeared in the month of July, 1840. Then, as he had come into possession of the score of *La Favorite*, performed in December of the same year, he gave Wagner the task of making a transcription of it for the piano,—a thankless undertaking certainly, if not a complicated one ; but Wagner was only too happy to do anything that would enable him to exist. He continued to knock at every door, and after repeatedly importuning the director of the Variétés, and possibly with the aid of Dumersan, the translator of *The Novice of Palermo*, he was asked to set to music a vaudeville which this same Dumersan had just written with Dupeuty, *La Descente de la Courtille* ; but at the first rehearsal the actors declared his music impossible to execute, and they were obliged to renounce it. This carnival folly was played Jan. 20th, 1841, and did not even contain the song, *Allons à la Courtille*, popular at the moment, and which everybody, one after another, attributed to Wagner: a double error, so it appears.

Among other things, he tried composing ballads for French words. He aspired to the fame of Madame Loïsa Puget, to the reputation of Schubert, and put to music first a translation, made expressly for him, of the *Two Grenadiers*, by Heinrich Heine, a composition somewhat labored, very inferior to that which Schumann had written the previous year for the same poem, and which the artists did not like. Afterwards he wrote *L'Attente*, by Victor Hugo, *Mignonne*, by Ronsard, *Dors, mon Enfant*, all of them simple and charming within their small limits, and which we admire to-day, but which he

was not able to have performed then, for lack of singers to
sing them, and publishers to publish them.   They were,
literally, too good for the public taste.   He did get a
small return from *Mignonne* when it was printed in the
Gazette Musicale ; and this melody was afterwards republished
with the two others in the supplement of Lewald's *L'Europa*.
In this connection it should be noticed in what pressing
terms Wagner, in a letter dated April 1841, submits these
three songs to the editor of the journal, and asks that he
shall be paid for them as quickly and as much as possible,
since the price for such productions varied from five to nine
florins ($2.00 to $3.75).

Meanwhile, his articles, which showed an original and
energetic personality, were having quite a success in a limited
circle, and his story entitled *A Pilgrimage to Beethoven*, published toward the end of 1840, was such a striking mixture
of poetry and jest, enthusiasm and bitterness, that Berlioz, a
good judge of such things, thought it worthy of a review in
the *Journal des Débats*.   He gives an account of a concert
organized by the *Revue et Gazette Musicale*, that indefatigable
journal which gives so many good things to its subscribers, —
beautiful concerts, good criticisms, fine portraits of artists,
and charming stories; and he adds, " For a long time to
come will be read one by M. Wagner, entitled *A Pilgrimage
to Beethoven*." [1]   Little did Berlioz know how truly he spoke.

Whilst working for Schlesinger he pursued without ceasing the composition of *Rienzi*, aiming no longer at the Opera
of Paris,— he denies afterwards ever having thought of it,— but
at the Dresden Opera, where there were artists of the first

---

[1] The articles by Wagner for the *Gazette Musicale* were translated by Dues-
berg, who was intrusted with editing all the German stories for this journal.   As
for knowing how much his articles or his arrangements paid him, that would be
quite impossible ; for Wagner, always short of money, has perhaps received four or
five times the price stipulated for his labor.

rank, Schroeder-Devrient, Tichatschek, etc.; he arrived at the end of his task in November, 1840. Then, encouraged by his success as an author, and driven by the direst poverty, he wrote with all his might to earn a living.

It was just at this time, in the beginning of 1841, that he published the story, so bitter and so sad, called *A Foreign Musician in Paris*, where, putting himself in the scene, with his well-loved Newfoundland dog, he describes with a virulent pen, the hopes which he had foolishly cherished, all the disappointments which he had encountered, including the loss of his dog, before arriving at the final discouragement, awaiting the liberating death of his hero. Said he, in speaking of this hero, who is no other than himself, " He was an excellent man, a worthy musician, born in a little town of Germany, died at Paris, where he had suffered so much. Possessed of a great tenderness of heart, he never could see the unhappy horses maltreated in the streets of Paris, without shedding tears. Naturally gentle, he suffered himself without anger to be dispossessed, by the gamins, of his share of the narrow sidewalks of the capital. Unhappily he joined to all that, the conscience of an artist of scrupulous delicacy. He was ambitious, without talent for intrigue. Moreover, in his youth he had once seen Beethoven, and this excess of good fortune had so turned his head, that he had never been able to regain his balance during his stay in Paris." This imaginary person is so plainly copied from himself, with his love for animals, that in the dialogue which follows, and which one would call inspired by the *Neveu de Rameau*, as much from the form as from the place of the scene, the *café de la Rotonde*, one recognizes perfectly all that he undertook to do in Paris, to no purpose; long waits in the ante-rooms of the directors, melodies written in the style of Schubert which nobody was willing to try; refusal of an overture composed by a disciple of Beethoven, by those who seemed most to admire that grand master, etc. To which a sceptical and disillusioned friend, into whose mouth he has put some of the counsels which Meyerbeer had given him, responds with warmth, "Allow me to interrupt you. Beethoven is deified, you are perfectly right, but mark well that his reputation and his name are now accepted and permanent things. Give an idea that a piece proceeds from that great master, and his name will be a talisman powerful enough to reveal beauties on the instant, and as if by magic ; but substitute for that name any other, and you will never be able to attract the concert director's attention to the most brilliant passages of that same piece." Wagner rebelled at this idea.

Meanwhile, Maurice Schlesinger, thinking only of how he could console the poor musician for his ill-luck at the Conservatoire, decided to have a composition by him performed at one of the concerts which the *Gazette Musicale* offered its subscribers ; and this fine project was put in execution on Thursday, February 4, 1841. His choice was fixed on the overture of *Columbus*, which was modestly put at the head of the program. Naturally it was noticed in the same journal of Schlesinger's. "Does this piece, which has rather the character and form of an introduction," said the critic Henri Blanchard, "deserve the name of overture, which the author so well defined recently in his articles in the *Gazette Musicale?* Has he wished to depict, by the high tremulo of the violins, the infinity of the deep, of the horizon which seemed without limit to the companions of the celebrated navigator? The appearance of the brass instruments recurs too uniformly and too persistently ; besides, their discordance, which shocks trained and sensitive ears, prevents a proper appreciation of M. Wagner's composition, which notwithstanding this misfortune, has appeared to us the work of an artist having large ideas, and knowing well the resources of modern instrumentation."

Thus it is curious to observe that in this work, written at the age of twenty-two, Wagner already made use of the high tremulo of the violins, and of the sharp attacks of the brasses, which have since served him so often and so marvelously.

This very modest execution was slightly echoed in Germany, thanks to Schumann, who mentioned the concert in his journal, calling attention to the fact that among the numbers on the program there was an overture by Richard Wagner, "a young Saxon," wrote he, "who remained silent for a long time, and who, by good luck, has begun to compose again." Encouraged by this little success, Wagner hastened to send his overture to London, hoping that Jullien might perform it in his promenade concerts; but the eccentric leader did not want it, and when the postman of the coach establishment of Lafitte and Caillard brought back the roll to the composer, the latter was too poor to pay for carrying it from London to Paris, and the postman calmly replaced the roll in his pack; thus was the overture lost forever.[1]

Wagner, in his distress, went so far as to present himself as chorus singer at a little theatre in the boulevard. "I came off," said he, "still worse than Berlioz, when he found himself in a similar situation. The leader of the orchestra, whose duty it was to examine me, suddenly discovered that I knew nothing at all about singing, and declared that he had nothing there for me."

Happily for him, there was at that time in Paris quite a numerous colony of Germans — artists, scholars, literary men — for the most part poor enough, but full of kindly feeling, and who certainly contributed to sustain Wagner and his wife through that terrible winter. But outside of that circle he felt

---

[1] This unhappy incident was related by Wagner himself in 1880, to one of his friends, who wished to find out what could have become of the overture during the forty years. The coaches existed no more; after having searched all over Paris, he discovered that the old M. Caillard, very aged, but in his right mind, was living next door to him. He determined to call on him, neglected it for several days, and when he went down one morning, he saw that they had put black on the neighboring house. He knew then that the old man was dead.

himself completely isolated in Paris, and it was among musicians that he counted the fewest friends, each busying himself with his own affairs, and having no time to join fortunes with another. Besides, he did not feel himself drawn toward any one of them. Of Meyerbeer, then sovereign master at the Opera, with *Robert le Diable* and *Les Huguenots*, he had from the first, without showing it, the opinion which he afterwards expressed, when he believed that such sentiments would no longer hinder any one from distinguishing between the man and the artist. As for Halévy, he judged that his lofty enthusiasm had lasted just long enough to obtain for him a great success, after which he had thought only of making a fortune out of his operas, imitating the negligence and indifference of Auber. Alas! if he had only been able, like his model, to acquire an appearance of style, appreciable in the loosest productions. As to Auber himself, he did not regard him more favorably, although at the time of *La Muette* he had defended him out of opposition to Rossini and the Italian school. He had no sympathy with him; however, he attempted once to praise him in the *Gazette Musicale*, to the detriment of Donizetti, Rossini, etc., but the director, Edouard Monnais, refused his article, not wishing to have French patriotism mixed up with a question purely musical, or rather commercial, since Schlesinger, publishing at the same time *La Muette*, *Guillaume Tell*, and *La Favorite*, desired that his journal should extol equally the three composers. The only one whom Wagner admired, in spite of his repellant nature, was Berlioz. "There is between him," said he, "and his colleagues in Paris, this essential difference, that he does not compose his music for money. But he cannot write for pure art either; the whole sense of beauty escapes him. He stands quite by himself in his peculiar line; he has nobody on his side except a troop of adorers who, stupidly, and without the least judgment, salute him as the creator of a brand-new system of music, and have completely turned his head. With this exception everybody shuns him as a madman."

It was at Paris that he for the first time met Franz Liszt, and the first relations between these two artists, who in course of time became such great friends, were most reserved, and by no means promising. Wagner showed a frank disdain for the noisy reputation of the great pianist. He held mere virtuosity in contempt, and felt that Liszt suffered himself to be governed by the public, even to giving proof of the worst possible taste, even to executing, for example, a fantasia on *Robert le Diable* at a concert organized for the purpose of raising a monument to Beethoven. He deplored the difference between the situation of a dramatic composer who can only disclose himself to an audience partly composed of amateurs, and that of a virtuoso, who easily triumphs before no matter what assembly. Then he compared himself with the celebrated pianist, and came to regard his own isolation before the public, not as an evil, but as a blessing, as a safeguard against the dangerous friendship of outsiders. And when he had turned these ideas well around in his mind, he went up to his room, and there, all alone, put them on paper. He boldly entitled this article *The Vocation of the Virtuoso and the Independence of the Composer*, and carried it to the *Gazette Musicale*, where it appeared in 1840. Out of conceit with the musical world of Paris, he renounced in these moments what had been his fondest hope, to conquer Paris, and he fell into a painful despondency, wearied alike by the performances of Liszt and Chopin, the songs of Duprez and of Mme. Dorus-Gras, the everlasting trills of Rubini. Duprez and Rubini had completely disgusted him with the bad music which they wrote ordinarily, and which was confidently applauded by an audience which called itself select, being gathered from the wealth and aristocracy of Paris. He found no interest in the luxurious representations at the opera, which, to be sure, he frequented but little, for lack of money, and saw there only a pretext for staging and scenery. " Whoever," said he, " has seen Halévy's *La Juive*, only in a German town, will never succeed in picturing to himself how and why that work has been able to charm the Parisians." The Opera Comique, on the whole, would have pleased him better than the Academy of Music and the Italiens, at least on account of the singers ; but everything that was written for the theatre then seemed to him absolutely detestable. "Where has fled, alas! the grace of Méhul, of Nicolai, of Boïeldieu, and the young Auber, before the ignoble quadrille-rhythms which are the rage at present?"

Notwithstanding a few passing gratifications, like the success of an article, or the execution of an overture, which brought small relief to his poverty, Wagner, crushed in his aspirations, suffered keenly in every way from the hardships and privations of the material life and from the cruel deceptions of a legitimate self-love. A ray of light suddenly brightened his existence, and the down-trodden artist felt a new life awaken within him. With the letter of recommendation from Meyerbeer to Habeneck, he had found a ready welcome at the Conservatoire, and the concerts of the Conservatoire, consecrated to the worship of Beethoven, brought him sweet consolation. He could at least attend the rehearsals, and each time he delighted in a symphony by Beethoven, rendered to perfection. That was the only thing, he said, which gave him an unalloyed satisfaction. And behold one day, he hears, oh marvellous! an incomparable execution of the *Choral Symphony*, the like of which he had never even suspected at the concerts of the Gewandhaus at Leipsic. Aroused, enchanted, breathless with enthusiasm, he feels himself carried back ten years in listening to this work, the favorite of his adolescence, and he thinks now to understand it for the first time, so deeply does he penetrate into its infinite beauties.

He feels a light enter his soul, he banishes the idea of creeping along in the beaten paths of *Rienzi*, he rejoices in being spurned by the Académie de Musique, where he would be forever lost in a style inferior and conventional; he perceives a glimpse of the ideal of his life in this masterpiece of Beethoven.[1] "It was," said he, "as if a scale had fallen from my eyes, as if a curtain had just been lifted."

He did not know which to admire most, the admirable application of the performers, or the energy displayed by Habeneck, who, after having worked all one winter on this symphony without succeeding in making it any clearer to his orchestra, had kept at it for two or three winters, and never left it until it had thoroughly penetrated the sensibilities of his musicians.

"Besides," adds he, "Habeneck was a leader of the old school; he was unmistakably the master, and all obeyed him." As an additional good fortune, *Der Freischütz*, in its original form, was represented for the first time in Paris, on the 7th of June, 1841, a *Freischütz* modified, it is true, by the laws of the French Grand Opera, augmented by recitatives and ballets, but without a note of it changed, and put on the stage with a religious respect by Berlioz; the *Freischütz*, in short, to which he had owed the first ravings of his youth. Ah! this time he hesitates no longer, and this double apparition of the German fatherland incarnate in Beethoven and in Weber awakens in the exile, as by a miracle, all his energy.

"Oh, my splendid fatherland, how must I love thee, how must I dream of thee, were it only that *Der Freischütz* was born under thy skies! How must I love the German people

---

[1] The concerts of the Conservatoire entered on their thirteenth year in 1840. There were then eight concerts in the season, one every fortnight, starting from January. It was at the concert of the 8th of March, 1840, that Wagner first heard the *Choral Symphony*, and he heard it again on the 2d of March, 1841, and the 9th of Jan., 1842, for they played it once a year during the three winters that he spent in Paris. After that, they did not play it again until 1849,

which loves *Der Freischütz;* which believes even yet in the
wonders of the most simple of the legends, which feels even
yet, in its manhood, the mysterious and fascinating terrors
which agitated its youthful breast!   Oh, thou bright dream of
Germany!   Reveries of the woods, reveries of the evening,
of the stars, of the moon, of the village bell which sounds the
curfew!   How happy is he who can comprehend and believe,
feel, dream, and ramble with thee."[1]

And immediately he put himself to work.   He felt that he
must give vent to the ideas which were confusedly boiling
up in his brain, and which he had already put on paper, auda-
ciously lending them to the author of *Fidelio*, in his imaginary
visit to Beethoven.

" The sounds of the instruments, although it is not possible
to state their true signification, pre-existed in the primitive
world, as organs of created nature, and even before there
were men on the earth to receive these vague harmonies.   But
it is quite otherwise with the genius of the human voice ; that is
the direct interpreter of the human heart, and explains its
sensations, abstract and personal.   Its domain, then, is essentially limited, but its manifestations are always clear and precise.   Now unite these two elements; construe the vague and
abrupt sentiments of nature by the language of the instruments, in opposition to the positive ideas of the soul, as represented by the human voice; and the latter will exercise a
luminous influence over the former, by regulating their outbursts, and moderating their violence.   Then the human
heart, opening to receive these complex emotions, enlarged
and expanded by these infinite and delicious presentiments,
will receive with enthusiasm, with conviction, this species of
intimate revelation of the supernatural world.

"The opera is not my business (let us not forget that it is
Beethoven who is supposed to be speaking) ; at least, I do not

---

[1] Richard Wagner d'après lui-même, p. 131.

know of a theatre in the world for which I would engage to compose a new work. If I were to write a score conforming to my own instincts, nobody would listen to it, for I would put into it no little airs, nor duets, nor any of that conventional encumbrance which serves at present in the construction of an opera, and that which I would put in its place would shock the singers no less than the public. They know only the delusion and the musical emptiness disguised under brilliant exteriors, the nothingness arrayed in tinsel. He who would write a lyric drama truly worthy of the name, will pass for a madman, and he would be one indeed, were he to expose his work to the criticism of the public, instead of keeping it to himself."

And that which Beethoven apparently would not have dared to attempt, Wagner undertook. A feeling of rebellion against the destiny which overpowered him, had made him a writer; at that time he was on the point of giving himself up to satirical writing, but the awakening of his conscience and the realization of his ability, led him to return to his natural calling, and to devote himself to music. During nine months he had made only common arrangements of operas, and written some magazine articles, which appeared at Paris in the *Gazette Musicale*, at Dresden in the *Courrier du soir*, or in *l'Europa* by Auguste Lewald, to which he sent, under the pseudonym of Freudenfeuer, a series of letters entitled now *Parisian Amusements*, and now *The Misfortunes of a German at Paris.*[1]

For a moment he had believed that fortune was going to

---

[1] In one of these articles he rails good-naturedly at Scribe, whom he represents taking his morning chocolate and giving audience to a number of visitors, while carrying on at the same time the construction of twenty pieces with as many different collaborators. In another, he speaks at length of Berlioz, whom he designates as a genial musician. He says, "He who would listen to his music must put himself out to go to him, for he will not find it anywhere else, not even in the places where one encounters Mozart and Musard side by side."

return to him with Meyerbeer. The latter returned to Paris just as Wagner had reached the last stage of his misery. He took pity on the young German, and recommended him to Leon Pillet, with so much persistence, that Pillet allowed Wagner to entertain the hope of writing a score for the opera. This time Richard Wagner could not contain his joy. He went to his home in a fever, and took no rest until he had finished at least the outline of the work, for which he already caught a glimpse of the most marvellous stage-setting, — such as could not be realized except in Paris.

After having obtained permission from Heinrich Heine to utilize the treatment which he had made of an English piece of the same title, he wrote with good success the rough sketch of *The Flying Dutchman*, which legend he had heard from the sailors on the open sea, at the height of the tempest. He made all haste to carry the sketch to Leon Pillet. But Meyerbeer had departed in the interval, and the director, struck by the poetic coloring and the originality of the subject, proposed simply to buy it of him, and get somebody else to set it to music. It would be quite to his advantage, added this seeming saint, as such an opera could not be put on the stage for four or five years, owing to previous arrangements. Now Wagner was tired of hawking himself about on all sides ; whereas, having before him all the necessary time, he could compose another, and easily console himself for this trifling sacrifice. Spent with fatigue, Wagner felt that it would be useless to argue, and replied that he would reflect. While he was reflecting, he learned that Leon Pillet had already spoken of this sketch as belonging to himself, and that if he did not give it up with good grace, he would probably be relieved of it through trickery. After all, the money which he would receive in exchange, would insure his existence for a little time, at least, and permit him to compose with a mind free from care, since he had decided to return to music. Therefore, reserving all rights in Germany, he accepted Leon Pillet's proposition and sold his sketch for five hundred francs.[1]

So then he threw criticism to the winds, and devoted himself to composition. The spring of 1841 was at hand; as much to flee his creditors, who were becoming unmanageable, as to be able to compose with more freedom, far from the annoyances and bustle of the city, he went to live at Meudon, near some fine woods which attracted him, in a little house, partially occupied by the proprietor, an old man of eighty, who looked no more than forty; an ardent legitimist, who loved to talk about the ancient court, and who had lost at the revolution of July a pension on the royal exchequer of a thousand francs. He occupied himself with painting pictures, execrable, it is true, but Wagner felt reassured, since painting was not a noisy trade.

Behold then, one fine day, as he is serenely tasting the tranquillity of the country, he hears appalling sounds proceeding from the cellar. He hastens to the spot, and finds the old man engaged in manufacturing a machine to combine the sounds of the harp with those of the piano; the painter was a collector and inventor of instruments! Wagner had a great deal of difficulty in dissuading him from this abominable combination, but he finally succeeded, and was able to proceed in peace with the composition of *The Flying Dutchman*. His first idea had been to treat this subject as a concert piece with a single scene, a "dramatic ballad"; he now took it in hand again, cut it up into three acts for the theatre, and the poem once completed, he set to work on the music. But when he

---

[1] *The Flying Dutchman*, arranged as a French opera in two acts by Paul Foucher, and become *Le Vaisseau Fantôme*, with music by Diestch, was performed at the Opera on Nov. 9, 1842. Wagner had already left Paris, and only learned from a distance of its failure, which, it must be confessed, gave him a certain satisfaction; it was played only eleven times.

found himself face to face with the piano, which he had
brought with him for his work, he was seized with a painful
disquietude; after so many months spent in writing, in criticis-
ing or arranging the works of others, was he himself still capable
of composing? He walked about the instrument with a veritable anguish. At length he opened it, tried it, and produced
at the first effort the Spinning Song and the Chorus of Sailors.
Wild with joy, he jumped up, and raised to heaven a cry of
triumph; he was a musician forever! In seven weeks the
whole opera was composed; but when he had arrived thus far,
material annoyances again overtook him, and although he had
the overture nearly finished in his head, he was obliged to wait
two long months before he could put it on paper.

Were not the unpleasant predictions, which the preceding
year he had put into the mouth of his friend, the giver of
counsels, now completely realized! "The public! you are
right. I am of the opinion that with your talent you might
hope to succeed, if you had to deal with the public only; but it
is in thinking it an easy matter to reach this point, that you
most sadly deceive yourself, my poor friend. It is not competition of talents against which you will have to struggle, but
that of established reputations and personal interests. If you
are assured of an open and influential protection, then enter
the lists; without that, and above all if you lack money, keep
yourself carefully out of the way, for you can only fail, without
even having drawn to yourself the attention of the public. It
will not be a question of putting to the test your talent and
your productions. Oh, no! that would be an unparalleled favor!
One will merely think to inquire what name you bear, and if it
be a name without reputation, particularly if it be not found on
any list of proprietors or land owners, you will be obliged to
vegetate unperceived, you and your talent. In short, either
they will allow you to waste your time awaiting in vain the
execution of your music; or else, if your compositions are

conceived in the daring and original spirit which you admire so much in Beethoven, they will not fail to find them turgid, incomprehensible, and they will rid themselves of you by this fine judgment."

As soon as he had finished his *Rienzi*, in November, 1840, Wagner had addressed it to the Opera at Dresden. A letter from Meyerbeer to the royal intendant, Baron von Lüttichau, under date of March 18, had been decisive, and on the 18th of July, 1841, the *Gazette Musicale* announced the reception of the work, adding that it would be put under rehearsal at once, in order to be performed before the end of the year. "It is certain," added the journal, "that the management is going to a considerable outlay in order to mount with an unusual sumptuousness this opera, 'which contains scenic effects of great beauty,' for the people who have examined the score are speaking well of it, and are counting on a grand success." *The people!* Was it not rather Wagner, and himself alone? After he had finished *The Flying Dutchman*, he had endeavored to get it accepted at Leipsic, and at Munich. But these two cities replied by a refusal, even adding in the case of Munich, that an opera like that could never be admitted on the German stage ; and Wagner, in transcribing this decree to the director, M. de Küstner, added bitterly, "And I had believed all the time that it would be received *only* in Germany, for it struck chords which vibrate in the German heart alone."

He then sent his manuscript to Meyerbeer, who occupied at Berlin the position of capellmeister, and the latter, always interested in his young friend, managed so that he was soon able to send a favorable response to Wagner. On the 2d of April, 1842, the *Gazette Musicale* announced this news, profiting by the occasion to explain that if the representation of *Rienzi* at Dresden had been subject to delays, it was wholly due to the importance of the stage setting; it was very important, in Wagner's eyes, that no shadow of doubt should be felt on this point.

At the time that he had learned that *Rienzi* would be performed at Dresden, he would like to have departed for his beloved Germany, where it seemed to him all must smile upon him; but his last resources had been absorbed during his retreat to the country; he was no longer worth a sou. He returned miserable to Paris, took modest lodgings at No. 14 rue Jacob, in a house formerly inhabited by Proudhon; then he went again to Schlesinger to demand work of him, — and such work! He arranged for the piano *Le Guittarero*, *la Reine de Chypre*, taking from it all the fantasias and qua-drilles that could by any possibility be found in it; and thus he spent one whole winter working hard to save up enough money for the voyage. As soon as he had gained it, he departed speedily for Dresden, and felt his heart overflow with joy on touching foot to German soil. He forgot in this sweet transport the three long years of poverty which he had spent in Paris, and in which, in his eyes, he had lost more than life; he had lost creative force and moral energy.

HERR RICHARD WAGNER TRIES HIS "MUSIC OF THE FUTURE" ON THE SENSITIVE EARS OF JOHN BULL.

CHAPTER III

IENZI was represented at Dresden on the 20th of October, 1842. From the moment that Wagner had set foot in this city, he had felt himself rightly placed, surrounded by friends, and people prompt to help his opera over the difficulties which always hamper the work of a beginner. The opera at Dresden was one of the best in Germany, and the theatre, newly reconstructed by the architect Gottfried Semper, was large enough to hold sixteen hundred people. They had left nothing undone in trying to make it as nearly as possible like the opera at Paris, and had even engaged French artists to decorate the *salle* and paint the scenery. At its head was the royal intendant, Baron von Lüttichau, an amiable man, but with mediocre talents for the fine arts, and the troupe counted at that time at least three artists of the first rank; the baritone Waechter, the celebrated tenor Tichatschek, and finally the illustrious Schroeder-Devrient, that artist of genius and woman of soul, whom Wagner dreamed so long of having for an interpreter. Unfortunately she was already advanced in her career, and while travelling about, by dint of singing indiscriminately masterpieces and worthless music for twenty years, she had contracted certain faulty tendencies, which Wagner and Berlioz have both pointed out, — like the habit of introducing spoken

45

interjections into a song, of exaggerating her importance in a scene, in order to eclipse all by her personality, etc. ; — nevertheless she remained, notwithstanding these defects, which increased with age, an artist of superior inspiration, and thoroughly imbued with the tragic genius; she was precisely the one to sing in *Rienzi*.

But how had this opera, signed by a German composer, been able to find favor with its judges in a city where they liked only that which proceeded from France, or from a foreigner? "When the manuscript of *Rienzi* was received at Dresden, it came near being rejected without examination. The Paris postmark puzzled the royal intendant, who decided to look into the manuscript, together with the capellmeister Reissiger, the leader of the chorus Fischer, and the tenor Tichatschek. The name was unknown, the score enormously thick; so the director and the capellmeister were inclined to refuse it. But the tenor, whom the journals of Dresden compared to Duprez, was attracted by the heroic tone of the composition. He foresaw for himself a creation after the manner of the great roles in *La Muette* and *William Tell*, and with the support of Fischer, he finally succeeded in obtaining an acceptance of the work." [1]

And Wagner, on his arrival at Dresden, had been received by these two partisans with a sympathy and cordiality which seemed all the sweeter to him after so many disappointments and humiliations. "I will never forget," he has said, "the good which this reception did me ; it was the first encouragement which had ever come to the young artist so rudely shaken by destiny."

This opera, which Wagner had so well succeeded in fashioning after the model of the French opera, with fine decorations, grand ballets, stately processions, hymns of war,

---

[1] *Richard Wagner*, by L. Bernardini, after *Richard Wagner's Leben und Werken*, by M. Glasenapp (Leipsic, 1882).

and religious invocations, was accordingly in the taste of the day at Dresden, where they desired, as in most of the large cities of Europe at that time, only imitations of the French opera, set off with music sufficiently commonplace, but developed at length, and of a powerful sonority. Everywhere and always the cry was Halévy.

From the time that the rehearsals commenced, Wagner experienced a satisfaction quite new to him, on observing the interest which the singers took in their roles, the zeal which they manifested, and the compliments which they bestowed upon him more warmly from day to day. At length arrived the day for the representation (Oct. 20, 1842) : this was a real triumph, both for Wagner and for the principal interpreters; for the tenor Tichatschek, admirable in the role of tribune; for Mme. Schroeder-Devrient, a very pathetic Adriano ; and for Mlle Wüst, a touching and seducing Irene. The roles of Stefano Colonna and of Paolo Orsini were taken by Dettmer and Waechter; those of Raimondo, Baroncelli and Cecco del Vecchio by Reinhold, Joachim Vestri and Carl Risse. On the next morning, Wagner, dismayed at the length of the performance, which lasted six hours to a minute, went to the theatre for the purpose of indicating the portions to be omitted ; but when he returned in the afternoon to make sure that it was being well sustained in all the parts, the copyist excused himself for having done nothing on account of the indignant objections of the singers. " I will allow nothing to be taken from my role," cried Tichatschek; "it is too charming." And the others, all said the same thing. During the next ten days two representations were given before crowded houses, with increased prices; and when, at the third, Reissiger laid down the baton in honor of the young musician, there was a wild enthusiasm in the house. In a word, Wagner was the hero of the day, — at least in Dresden.

At Leipsic, where reigned the classic influence of Mendelssohn, his success was less pronounced. On the 26th of November, 1842, at a soirée given at the Gewandhaus by Sophie Schroeder, the niece of Madame Devrient, Tichatschek and Mme. Devrient sung, one the prayer of Rienzi, the other the air of Adriano. Immediately Henri Laube undertook to extol his friend. By a mischance, as these selections were preceded by a duet from the *Templier*, by Marschner, he confounded them, and bravely announced that "these three pieces were very dry, and wanting in character." To make amends, he demanded of the young author some notes on himself, — this was the nucleus of his autobiography, — and he published them in the *Journal du Monde Élégant*, with a portrait of Wagner by Kietz; this was a seal put upon his fame. "What!" said he later, in his *Communication to my Friends*, "I, so lately isolated, abandoned, without hearth or home, I found myself suddenly loved, admired, even regarded with astonishment! Moreover, from the effect of this success, I found a solid and durable basis for well-being in my nomination, as unlooked for as it was surprising, of royal capellmeister of Saxony. Was it not natural that I should abandon myself to sweet illusions, destined, however, to be dissipated by a sad awakening?"

On the 30th of October, the *Gazette Musicale* of Paris announced that the opera of its former collaborator had borne away a brilliant success at Dresden, and that never before had public enthusiasm manifested itself with such ringing applause, the author being called before the curtain three or four times; then, in a following number, the same journal inserted a long letter, to which it may be supposed without too much improbability that Wagner was not an entire stranger. The enthusiasm of the public steadily increased, it said in substance, and people could not get over their surprise at seeing a young man, hitherto unknown, spring so high at a single bound, and place himself instantly by the side of illustrious musicians;

but what was most amazing was to find, united in the same artist, two qualities so different as those of poet and musician. It would take a long time to recount the annoyances and disappointments endured by the author before he was able to see his piece performed, as from the time it was first rehearsed at the piano, a cry was raised against the excessive difficulty of the music. A similar thing had been already seen, and people would remember the interminable discussions raised by *Fidelio*, of which several portions had been declared inexecutable; but Beethoven was at that time in the meridian of his glory: he overpowered by his name and his will everything that opposed itself to him ; whereas a young composer, without reputation, found himself disarmed when facing artists who inveighed against a work and refused to execute it. Notwithstanding all, he was not discouraged : he succeeded in transforming this ill-will into zeal, into extraordinary enthusiasm; and the colossal success of the work finally recompensed all his efforts, for in spite of the increase of prices maintained until after the seventh evening, no diminution was perceived in the audience. Excellent singers, admirable stage settings, enormous receipts, everything that could be desired, they had, according to this correspondent. And the music? He does not say much, it is true, but it is carefully written. " In order to give a description of its many beauties, it would be necessary to make a thorough analysis of the score, — a difficult task, which others can fulfill better than I. I will confine myself to saying (and this is the unanimous opinion of the connoisseurs of whom I am the organ), that this music bears throughout the stamp of originality, that it abounds in new and inspired motives. The instrumentation, very rich, displays all the resources of the orchestra, without, however, drowning the voice. On the whole, it is the work not of a beginner, but of a finished master."

This judgment, with its modest reserve at the outset, its

reference further on to *Fidelio* and Beethoven, is tantamount
to a signature at the foot of the article, — and it would be
that of Richard Wagner.[1]

Rienzi differs in no respect from the great French works
then applauded, the plan of which, with the airs, duets, trios,
etc., he reproduced exactly; but, even if it be an imitation, an
exaggeration of the operas of Spontini, with whom Wagner
is evidently inspired for the recitatives and the general
declamation, it must also be recognized that this imitation is
marked, in certain parts, with an individuality, and that the
style of the composer begins to dawn here and there throughout the opera. The work, as a whole, is modeled on all
those of the same epoch, and yet the author attempts several
forms to which he will often have recourse later on, such as
the frequent use of the high tremulo on the violins, and the
melodious progressions, falling back into a delicious *pianissimo* after having reached their maximum crescendo; one may
already detect a marvellous skill in wielding the orchestra, and
of obtaining from it unusual effects; but more than these,
certain pieces, like the beautiful prayer of Rienzi, different
episodes, like the scene of the interdict, magnificent in every
particular, both as to the music and the situation, reveal a
future master in this beginner.

This is what the Parisian hearers might have recognized
in 1869, instead of jesting; this, so it would appear, was realized by some amateurs of Dresden in 1842, since they confessed " to have undergone a transport of enthusiasm, caused

---

[1] The portrait given here is probably the first one of Wagner, engraved on
wood by Kietz in 1843, and reproduced later by lithography at Zurich, during his
sojourn in Switzerland. It was then that the master would have added beneath it
this manuscript thought, of which we may thus render the spirit, if not the exact
text : " The creator of the work of art of the future is no other than the artist of
the present, who embraces the life of the future, and desires to participate therein.
He who, conceiving this desire, finds within himself the means of realizing it,
perceives already a new life ; only the artist has this power."

RICHARD WAGNER, IN 1843.

by the strangeness of his methods, which had appeared to them to announce a creative genius, destined to direct art into new channels." And Fétis, in his hatred against the author, quotes this estimate, in order to show how signally Wagner had failed to live up to the prediction of these connoisseurs; and after all they had not judged so badly.

"This work, in which is found the ardor, the splendor which youth strives after," writes Wagner in his *Letter on Music*, "is the one which has obtained for me in Germany my first success, not only at the Dresden theatre, where it was first represented, but at many of the theatres where it has been given since then, with my other operas. I have conceived and executed it under the sway of the emulation excited in me by my youthful impressions of the heroic operas of Spontini, and the brilliancy of the Grand Opera at Paris, where were borne down upon me works bearing the names of Auber, of Meyerbeer, and of Halévy. I am to-day far from attributing to this composition a particular importance, for it does not mark very clearly any essential phase in the development of the views on art which dominated me later. Moreover, it is not my purpose by any means to parade here, before your eyes, my triumphs as a composer, but rather to give you an explanation concerning the problematical tendency of my ideas.

"This *Rienzi* was finished during my first stay in Paris. I had before me the splendors of the Grand Opera, and I was presumptuous enough to conceive the desire, to flatter myself with the hope, of seeing my work represented there. If ever this desire is to be accomplished, surely it would seem strange to you, as it did to me, that fate should have allowed so long a time to slip by between the desire and the realization, and heaped up disappointments which drove all hope from my heart."

Immediately after the success of *Rienzi*, the Dresden

theatre began rehearsing *The Flying Dutchman*, and although the singing personnel was in Wagner's opinion insufficient, particularly the tenor charged with the role of Erik, the first representation was given on the 2d of January, 1843. The baritone, Waechter, gave an artistic representation of the Dutchman, and Mme. Schroeder-Devrient held the role of Senta, which was one of her most powerful creations.[1]

It met with a success which at first it seemed must equal that of *Rienzi*, but which soon died away for the good reason that the public did not find in it that degree of theatrical pomp and musical uproar with which it was so charmed in the preceding work. At Paris, the *Gazette Musicale*, always prompt to eulogize anything concerning Wagner, at once proclaimed the success in a notice in which it was a question of nothing less than "genius." At the end of February, when the failure was a settled fact, it published a short article, explaining that the second opera of Wagner had achieved a success at least equal to the first, greater, perhaps, in regard to the means of execution which the author had been able to command. " In *Rienzi*, the pomp of the spectacle, the grand concerted pieces, and the dramatic effects of a more complicated action, would naturally dazzle the public, and militate in favor of the author. There is nothing of all that in *The Flying Dutchman*, where, save the final scene and the appearance of the fantastic ship, all is simple, and quite devoid of the effects which the public is accustomed to see in the operas of the day. It is in reality a ballad put in action. One would suppose that music of this kind would be little liked, but it has been quite otherwise. It has made a vivid impression on the large numbers who have witnessed it, and in the second act, which was a decided triumph, enthusiasm knew no bounds. Author and actors were called for, and received with acclama-

---

[1] Daland, Erik, and the nurse Mary, were Dettmer, Reinhold who had already played in *Rienzi*, and Mme. Waechter.

tions which amounted to a frenzy." It is easy to embellish
when writing from afar.

In order to console Wagner for this failure, they made
haste to put *Rienzi* on again ; but the success of a work which
he considered at best an imitation, could not lessen the
author's disappointment at seeing come to naught the first, the
only opera in which he had really put something of himself.
However, five months had not elapsed before the *Flying
Dutchman* was played at Riga with success, in May, 1843,
and at the same time there appeared in Schumann's
Journal, the *New Musical Gazette*, an article in which the
new opera was saluted " as a signal of hope that the German
genius would soon cease to be forever tossed about on the
seas of foreign music, and that it would find at length a hospitable haven on German shores."

Moreover, the poem had been submitted to Spohr, who
had judged it a " masterpiece," and who had desired to become
acquainted with the music; after having seen it, he arranged
to have this opera performed at the theatre at Cassel, on June
5th, and immediately announced the success to Wagner, while
urging him " to persevere in the right path."   One recognizes
there the old champion of pure German art, against the music
from beyond the mountains and beyond the Rhine.   Spohr was
the only musician, representing the former generation, who
from the first recognized and saluted in Wagner a musician
of genius. " *The Flying Dutchman* interests me most deeply,"
he wrote to his friend Lüder, while the opera was being
rehearsed. "This work is full of imagination, of noble invention, well written for the voice, very difficult, and too much
loaded with instrumentation, but overflowing with new effects ;
on the stage it will surely appear clear and intelligible. . . .   I
have come to think that of all the composers for the theatre,
Wagner is actually the most richly gifted." This double success, at Riga and at Cassel, at length decided the directors of

the theatre at Berlin to play an opera which they appeared to
have received solely out of politeness towards Meyerbeer, and
for which Wagner was much put out, going personally to Berlin without obtaining anything. Finally, *The Flying Dutchman* was represented there in the early part of 1844; but on
the second evening the house was empty, and they could not
proceed with it.[1]

In *The Flying Dutchman* Richard Wagner has unquestion-
ably done the work of a creative poet, since he had no other
materials to utilize than the five or six pages in which Heine
had summed up the melodrama by Fitzball, which he had seen
played at London, and the legend itself, recounted to him by
the credulous sailors during the tempests which retarded his
voyage from Pillau to London. His first intention was to
make this opera in one act, from which it will be seen that the
splendors of his Parisian ideal had already paled before his
eyes, and that he had begun to draw rules for the form of his
conception from another source than that of the broad sea of
official publicity. " I do not know what poetic value may be
attributed to this poem," adds he, " but what I do know is that
while composing it, I felt a freedom which I did not know
when working out the libretto of *Rienzi*; for in the latter I
had in mind only the plan of opera which would permit me

[1] Here is what the Paris *Musical Gazette* says in its issue of February 4, 1844:
" They have represented at Berlin the new opera of Wagner, *The Flying Dutchman*. This work has met with some success. The first representation was directed
by Meyerbeer, the second and third by the author." Note that according to this
article, proceeding from we well know whom, the third representation had already
taken place, but in the following number (February 11), the journal, perceiving that
it had been premature in its announcement, rectified it incidentally, in a paragraph
extremely flattering : " The good fortune of our former collaborator, Richard Wagner, increases every day in Germany. They are mounting at Hamburg his opera
of *Rienzi*, for a representation which will be given by the celebrated singer Tichatschek, of Dresden. The third representation of the *Wandering Dutchman* (*Hol-
landais errant*) is expected at Berlin, and the young composer has just finished a
work entitled *Tannhäuser*.

to unite all the forms allowed in, and even demanded by, the grand opera, properly called: introductions, finales, choruses, airs, duets, trios, etc., and to employ therein all the magnificence possible. In *The Flying Dutchman*, the thing which principally concerned me was, not to depart from the most simple lines of action, to banish all superfluous detail and low intrigue, and on the other hand to give unusual attention to developing the features calculated to show in its true light the characteristic coloring of the legendary subject; that coloring seeming to me quite appropriate to the inward motives of the action, and consequently identified with the action itself."

It is dating from this opera that Wagner instinctively made a change in the character of his subjects, and that abandoning, not without a mind to return, the field of history, he made a first excursion into that of the legend. He has been pleased to say that this resolution was thenceforth final, but he forgot, in thus speaking, that he always experienced a hesitation in choosing between a subject of the legendary order and one of a historical character, each time that he undertook a new work. In adopting the legend, he freed himself from all detail necessary for describing and representing historical fact and its vicissitudes, and found himself thenceforth rid of the obligation to treat poetry, and above all, music, in a fashion which he judged incompatible with the means of expressing these two arts. The legend of any epoch or nation to which it might belong, seemed to him to contain exclusively all that was purely human in that epoch or that nation, and to present it in a form very forcible, and therefore intelligible at first sight. "It is thus that a ballad, a popular refrain suffices," said he, "to show in an instant this character with the greatest distinctness. In short, then, the legendary character assures a double advantage of great importance in the execution; for on the one hand the simplicity of the action enables the eye to take it in easily at a glance, permitting no

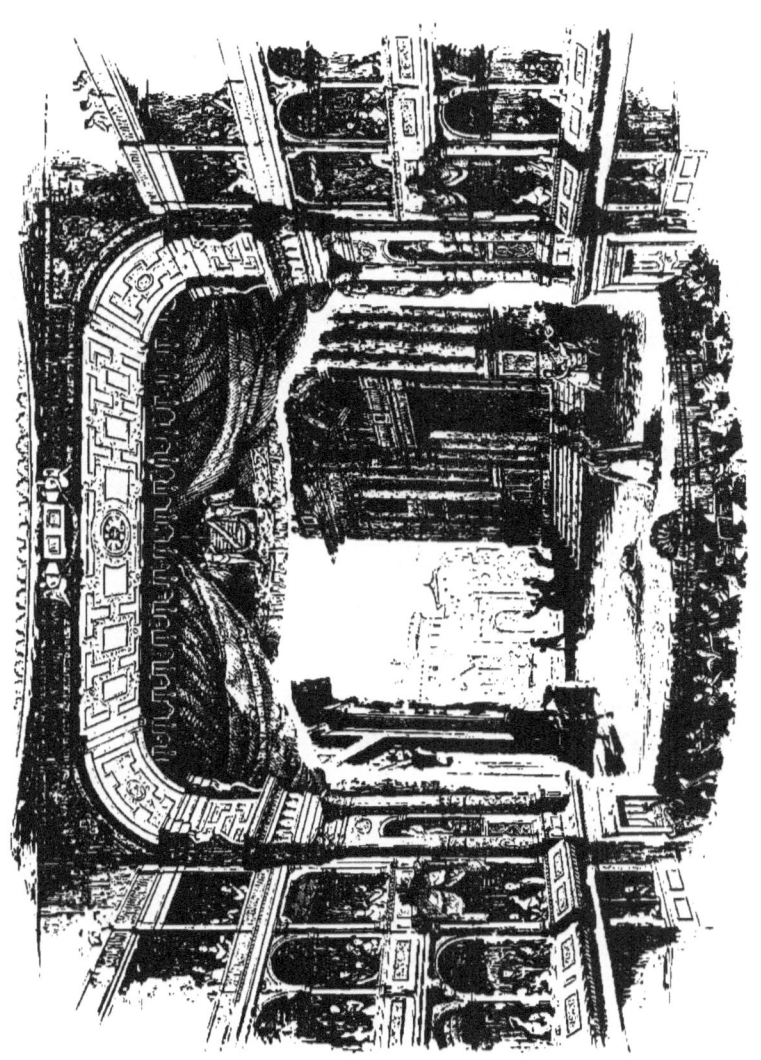

REPRESENTATION OF "RIENZI," AT DRESDEN, OCT. 20, 1842.
(Act IV, last scene).— After an engraving of the time.

distractions in the way of explanations of exterior incidents,
and on the other, the greater part of the poem may be thus
devoted to the development of the inner motives of the drama,
because these motives awaken sympathetic echoes in the
depths of our heart."

So much for legend in general, replacing history in Wagner's mind, as a frame-work for musical drama; but what particular motive, what secret attraction had induced him to
choose the legend of *The Flying Dutchman?* One may discover there in another form the myth of Ulysses in former
ages, the legend of the *Wandering Jew* in the Christian
world, both myth and legend resting on an essential trait of
human nature, namely, the ardent desire for eternal repose amid
the repeated storms of life. "Thus," said he, "in *The Flying
Dutchman* we find again, prodigiously developed, the fundamental trait of the old Grecian myth. The tale of the sailors
dates from the period of the great voyages of discovery. In
it the people have wrought a remarkable fusion of the two
preceding types. The Dutch navigator is condemned by the
devil (visible symbol of the winds and waves), to wander
without rest for all eternity upon the sea: that is the punishment of his temerity. The end of his suffering is death, to
which, like Ahasuerus, he aspires. But this deliverance,
refused to the wandering Jew, he may obtain through the
sacrifice of a loving and courageous woman who shall conse-
crate herself to him. The desire for death leads him forth in
search of the woman. But this woman is not Penelope, the
wife, the guardian of the domestic hearth; it is the woman in
general, as yet unknown, but desired and foreseen, in whom
the instinct of the feminine heart shall be infinitely developed,—
in a word, the woman of the future." Lost as he was then in
Paris, which roared about him like the ocean, Wagner recognized in himself this unhappy navigator, beaten by the storm,
and he was himself consumed by the same thirst for rest as his

hero, for final rest with a true woman, symbol of the domestic hearth and of the ideal fatherland.

"Such conditions," says Wagner, "I did not yet know; I could only long for them. However, my Hollander had not discovered the new world; his wife could save him only by dying with him. *En route, donc, et en avant.*"[1]

How had he arranged for the stage this myth in which he himself reappears, the only work of his which then merited the name of poem, and the first of a long series which extends from *The Flying Dutchman* to *Parsifal?* From a frightful tempest, two vessels seek shelter in a hospitable harbor. The first which nears the shore has for a captain a Norwegian navigator, whom the winds have taken seven miles out of his course. "The storm nears its end," says he to his sailors. "Go to rest; to-morrow we will depart." And all the crew fall asleep, lulled by the song of the pilot watch, who dreams of home, of the joy of returning, and soon gives way to sleep while thinking of the absent loved one. Then the storm returns with a terrible violence, and another ship, shaken by the fury of the sea, a black ship, with blood-colored sails, approaches in its turn, and casts anchor. A phantom crew noiselessly executes the manœuvre; a man descends to the shore and sadly cries, "The term is passed; seven years have fled! The sea has cast me on the earth with loathing. Oh! proud ocean! In a few days thou must bear me away again! No tomb! no death! Such is my terrible sentence of condemnation. Day of judgment, day supreme! When wilt thou dawn upon my night?" It is the Flying Dutchman, the Wandering Jew of the sea; it is the ancient blasphemer, condemned to wander on the deep until he shall have found a woman faithful unto death. In seven years the sea has cast him ashore for only one short moment. The two captains

---

[1] Richard Wagner, d'après lui-même.

accost each other, and the Hollander asks shelter of the Norwegian Daland for several days, causing to glitter before his eyes the bait of unnumbered treasures. Finally he says, " Hast thou a daughter? Would that she might be my wife! I would never return to my country. What does it profit me to amass riches? Be convinced, consent to this alliance, and take all my treasures." The old mariner agrees at least to bring him face to face with his daughter, and the sea having calmed, the two make their way to the port, where they wait on the daughter of Daland.

In the house of the Norwegian, near a cheerful fire, the pensive Senta, with her nurse and her friends, sigh for the return of the seafarers; but while the young girls sing, and gaily turn the spinning wheel, Senta alone, absorbed with sad musings, does not once take her eyes from a certain sombre portrait hung upon the wall. They question her; then, as in an ecstasy, with a passion which thrills and transfigures her, she points out to her companions the horrible destiny of the mariner condemned by fate to wander always on the sea, and never to die. The unfortunate man, driven back by the tempest each time that he wished to weather a dangerous headland, had one day cried in anger, "Well, I will overcome this unsurmountable obstacle if I struggle through all eternity." And Eternity had accepted the challenge of the audacious mariner.

Neither the rallies of her companions, nor the anxious prayers of the hunter Erik, her lover, can calm the ardent desire for sacrifice which seizes this young girl, and bears her irresistibly towards the condemned one. Suddenly she cries, "Oh! that he might appear! I would love him faithfully unto death!" The door opens; Daland appears conducting his guest by the hand, and Senta, recognizing her mysterious loved one of the sombre mien, flies quickly towards him. When her father has left her with the stranger, she devotes herself to his comfort, and swears fidelity unto death. The

brief respite expires. The condemned must again take to the
sea, and already the silent preparation for departure has commenced. Then Senta feels herself weaken, while listening to
the tender reproaches of Erik, whom she fondly loved before
learning what a fatality rested upon the poor mariner. She
yields to the sweet remonstrances of the young lover, and
when the Hollander comes to take her away, she falls into the
arms of Erik. It is then settled; there is no redemption pos-

FINAL SCENE OF THE "FLYING DUTCHMAN," AT DRESDEN (1843).

sible for the despairing mariner. He goes back to his ship,
and again takes up his eternal voyage. "To the sea! to the
sea!" cry the sailors, and the merciless tempest resumes its
fury. The ship departs. Then Senta desires to follow it; her
father, Erik, her friends try in vain to hold her back; she
escapes them, scales a cliff, and precipitates herself into the
waves. Suddenly the accursed vessel is swallowed up by the

sea, and the hero and Senta are seen to appear in the clouds, transfigured by love and devotion.

In the score of *The Flying Dutchman*, operatic melody dominates still, but there is a manifest tendency, in each separate page, as well as in the work as a whole, to merge the different parts into a musical and poetical unit, entirely homogeneous. The author had yet to abandon the practice of cutting up his music into definite parts, although the point of connection with the recitatives already tends to disappear; he had yet to give up making his personages sing together, to repudiate cavatinas and cadenzas, and to avoid subordinating everything at times to mere vocal effect; but notwithstanding these numerous traces of conventional opera, this work leaves on the mind a deep impression.

This proceeds at least as much from the poem as from the music, and especially from the attempted fusion between these two elements of the opera; I repeat, of the opera, for Wagner, it must be emphatically stated, never employed any other title until after the completion of Lohengrin. Here there is no longer mere juxtaposition, as in the case of Berlioz, who also composes both his verses and his music, but not together. With Wagner, the birth of the two is simultaneous, and one clearly perceives in *The Flying Dutchman* that the germs of the poet and the musician, unfolding successively in the same individual, and developing singly, are here forever joined, that they will henceforth move on together, indissolubly united in the pursuit of a common ideal, dreaming, conceiving, laboring, and creating from one and the same impulse. And precisely herein consists the great originality of Richard Wagner.

Assuredly, however, he does not yet detach himself from Gluck, since he does not hesitate to repeat words in order to produce a purely musical effect, and his declamation very plainly proceeds from this model. Neither is he freed from the influence of Weber, which is especially felt in the admir-

able handling of the orchestra, in the terrific color of the supernatural episodes and in the fresh simplicity of certain melodies ;
but these reminiscences are already becoming blended with
a powerful personality, not merely reproductive, but creative
in character. The true superiority of *The Flying Dutchman*
over *Rienzi*, consists in the author's rejection of everything
not directly related to the drama and which if introduced
could serve only to dazzle or to bewilder ; here again he employs
the forms of the opera, but he subordinates them irrevocably
to the drama. To this he was tending when he adopted the
myth as subject matter in the place of history, and to this he
will attain.

Another new element which should be noted in the *Flying
Dutchman*, is the first appearance of the characteristic melody
which was to be of such material aid to Richard Wagner in the
attainment of his ideal. And, as he repeatedly asserted afterwards, what has always been called his " system " was so little
the result of preconceived ideas of a *parti pris*, that this
innovation was, in the beginning, the effect of chance. He
himself has related that when he composed the *Flying Dutchman*, he wrote first the ballad of Senta, which became, as it
were, the musical pivot of the whole work; and that later, as
he approached the different situations of the drama, they
evoked in him the same melodies which they had at first suggested, melodies which tended to modify or develop themselves
according to the feelings excited. By following this natural
impulse, it would then have been possible for him to build his
whole work upon the development of two or three essential
melodies ; this is what he was to arrive at afterwards, but he
was still too much imbued with the operatic methods of the
day not to follow the ordinary course and force himself to find
almost as many different motives as he had pieces to compose.
However, the idea had appeared, and it had now only to
germinate.

If a new charm, a powerful impression of strength and of individuality is imparted by the *ensemble* of *The Flying Dutchman*, it must also be said that certain fragments, such as the overture, the chorus of the sailors, the ballad of Senta, the song of the pilot, and, above all, the bursts of despair or of love on the part of the unhappy condemned, are absolutely original creations of Richard Wagner. And, notably, the overture, a true masterpiece, is based upon the struggle between two opposing motives, which we may call, as we will, damnation and deliverance, perdition and salvation, sensual pleasure and redeeming love, or pedantic science and free genius. In any case, the good finally prevails over the bad, and the same conflict was often to be represented later, always with incomparable grandeur. It would have been very singular if a work so individual, while it repelled its hearers taken in a mass, had not found some zealous admirers, — strange, whimsical people, it is possible, but endowed with minds open to new impressions. Such admirers Wagner found, and the faithful adherence of these unknown friends was so gratifying to him after the grievous blow which he had suffered, that he immediately formed a new resolution. " From Berlin, where I was entirely unknown," he says in his *Communication to my Friends*, " I received from two utter strangers, who had been attracted towards me by the impression which *The Flying Dutchman* produced upon them, the first complete satisfaction which I had been permitted to enjoy, with the invitation to continue in the particular direction I had marked out. From this moment I lost more and more from sight the veritable public. The opinion of a few intelligent men took the place in my mind of the opinion of the masses, which can never be wholly apprehended, although it had been the object of my labors in my first attempts, when my eyes were not yet open to the light. I now arrived more and more at a clear understanding of my aim, and, in order to make sure of being

FINAL SCENE OF THE "FLYING DUTCHMAN."
at the Lyceum Theatre, London.   (1876.)

followed, I no longer addressed myself to the masses, which had nothing in common with me, but rather to the individuals, whose dispositions and sentiments were analogous to my own. This surer position with reference to those who were to receive my communications, exercised thenceforth a very important influence upon my artistic nature." Then let Fétis laugh; it will not prevent a really superior artist from always acting thus more or less radically. In order to please everybody at once, it is necessary to compromise; and in questions of art, he who compromises is sure to disappear in a short time.

RICHARD WAGNER IN HEAVEN

Richard Wagner addressing the Angels: " A very pretty welcome, my dear angels, but without kettledrums and trombones you can never produce an effect." (*Kikeriki* of Vienna, Feb. 18, 1883.)

CHAPTER IV

HE representation of *The Flying Dutchman* was given Jan. 10, 1843, and within eight days thereafter, Wagner had achieved, as orchestral leader, a great personal success, which was to result in his being established at Dresden in much easier circumstances. Since *Rienzi* had first seen the light, the death of the deputy capellmeister Morlacchi, and that of the musical director Rastrelli, had caused two vacancies. Reissiger, left alone with the double duties of capellmeister and theatre manager, had accepted Morgenroth as deputy capellmeister; furthermore it had been decided that in view of the importance of the work at the theatre, the new capellmeister who should be appointed, should devote himself exclusively to the orchestra. The qualities of which Wagner had given proof while directing *Rienzi*, and also the success of this opera, seemed to point him out as a likely candidate for this office; but he hesitated to present himself, so thoroughly disgusted was he with his former hard and thankless labors at Königsberg and at Riga. However, the necessity of living somewhat dimmed these recollections; his wife and friends represented to him that he could ill afford to let escape him a permanent employment with a fixed salary. Accordingly he decided to try his chances against Ludwig Schindelmeisser, Dorn's brother-in-law, whom he had formerly known at Leipsic, and who believed himself sure of success. The latter chose for his *concours* representation *La Vestale*; Wagner, perhaps in remembrance of his early adoration for Weber, chose *Euryanthe*, and Weber brought him good luck. He aspired at first, so it appears, to the post of musical director only, at nine hundred dollars; but through the influence of Baron von Lüttichau, he obtained that of capellmeister at eleven hundred and twenty-five dollars, and the commission was delivered to him at the end of January, 1843.

The ceremony of his presentation at the chapel where he took the oath, took place on Feb. 2, the next day after Berlioz had arrived at Dresden on his first journey through Germany, finding his friend all aglow with a very natural joy. It is before Berlioz, who was present at his rehearsals, that Wagner was to exercise his authority for the first time, which he did with great zeal and courage; Berlioz himself bears witness to this, and his word is not to be doubted. The French master heard *The Flying Dutchman*, and the last three acts only of *Rienzi*, which they had decided to perform in two evenings, owing to its length. He does not appear to have paid much attention to this work, and its subject did not make a lasting impression on his mind; he remembers only " a beautiful prayer in the last act, and a triumphal march modelled, but not servilely, after the magnificent march *d'Olympie*." He appreciated " the sombre coloring, and certain stormy effects well suited to the subject" in *The Flying Dutchman*, but he remarked an abuse of the tremulo, which he considered a sign of laziness and lack of invention on the part of the author. On the whole, the interpreters seem to have impressed him more than the works themselves. Mme. Devrient, ridiculous enough as a young boy in *Rienzi*, raised herself in his eyes in *The Flying Dutchman*; Tichatschek was, said he, passionate, brilliant, heroic, captivating in *Rienzi*, while Mlle Wüst had been appropriately given the insignificant role of Irene; finally, the baritone Waechter had produced a most profound impression upon him, with his pure and perfect talent; his voice, exceptionally beautiful, had a smooth and vibrating *timbre*, and also great power of expression, though the artist put ever so little heart and sensibility in his song, and these two qualities, said Berlioz, Waechter possessed to an extraordinary degree. Berlioz departed, but his memory was cherished at Dresden, for, some time afterwards, when Wagner had his overture to *Faust* performed, they took it for a fragment of the *Damnation of Faust*, and applauded it accordingly. Which of the two should be the more displeased at this mistake?[1]

The position held by Wagner was far from constituting a sinecure. There were performances to conduct every evening in the year, at least three pieces, and generally three or four different operas a week, to say nothing of the ordinary music, and the exceptional court concerts; such was the labor to be divided between the musical director and the two capellmeisters, the first directing the representations and superintending the church music during the week; the two others conducting at the church on Sunday, and each being responsible for the good execution of certain operas. In accepting these heavy duties, Wagner had not only yielded to the desire to assure to himself an honorable living; he was also possessed of the hope that he might exert a happy influence upon the opera at Dresden, and by reaction, upon art in general. But he had no sooner put his hand to the work, than he encountered the same indifference, and the same prejudices, which he had been unable to overcome elsewhere. He had occupied his

---

[1] At this concert, given on July 22, 1844, for the benefit of the poor, he had performed, besides his overture to *Faust*, the *Pastoral Symphony* and Mendelssohn's *Walpurgis Night*.

post scarcely three months, when he underwent a first attack, *apropos* of a representation of *Don Juan*, which he had directed April 26, 1843, with a profound admiration for Mozart, but with an execution according to his own convictions. He found that his rendering departed sensibly from the current tradition at Dresden; tradition good or bad, coming from Mozart himself, or introduced by the capellmeisters, Morlacchi and Reissiger, it mattered little, but a tradition all-powerful, and which no one but a madman would wish to modify. They took pains to let him see it; the old amateurs exclaimed at the scandal, and a certain critic, outdoing them, declared that the author of *Rienzi* and *The Flying Dutchman* was a barbarian incapable of comprehending Mozart. This cry goes back far enough, as you see, and it is not a thing of yesterday that people have sought to characterize Wagner as a savage, fond of hub-bub, while opposing to him the seraphic and melodious master of Salzburg.

Wagner, through his position, was in the pay of the court, and was required to play a role in the official fêtes; it is thus that he wrote the music of a hymn composed by the advocate, Hohlfeldt, for the inauguration of the statue of the late king, and directed the execution of it, on June 7th, 1843, in the presence of the sovereign, the body of the state, and the deputations of the kingdom. A year later, when Frederick Augustus returned from a voyage to England, he composed the words and the music of a cantata, entitled *Salute to the King*, which was sung on the 12th of August, at the summer residence of Pillnitz. Meanwhile, he had written a more important work, dedicated out of gratitude to Madame Charlotte Weinlig, the widow of his first master who had just died, and these are the circumstances under which he had composed this grand biblical tableau of *The Last Supper*. In his capacity as leader of a men's choral society, the Liedertafel, he had been chosen with Reissiger to organize and direct a general reunion of all the singing societies in Saxony. The Fête commenced on July 6, 1843, with a monster concert at the Frauenkirche, the largest church in Dresden; the singers, twelve hundred in number, were grouped upon a platform erected in the choir, and behind them, higher yet, was the orchestra, composed of five hundred artists and amateurs. The sovereigns arrived precisely at midday, and immediately the festival commenced. The piece by Wagner came last; this is how he had conceived it: the Disciples being assembled together to celebrate the Lord's Supper, the Apostles arrive bearing the news that it is forbidden them, under pain of death, to teach in the name of Jesus. All feel their courage weaken, and in their distress they supplicate the Father to send the Holy Spirit to succor them. Then are heard voices from on high; they announce to the suppliants that their prayer is heard; the wind roars, the earth trembles, and, filled with the divine spirit, the Apostles and the Disciples go forth to convert the world. A chorus of forty men represented the forty Disciples assembled, and in order to better render the effect of the heavenly voices, Wagner had arranged to have this invisible choir sing from the height of the cupola. This arrangement, purely material, and of which the author later on made good use in his *Parsifal*, was all that criticism touched upon in this new work; it was agreeably diverted by it, and remained deaf to the admirable crescendo which announced the descent of the Holy Spirit, and which the orchestra, silent until then, construed with marvellous power. To what end does one possess genius prematurely?[1]

The management of the theatre had decided to make a

---

[1] " This last work, the conception of which is most daring " — writes at Paris the habitual correspondent of the *Gazette Musicale* — " has produced an extraordinary effect, and one which it is impossible to describe; the king, after the concert was over, summoned the young author to him, and testified his satisfaction in the most affectionate terms."

formal revival of *La Vestale* during the autumn of 1844, and since it appeared certain to succeed with such a Julia as Mme. Schroeder-Devrient, Wagner, moved by a feeling of admiration for Spontini, who had just left the direction of the opera at Berlin under circumstances painful for his self-love, had persuaded the Baron von Lüttichau to invite the old master to come and direct his opera. This being agreed upon, he would allow no one but himself to extend the invitation, and accordingly wrote a letter to Spontini in French, which produced the desired effect, for the master replied that he accepted with pleasure, and had no doubt of the excellence of the interpretation. Unhappily, he naïvely indicated such unreasonable requirements regarding the number of performers and musicians in the orchestra, that Wagner, quite distressed, hastened to the intendant and to Mme. Devrient, to acquaint them with his embarrassment. The latter, who knew Spontini very well, laughed goodnaturedly at the imprudence committed, but offered at the same time to repair it. and as the old master had shown in his letter a desire to return to Paris as soon as possible, it was agreed to notify him of an indefinite postponement, occasioned by an indisposition of Mme. Schroeder, who served thus as scapegoat. This was done, and they went on rehearsing, troubling their heads no further about Spontini, until, just on the eve of the general rehearsal, he unceremoniously tumbled in upon Wagner, and demonstrated to him, letter in hand, that in arriving at that date he was conforming strictly to the instructions sent him, and that he was thenceforth at the disposal of his friends at Dresden ; he would not go away until after the opera had been played.

Notwithstanding this unexpected blow, Wagner thought at first only of the pleasure of having the great composer near him, and of hearing one of his operas under his own direction ; he persuaded himself that all would go wonderfully well, and in order to remove from his mind the last mental reservation, he proposed to him to direct the general rehearsal fixed for the following day. Spontini's face fell; then, after a moment's hesitation, he asked Wagner what style of baton he was accustomed to use for conducting. The latter indicated the size of an ordinary baton; then the master sighed, and asked if between that time and the morrow it would be possible to have made for him an ebony baton, of an extraordinary length and thickness, finished off at the two ends with large ivory balls. Wagner replied in the affirmative, and Spontini retired perfectly satisfied. As soon as possible Wagner hastened to spread the alarm, and to interview the carpenter, who promised to construct an ebony baton according to the required conditions. The following day at the desired moment, Spontini had his baton; then, instead of taking it by one end, like any other leader, he grasped it with his full hand around the middle, and brandished it like a marshall's baton.

From the first scenes it was evident that nothing went according to the taste of the composer, and that he intended to make a fresh study of the whole opera. He attempted, while jabbering the most outlandish German, to correct the faults of the orchestra, the shortcomings of the chorus, and even the manœuvres of the supernumeraries, whom he made begin all over again, directing them himself with an indefatigable perseverance. Then Wagner recalled the analogous evolutions executed at Berlin, which had so impressed him in *Fernando Cortez*; he understood also that at Dresden they would never adopt that mechanical precision, which produced almost a startling effect. In short, at the end of the first act, singers, musicians, manager, all begged a release. Wagner took Spontini aside, and spoke some words of deference, assuring him that his wishes should be carried out, and that in order to more easily accomplish them, they would send at once for Edouard Devrient, who was perfectly familiar with *La Vestale* as produced at Berlin.

All was to commence anew. The *personnel*, especially the leader of the chorus, was furious; Wagner alone had not a black look for Spontini, so thoroughly did he admire the extraordinary energy which the latter evinced in " pursuing and maintaining a goal in dramatic art nearly forgotten in his day." He was struck by his habit of treating without consideration the most famous of the singers; he profited by his demands to improve upon the former arrangement of the orchestra; he laid before him certain doubts, and profited by his judicious explanations; he noticed the energy with which he insisted on making the rhythmic accents very conspicuous; in short, he was much interested in the master's representation of the lyric tragedy, and showed him a respectful devotion. Thus Spontini conceived an affection for him, and desired to reward him for his zeal by giving him a bit of charitable advice; he counselled him to renounce dramatic music. " When I heard your *Rienzi*," said he one day, when they were dining at the house of Schroeder-Devrient, " I thought, this is a man of genius, but he has already done more than he can do." And by way of explaining this paradox, he proceeded thus: " After Gluck, it is I who have made the grand revolution, with *La Vestale*; I have introduced the prolongation of the sixth in harmony, and the big drum in the orchestra. With *Cortez* I have taken a step forward; I have taken three with *Olympie*, and one hundred with *Agnes de Hohenstaufen*. After that I might have composed *The Athenians*, an excellent poem, but I have renounced it, despairing of out-stripping myself. Now, how do you imagine that it is possible for anybody to invent anything new, when I, Spontini, realize that I am unable to surpass my preceding works? and furthermore, it is very evident that since *La Vestale*, not a note of music has been written that has not been stolen from me." And Spontini supported this last affirmation with scientifically verified facts. Quite stunned by this discourse, Wagner risked a timid objection, and asked if he did not feel himself impelled to create new forms, when approaching an entirely new subject. Spontini gave him a smile of pity. " In *La Vestale*," said he, " I have treated a Roman subject; in *Fernando Cortez*, a Spanish-Mexican subject, in *Olympie* a Græco-Macedonian subject; and finally, in *Agnes de Hohenstaufen*, a German subject; all the rest is worth nothing."

Notwithstanding this phenomenal egotism, exasperated at seeing himself supplanted by worthless musicians, Spontini, ridiculous and old as he was, ended by regaining the sympathies of the artists, by dint of energy and confidence in himself; and when he finally demanded the re-establishment of the final scene, with ballet and chorus (which they had habitually suppressed, finishing with the duet of Sicinius and Julia after their deliverance), he found nobody to object to this additional labor. It was labor lost. The performance was not a success, principally through the fault of Schroeder-Devrient, who, feeling herself too heavy for the role, by the side of a high priestess so young and charming as Johanna Wagner, aspired to counteract this disadvantage by dint of pathos, and her redoubled efforts carried her clear beyond the mark. The audience was cold, and the applause which terminated the performance was only homage rendered to the glory of the author. Wagner experienced a painful sensation at seeing him advance upon the scene, loaded with decorations, and making no end of acknowledgment for so feeble a recall. In order to escape from a more glaring discomfiture, Mme. Schroeder-Devrient still clung to the pretext of an indisposition in order to put off a second representation of *La Vestale*, Spontini having given evidence of a secret desire to be invited to prolong his stay at Dresden, and to mount there the complete series of his operas.

But suddenly he was in great haste to get away from Dres-

den ; he had just learned that the king of Denmark had conferred upon him a patent of nobility, and that the Pope had
honored him with the title of Count of San Andrea. He
instantly forgot *La Vestale*, to the great relief of his hosts,
and departed almost immediately for Paris ; he left in Dresden
a champion, at once skeptical and enthusiastic, in the young
musician, who promised, at the moment of parting, to meditate
at leisure upon his advice regarding the dramatic career —
and who followed his counsels so badly.

A short time after, about the 14th of December, 1844, the
ashes of Weber were brought back to Dresden, and this event,
Wagner himself says, had a great influence upon the mood in
which he found himself at the time of composing *Tannhäuser*.
A committee had been appointed, some time since, for the
purpose of bringing back to Dresden the remains of Weber,
who had died at London, whither he went to conduct his
Oberon; but the propaganda was insufficient, and furthermore, they encountered the religious scruples of the king,
who was unwilling to disturb the last sleep of death. Wagner, once in office, again agitated the project with an incredible energy. He was moved by a desire to render a supreme
homage to a German musician *par excellence*, to him who had
stirred his breast with its first musical raptures, whom he had
been pleased to salute as his master, and who, during his time
of trial in France, had brought him a breath from the German
fatherland with *Der Freischütz*. There was nothing to be
expected except through his personal effort, and furthermore he
must conquer, before all, the opposition of the royal intendant,
who, seeing in Weber only an ordinary capellmeister, feared to
create a precedent which would oblige them thereafter to
bring back to Saxony with great honors all the capellmeisters
who might die in foreign lands.

Wagner, having accepted the title of president of the
committee, launched his appeals on all sides, received sub-

scriptions, organized concerts, persuaded certain second-rate theatres to give performances for the benefit of the under- taking, and obtained one at the opera of Berlin, through the influence of Meyerbeer, which brought in two thousand thalers. He manœuvred so well, that the opera of Dresden could not very well remain behind, and they soon made up the sum necessary for transporting the ashes, and for erecting a monument.

The eldest of Weber's two sons went to London in quest of the mortal remains of his father; the coffin arrived at Magdeburg on the morning of the 14th of December; in the evening, at eight o'clock, a boat, draped in black, decorated with lyric trophies and illuminated with many lanterns, trans- ported it to the right bank of the Elbe. Then they deposited it upon a magnificent catafalque, in the centre of a circle formed by three or four hundred artists and amateurs, each holding a wax taper and a laurel wreath; then four hundred and fifty performers and singers executed a funeral hymn by Richard Wagner. After that they formed in procession and marched to the Catholic cemetery, amid the tolling of all the church bells in the city. The streets through which they were obliged to pass were illuminated by means of innumerable candles placed at the windows, and all the artists, friends and admirers who followed the coffin, together with five hundred foot soldiers of the royal guard, carried torches in their hands. Wagner had composed for the ceremony a funeral march with two motives from *Euryanthe :* the theme which in the over- ture describes the appearance of the phantom, joined to the cavatina from *Euryanthe*, transposed into *B flat major*. This symphonic piece, written for eighty wind instruments, to which he had added twenty muffled drums, in order to render *pianissimo* the tremulo of the altos in the overture, was of a superb grandeur, and produced an indescribable effect. At the chapel of the cemetery, Mme. Schroeder-Devrient awaited the body, upon which she placed a magnificent wreath of flowers. The interment did not take place until the next day. When the grave had been covered, the assistants formed above it an enormous pyramid of laurel wreaths; then Richard Wagner, speaking for the first time in public, delivered an address, in which he recalled the recent death of Weber's younger son, and passed by a very natural gradation into an invocation to German national art. "There never lived a musician more *German* than thou! England renders thee justice, France admires thee, but Germany alone can *love* thee; thou art hers, thou art a beautiful day of her existence, a warm drop of her blood, a portion of her heart! Who then can blame us for having desired that thy ashes should become a portion of her soil, of the soil of the dear German fatherland?"

Every year, on Palm Sunday, they were accustomed to give a grand concert at Dresden, for the benefit of the musicians. The concerts included a symphony and an oratorio, conducted alternately by the two leaders of the chapel, who were free to choose the work which they wished to direct. Reissiger having to direct the oratorio for 1846, Wagner, who the preceding year had chosen *The Creation*, decided to play *The Ninth Symphony*. He had preserved a profound admiration for this work, and wished for nothing less than the return of the impression which he had experienced at Paris, at the concerts of the Conservatoire, while listening to Habeneck's execution of it.

But the musicians of the orchestra, besides feeling a repugnance for the considerable labor involved, feared that the announcement of this symphony, hitherto badly played and badly understood in Dresden, would have an injurious effect upon the receipts, and they waited upon M. von Lüttichau, in order to induce him to oppose the project of the capellmeister. Fortunately, the authority of the latter was absolute, and

Wagner remained obdurate. It was necessary then to leave out what he thought best, and to begin rehearsing at once. On this occasion Wagner gave a rare example of that tenacity, that authority, and those outbursts of enthusiasm, which always made him so much feared and admired by his interpreters. He devoted the whole winter to these studies. He made each part of the orchestra rehearse as many as a dozen times, and added to the chorus various singing societies, and the choirs of the Seminary and School of the Cross, attaining thus to the number of three hundred voices. He made a change in the arrangement of the platform, to the great disgust of the musicians, who would willingly have done away with the expenses of a carpenter. He drew up, and had printed, a program explaining the symphony, but more than all he undertook to act upon the spirit of his musicians, after the fashion of Habeneck, to make them feel keenly that which they executed; and as he was in thorough sympathy with this masterpiece, as he knew it by heart from the first note to the last, he succeeded in arousing these musicians to an enthusiasm equal to his own, and the execution which he obtained had the effect of a thunderbolt upon the musical world of Dresden. "It was worth the trouble of the voyage," said Niels Gade, "just to hear the recitative of the double basses." Now there were present in that enthusiastic audience of April 5th, 1846, a young man and a child, who were to be reckoned later among the warmest partisans of Richard Wagner; the young man was Hans von Bülow, then sixteen years of age, and the child, not yet ten, was the future tenor, Ludwig Schnorr von Carolsfeld, the inspired creator of *Tristan and Isolde*.

Whilst preparing the *Ninth Symphony*, Wagner also gave his assiduous attention to a revival of *Iphigenie in Aulis*, by Gluck; indeed he gave too much attention to it for the taste of certain critics, since he re-enforced, discreetly, it is true, the orchestration of it, and modified the conclusion of the poem, departing somewhat from Racine, in order to approach more nearly to Euripides and to Goethe. When Spontini was rehearsing *La Vestale* at Dresden, he had said one day to Wagner, "I have heard, in your *Rienzi*, an instrument which you call a *basse-tuba*; I do not care to banish it from the orchestra; write me a part for it, for *La Vestale*." And Wagner, not wishing to do less for Gluck than for Spontini, had fancied to himself that he could take the same liberties with *Iphigenie* and yet produce the same effect which was produced at the epoch when no other instruments were used save those employed by Gluck. He acquitted himself of this delicate task with extreme conscientiousness. He procured an authentic copy from Paris, for fear that the score in use at Berlin had undergone some retouches from the hand of Spontini; furthermore, he applied himself to a very careful revision of the German text; he condensed certain parts, added some connecting links, and, as we have said, changed the *dénouement*; in short, he abandoned his personal work for a time, in order to devote himself to Gluck, and to glorify him; and he succeeded therein, for *Iphigenie in Aulis*, thus retouched, was a very great success. Certainly, this zeal and this disinterestedness are to the honor of Wagner, but he made a mistake in undertaking a work which could not have lasting results. Surely Gluck is not so antiquated, nor his orchestra so rudimentary, that his masterpieces may not still put in a good appearance on the stage. Furthermore, it is not permitted to tamper with creations of this magnitude, which form the pinnacles in the history of musical art. Such corrections are only admissible for works of a secondary order; ephemeral, good for diverting the masses momentarily, but which one would never think of offering for the study and veneration of posterity. Moreover, a single word solves the question: would Richard Wagner ever have admitted the idea that at some future time, one should do, out of admiration for him, what he had done out of admiration for Gluck — that one should modify his orchestra, and marry Lohengrin with Elsa? Therefore, the simplest and best means for glorifying Gluck was to execute his opera just as he had conceived it. It was a doubtful honor that he rendered him, and Berlioz, on a similar occasion, has shown for the author of *Orpheus* and of *Armides* an admiration more intelligent, a zeal much more respectful.[1]

Wagner had not much to do with the music of the chapel royal, but even there the routine annoyed him, and he deplored the work which was done there. The court, being Catholic, wished only Catholics in the choir, and the soprano and alto parts were taken by young boys; in all twenty-six choristers, fourteen of them men and twelve children, besides a complete orchestra, which on great occasions could be increased to the number of fifty performers. "The echoes and reverberations in the building were deafening. I wanted to relieve the hard-worked members of the orchestra, add female voices, and introduce true Catholic church music *a capella*. As a specimen I prepared Palestrina's *Stabat Mater*, and suggested other pieces, but my efforts failed.[2]

"There was a singular relic of former days there; a *musico*, a mature and corpulent *soprano*, whose pretensions and utter stupidity amused me greatly. On fête days he refused to

[1] Berlioz, when he added some solos and a ballet to *Der Freischütz*, at least respected the orchestra of Weber, and made no changes in the score; on the contrary, he adhered to it to the extent of keeping the *dénouement*, long as it was. With respect to *re-orchestrations*, one always hears quoted those of the *Messiah* by Mozart, the *Danaïds* by Spontini, the *Deserter* and *Richard, the Lion-hearted* by Adolphe Adam, etc., etc., but not one of these cases is comparable to that of Wagner, in the first place, because he modified the score, and above all, because the instrumentation of Gluck is, even to-day, neither insufficient nor antiquated. This revival of *Iphigenie in Aulis*, with *dénouement* by Wagner, took place under his directions, February 22, 1847. Mme. Schroeder-Devrient played Clytemnestra; Mlle. Johanna Wagner, Iphigenie; Mlle. Marpurg, Arthémise; Mitterwurzer, Agamemnon, Tichatschek, Achilles; and Dettmer, Calchas.

[2] Conversation with M. Dannreuther, in Grove's *Dictionary of Music*.

sing unless particular airs were reserved for him, and it was
most laughable to hear this aged Colossus gargling with the
graces of Hasse ; one thought only of an enormous pudding,
with the voice of a cracked rattle.　But with all that, he had
one incomparable quality : with a single breath he could sing
as much and more than any other artist in two respirations."

Wagner, during his long sojourn at Dresden, had had
occasion for the first time to unveil his character, in putting
his ideas in practice, and at that time he had shown himself
what he continued to be through life : ardent for innovation,
dissatisfied with everything — which he called his highest
faculty — without consideration for the opinions or prejudices
of others, violent, difficult, proud to excess ; but also possessed
of a rare energy, and so much power, notwithstanding his
faults, that he was able to draw to himself many warm partisans from among those who had attacked him the most
violently at first.　Those of his colleagues who had the
requisite intelligence, appreciated and loved him ; but he
displeased almost everybody by his irritable humor, and by
his indefatigable and encroaching activity.　Nobody, to be
sure, came to an open quarrel with him, but he was made to
feel the effects of the jealousy and ill-will which existed under-
neath a calm exterior.　His manner of conducting himself,
and his overbearing temperament, had rapidly estranged from
him at Dresden — the same at Paris, Munich and everywhere
— the journalistic world, which pursued him with taunts and
published the most absurd anecdotes about him.　The ac-
credited critic of Dresden, a particular friend of Reissiger, was
posing just then as the champion of established customs,
which he decorated with the high-sounding title of " classic
traditions."　This Schladebach, who was not without some
education and merit, had begun by shielding Wagner ; then
he turned about and criticised everything in his operas which
wandered from the beaten path.　As he was the principal

correspondent at Dresden for the political and literary papers of Leipsic, Berlin, and other important cities, his judgment radiated through all Germany, and did considerable harm to Wagner. Most of the directors and musicians, taking their watchword from the journals, Wagner was pronounced, not without some truth, an eccentric person, insupportable, and difficult in temper; the pieces and scores which he presented were scarcely looked into, and more than once they had been returned to him without being opened. But these attacks, and these drawbacks had no power over a man of his stamp, so confident of his own genius, — and their violence only increased in him a natural disposition to pose as an artist not understood, beset by enemies, and much more unappreciated than he really was. What Wagner was in his country, Berlioz was in his.

WOTAN AND HIS MESSENGER RAVENS

The slipper which the ravens hold in their beaks expresses the power which the jealous Fricka exercises over her spouse Wotan ; the familiar German saying, "to put on the slipper," signifies that the woman is mistress of the household.

(Taken from the *Schultze and Müller Ring of the Nibelungen*, 1881.)

CHAPTER V

OWARDS the end of his stay in Paris, and while he was pretty well occupied in accumulating enough money to take him to his native country, Richard Wagner in his leisure moments read German history, with the hope of finding there a subject for an opera. For a long time he searched in vain; but what struck him the most forcibly was that the poet and musician in him were always of one mind about rejecting a subject, and when a historical subject appeared to him inappropriate for a dramatic work, it offended likewise his musical sense. This observation confirmed him in an idea which had already taken possession of him, namely, that legendary subjects lent themselves to music much better than historical ones, and yet he kept on searching through history. He had ended by selecting an episode from the latter part of the Hohenstaufen power, and had chosen for the principal personages, Manfred, son of Frederic II., and a supposed daughter of the latter, a young Saracen maiden, who raised again the fallen courage of Manfred, led him by victory after victory up to the throne, gave up her life for her brother's sake, and revealed to him, only in dying, the relationship which opposed their union. Wagner had even partially developed his plot, when one of his friends, a philologist, lent him the popular tale of Tannhäuser. It was not unknown to him, for he had formerly read the poem by Tieck, which, he said, had not by any means pleased him; he knew also that Weber had had an idea of treating this subject musically, and it had therefore a great attraction for him. In short, this old legend, in which the principal figure is brought out very clearly and simply, fascinated him to the last degree. He was particularly pleased that it could be easily connected with the poetical tourney of the Wartburg, an episode well calculated to excite his inspiration, since it responded so marvellously to his worship for old Germany. Therefore, however scornful he may have shown himself of Tieck's poem, it did not prevent him from making use of it. Tieck, indeed, had imagined that Tannhäuser, on his way to the concours of the *Minnesinger* opened at the Wartburg, had encountered Venus, and allowed himself to be seduced by her, and Wagner, in adopting this idea, has simply added the love between Tannhäuser and the niece of the Count, a love instantly forgotten for Venus, and which in the end saves the knight, by snatching him from his perdition, through repentance.'

In his haste to be present at the rehearsals of *Rienzi*, he had arrived at Dresden before they were ready to take it in hand, and in order to divert himself, he made a journey into the mountains of Bohemia. He returned to Teplitz, and built the plot of *Tannhäuser*, in the same spot where, eight years before, he had traced the plan of the *Love-Veto*. He immediately set to work with great earnestness; however, he had some days of doubt after the disappointing reception accorded to *The Last Supper*; he succumbed to the need which all artists feel, of immediate applause, and he considered the expediency of abandoning *Tannhäuser* and of returning to

---

' In undertaking to trace to its source the history of the tourney of the singers, Wagner touched upon the germs of *Lohengrin* and *Parsifal*. Indeed, one of the copies of the "Combat of the Singers," led to the poem of *Lohengrin*, and Wagner, drawn into reading the *Parsifal* and the *Rituel* of Wolfram von Eschenbach, "saw an entirely new world of poetry suddenly opened before him."

Manfred, which appeared to him more likely to suit the public taste, — to write, in a manner, a second *Rienzi*. He knew that Schroeder-Devrient would be marvellous in the role of the Saracen maiden, and he submitted to her his project for the drama, but she was not pleased with it, and persuaded him not to carry it out; besides, he hesitated to sacrifice his own ideas to the taste of the masses. He has himself depicted somewhat forcibly the internal struggles which then distracted him.

" The happy change in my surroundings, and the freedom of mind resulting from it, more than all, the intoxication of finding myself in contact with a new and sympathetic society, fixed in my heart a desire for immediate appreciation, which turned from its proper channel my inner nature, formed as it had been by the unpleasant impressions of the past, and the struggle into which they had thrown me. The natural inclination which leads a man after the pursuit of happiness, tempted me into an artistic path which was very soon to end in profound dissatisfaction. The fact was, I could find happiness only in acquiring the name of artist, and that was possible only on condition that I should sacrifice my true nature to the taste of the public. I must give myself up to the pursuit of the caprices of fashion, I must lend myself to all the meannesses of speculation, which, at the point where I had arrived, I felt sure would kill me with very disgust. Thus the positive pleasures of life presented themselves to me under the single form which our modern world has given them; and in order to obtain them, it was necessary for me to apply my artistic faculties to exigencies, the worthless character of which I knew only too well."[1]

He came out conqueror in this internal struggle, and once for all, he sacrificed *Manfred* to *Tannhäuser*, the work which

[1] Richard Wagner d'après lui-même, p. 176.

he would have made according to the taste of the public, to that which he aimed to make conform to his ideas upon art; but truth to say, he nourished a secret hope of reconciling the two, and of gaining the good will of the masses, without abandoning even one of his ideas. But this project, as we shall see, was doomed to failure. He had completely finished *Tannhäuser* in April, 1844, and submitted it to a first revision, which he had achieved in the month of December. He had worked at it with much animation, and had finished it in such a heat of inspiration, that he had risked having the complete score lithographed from the manuscript; in 1845 he sent a copy of it to Carl Gaillard of Berlin, with a long and interesting letter. "The piano arrangement has already been prepared so that the day after the first representation, I shall be free. My intention is to be idle for a year or two, to spend my time in reading, and produce nothing. A dramatic work, to be significant and original, must mark a step forward in the life and culture of the artist; but one cannot take such a step every six months."

Notwithstanding the failure of *The Flying Dutchman*, the management of the opera of Dresden received *Tannhäuser* eagerly, and took great pains to have it worthily represented; the decorations had been ordered at Paris from Dieterle, and the best singers were placed at Wagner's disposal. But the music baffled them. First of all, Tichatschek was given the role of Tannhäuser, all the high passages of which had to be modified, because he found them too fatiguing; an excellent baritone, Mitterwürzer took the part of Wolfram; the niece of the author, Johanna Wagner, made a gracious Elizabeth, and Mme. Schroeder-Devrient figured as a rather mature Venus; she had accepted this role merely to be obliging, declaring that she could make nothing out of it: "You are a man of genius, said she to Wagner, but you write such eccentric stuff that it is impossible to sing it." Dettmer and Schloss had the roles of the Landgrave and Walther; Waechter, Curti and Riss represented Biterolf, Heinrich and Reimer, and Mlle. Anna Thiele was the little shepherd.

The first representation was given on the 19th of October, 1845, before a crowded house, more curious than sympathetic; they particularly wished to know if the author had persevered in the path which he had entered with *The Flying Dutchman*, or if that set-back had decided him to return to the accepted style of opera, in which he had made so marked a success with *Rienzi*. Richard Wagner had persisted in his new ideas, and the public were greatly disappointed. The performance was a downright failure, notwithstanding the reports spread by certain French narrators, including Gasperini, who spoke of ovations, of recalls, of crowns, of triumph. And the principal cause for this serious failure, was the scene of the return from Rome, where Tannhäuser recounts his unhappy voyage, and his interview with the Pope; this being admitted to be the only drawback to an otherwise admirable creation. Until then, the performance had dragged along in a rather spiritless fashion, and the different scenes of the drama were received with more or less favor, according to the amount of melody and *éclat* which the hearers found in them. The scene of the Court of Venus, in particular, much less important than it was to become in course of time, and badly sustained by Mme. Schroeder-Devrient, who foresaw only too clearly that she would not do herself justice, had indifferently prepared the audience; they understood very little of it, in spite of the explanation of the legend of *Tannhäuser*, which the author had drawn up and had placed at the head of the libretti, which were sold at the door. After that, however, the final septet of the first act had made an excellent impression, and they had recalled the author with the singers. Then the march and some very clear melodies in the second act had been more warmly received, and Wagner was again recalled, a common enough occurrence in

Germany, where the author is usually recalled at the close of the performance. They had simply advanced the moment of this usual courtesy, and it was well they did. The last *entr'acte* indeed, having lasted for nearly half an hour, had put the people in a bad humor, and the long recitative of Tannhäuser coming on top of this, and lasting a quarter of an hour, completed the impatience of the audience. They had expected an honest melody, they had heard only a tedious recitative! Down with the donkey! This was the general outcry against a musician who, having at hand such a tenor as Tichatschek, could find nothing better for him to sing in the third act at the decisive moment for success, than an interminable recitative, and they immediately concluded that a musician capable of so grave a fault must be entirely devoid of melodious invention. Thus it was one of the most inspired pages, one of the grandest conceptions, which gave rise to that senseless criticism of weakness and want of melody, which has been re-echoed in every country during the past forty years!

The day after the performance, Wagner was above all crushed that the sweet illusion which he had cherished, of reaching the sympathies of the public without sacrificing his ideas of reform, had just suffered the rudest shock. "I was," said he, "overcome by this disappointment, and the isolation in which I found myself could not be concealed. The small number of friends who sympathized with me felt discouraged themselves, through a keen realization of my painful situation. A week slipped away before a second representation could be given, on account of the changes and the clippings which seemed necessary for a clearer understanding of the work. This week seemed to me like a life-time. It was not wounded pride which made me suffer; I was conscious of the absolute annihilation of all my illusions. I became aware that with *Tannhäuser* I had revealed myself to only a little group of my intimate friends, and not to the public, to which I involuntarily addressed myself in the production of the work. It did not seem to me possible to reconcile this contradiction." Notwithstanding this apparent resignation, Wagner had clung to the solitary hope that the second representation would be a little better understood; finally, after eight days of anxious expectation, the requisite changes being made and Tichatschek having recovered from the hoarseness from which he had been suffering, they played *Tannhäuser* again, on the 27th of October; this performance so impatiently awaited, had the same result as the former one. The house was more than half empty, and the stray spectators who wandered in did not show themselves quicker of comprehension than those of the previous evening. However, thanks to the perseverance of the management, and particularly to the zeal and the talent of the actors, they lent a semblance of life to the work, and by the end of the year, in nine weeks, they had given seven representations.[1]

The journals with one accord, had declared *Tannhäuser* insupportable and tedious; it had neither melody nor form. And then, this sort of music acted upon the nerves, to say nothing of a subject by far too fatiguing and sorrowful. Art, said the critics, should be gay and consoling; why did not Tannhäuser marry Elizabeth? So the royal intendant explained to Wagner, that his predecessor, Weber, managed things much better, since he knew how to terminate his

---

[1] " This work excited the liveliest enthusiasm, wrote the *Gazette Musicale* of Paris; the author was recalled after every act, and after the performance, the musicians of the orchestra, and more than two hundred young men, each furnished with a torch, formed in procession and marched to his house, in order to execute under his window a serenade composed of selections chosen from his works and those of Meyerbeer." (Nov. 2nd.) But a month later it was obliged to recognize the fact that this success was only visionary; " This remarkable score has caused heated and serious discussions among the masses, as well as among men of art; but everybody agrees in pronouncing it a capital work, and one which does great honor to the composer." (7 December, 1845.)

operas happily. Finally, the dissatisfaction was general. *The Evening Gazette*, of Dresden, exalted by comparison a certain opera by Ferdinand Hiller, *Christmas Night's Dream*, represented at Dresden in April, 1845, and which, it said, contained much more music, in the true sense of the word. *The Norddeutcher Zeitung* playfully said : " If it is true that Wagner has unknown heights in view, heaven grant that he may never attain to them. These heights are crowned with an ennui so heavy that they are inaccessible." Finally the *New Musical Gazette*, of which Schumann had given up the management, made up for its former praises by attacking both the poem and the music, the obscurity and improbabilities of which it brought out in bold relief ; Wagner knew by this that Schumann was no longer there.

The professional musicians were not more favorable than the press, to *Tannhäuser*. Mendelssohn, after hearing it, simply said to the author, " the canonical entry in the adagio of the second finale pleased me." Maurice Hauptmann who had replaced Weinlig at the Thomasschule, wrote to Spohr that the overture was quite atrocious, incredibly long, awkward and tedious. And Spohr, when he had had it played at Cassel in 1853, wrote to Hauptmann that this opera contained many new and beautiful ideas, but as many passages disagreeable to the ear ; then in a following letter he announced himself quite accustomed by repeated hearings, to the things which formerly grated upon his ears, and that it was only the absence of definite rhythms and the frequent lack of rounded periods which continued to trouble him. Schumann, for he had come to live at Dresden in the autumn of 1844, wrote to Dorn on the 7th of January, 1846: " I wish that you might hear *Tannhäuser*. Some parts of it are most profound, most original, in short, a hundred times better than the preceding operas, and other parts are musically light. Wagner is able to take a very important place at the theatre, and I am sure that he possesses the necessary courage. The technical means, for example the instrumentation, are quite remarkable, incomparably surer than formerly. He has already made a new libretto, *Lohengrin*." Schumann, at this period had almost entirely ceased to write long criticisms, but when a musical work struck him, whether favorably or unfavorably, immediately upon his return home, he rapidly noted down his impression on daily tablets : these brief mentions, covering the years 1847 to 1850, form a theatrical note-book. Now, one may read there under date of August 7th, 1847 : "*Tannhäuser* by Richard Wagner. It is impossible to speak of this work in few words. That which is beyond all doubt is that it has the color of a work of genius. If Wagner had as much melody as cleverness, he would be the privileged man of his time. This opera would furnish material for many observations. It deserves that I keep this task for some future time." [1]

He never returned to it. And moreover his opinions shortly suffered a change on the subject of Richard Wagner, for he wrote in a letter of 1853, " Wagner is not, if I may say the thing in few words, a good musician ; he lacks the necessary sentiment of form, and beauty of sound. Apart from the representation, his music is poor ; it is the music of an ama-

---

[1] This encomium from the pen of Schumann has all the more weight, since, three months before he had very severely criticised the retouches which Wagner had given to *Iphigenie in Aulis*. He had heard Gluck's lyric tragedy thus arranged on the 15th of May, and this is what he wrote in his theatrical note-book after leaving the theatre : " It is Richard Wagner who had put the work on the stage ; the costumes and decorations are worthy the interpreters. He has even added to the music, as I believe I have remarked elsewhere. I will say more : all the finale, " Nach Troja," is of his invention. This is too much. Perhaps Gluck would be justified in doing the same with one of Richard Wagner's operas, even to cutting it up and making radical changes in it. What would I say of the work in itself ? As long as the world lasts, music like that will always shine resplendent, and will never grow old." These are very sensible criticisms, for which Richard Wagner never forgave Schumann.

teur, empty, and unpleasant." Spohr and Schumann changed opinions at the same time, but in the contrary direction.[1]

Wagner gave a good deal of thought and speculation to the causes of this repulse, and came to the conclusion that the artistic taste of the public, spoiled by worthless productions, must be entirely refashioned ; moreover that any ordinary man would succeed but badly and that in order to undertake the work with any chance of success, one must have the protection of a power in the land, of a prince or a king. Just at that time there was a sovereign on the throne of Prussia deeply infatuated with the fine arts, with music in particular, very susceptible to new ideas, and very respectful to the masterpieces of the past, and who threw his capellmeisters into confusion by demanding of them off-hand, an execution of certain fragments from the old masters, forgotten by all, but not by him ; it was the king Frederick William IV. Richard Wagner thought that a sovereign who had given to music such an honored place in his domain, who had called to Berlin, Meyerbeer and Mendelssohn, who had ordered of the latter the choruses to *Antigone* in order to restore antique tragedy, would bring some sympathy, or at least some curiosity to the examination of new musical ideas, and perhaps aid them to carry the day. Far, then, from giving up to the recent failure of *The Flying Dutchman*, it was in this direction that he turned all his efforts, addressing first the intendant of the royal theatre, then venturing even to the intendant of the court music. The account of the replies which he received from these two dignitaries, is best given in his own words :

---

[1] In February 1846, the overture to *Tannhäuser* was executed at Leipsic under the direction of Mendelssohn, " who conducted it," said M. Glasenapp in his work written on the inspiration of Wagner, " with the moderate sympathy which he always felt for the efforts of Wagner. If it is true that he has had the intention of showing this overture there as a model to avoid, one may rest assured he has succeeded." The compliment is worth the price.

" I made some attempts to have my opera introduced, aiming especially at the Berlin theatre ; but I received a formal refusal from the intendant of the royal theatres of Prussia. The intendant general of the court music seemed better disposed towards it ; through him I begged that the king would interest himself in the execution of my work, and asked permission to dedicate to him the score of *Tannhäuser*. He made official response that the king never accepted the dedication of a work without hearing it; but that considering the obstacles which prevented the execution of my opera at the Berlin theatre, it might be possible to have it heard by the king if I would arrange some pieces for military music which would be played on parade. I could not have been more painfully humiliated, nor have recognized with more certainty my true position. Henceforth there was no more fame in art for me."

This is well enough to say afterwards ; but is an artist who is truly convinced of his worth and of the power of a new idea, ever disarmed before the public ? Such a weakness is only excusable in composers without conviction, and without conscience, and heaven knows there are enough of them in the world! Instead of lamenting at his failure, Wagner while projecting a new work in which he could develop his creative and inventive faculties (*Lohengrin*) also occupied himself with retouching and improving *Tannhäuser*. In its first form *Tannhäuser* differed in two important points from the work which was heard at Paris in 1861. In the first place, the opening scene of the Court of Venus, so indifferently rendered by Mme. Schroeder, was far from being the richly developed scene which Wagner afterwards made it, expressly for the Parisian public ; furthermore, the conclusion of the work was much shorter ; one saw neither Venus nor the funeral procession of Elizabeth. Tannhäuser remained alone on the stage with Wolfram, and the struggle between the voluptuous pagan and the virtuous Christian who disputed for his heart, was indicated only by the distant light in the grotto of Venus, and the funeral knells tolled by the bells of Wartburg; Wagner modified and developed this final scene in the second revision of his opera, finished in September 1846, but before the completion of this recasting, he had experienced a double pleasure. First, having gone to Cassel, he had encountered there the aged Spohr, whom the reading of *Tannhäuser* had confirmed in the high opinion which he had formed of Wagner's talent, after the representation of *The Flying Dutchman.* Then a revival of the work effected at Dresden in 1847, with the conclusion leisurely developed, had been more and more favorably received by the amateurs. The press was not disarmed, and still held that the work was as bad as ever; but the public itself showed such a general interest, that Wagner persuaded himself that except for the criticisms, he could easily secure the adoption of his new point of view and his most individual creations, by all sincere and unprejudiced people.

Humiliated as Wagner had been by the proposition made to him at Berlin to judge his *Tannhäuser* in the form of parade music, he had nevertheless, being pressed for money, renewed his solicitations, with the aid of Meyerbeer, and the king of Prussia finally designated *Rienzi* for the holiday representation to be given on the anniversary of his birthday, Oct. 15, 1847. The author went to Berlin in September, in order to direct the studies; he received a rather lukewarm welcome, and the journals immediately came out with ill-natured remarks and personal attacks which augured ill for the final result. At the theatre he was satisfied with the zeal of the orchestra and with the talent of the singers — Pfister as Rienzi, Mlle. Tuszek as Irène, and Mme. Schlegel-Koester as Adriano — but he could not succeed in conciliating the press. Furthermore he was not happy in his discourse, and in speaking of the grave of Weber had made some unfortunate re-

marks.   At the general rehearsal, while undertaking to thank
the *personnel* and particularly the orchestra, he so far forgot
himself as to say that *Rienzi* was the work of a beginner, the
tendency of which he repudiated, and that one ought not to
judge of his actual ideal by this totally insufficient production,
which he himself declared to be a " transgression of youth."
The performance, delayed by an indisposition of Mlle. Tuszek
did not take place until the 26th.[1]

Meyerbeer had departed a few days previously, and the
king, although he had designated the opera, had not deigned
to be present.   However the house was filled, notwithstanding
the doubts and preconceived notions of the press.   The overture, it is true, was received coldly enough, but the composer,
who directed the execution, was recalled after the second act,
and again at the end of the play.   There was probably more
civility than real enthusiasm in these recalls, and on the following day, the journals did their worst for the work, summoning to their support the author's own confession, and re-
proaching him for his noisy orchestration, his lack of melody,
of form, etc.   And this was the fate of *Rienzi* in Berlin because the author had not known how to curb his tongue.   An
unhappy speech had caused all the trouble, and more than
once in the course of Wagner's career, the orator in the man
has compromised the musician.

From *The Flying Dutchman* to *Tannhäuser* there was a
very perceptible progress, in the sense that Wagner disen-
gaged himself more and more from the forms of conventional
opera, such as Gluck and Weber, to his mind the greatest
masters, had treated it.   Certainly Gluck and Weber, as well

---

[1] Was this the true and only reason?   It has been said that the management
had found in *Rienzi* certain dangerous political expressions, — liberty, fraternity,
etc., which would have to be emphasized at the representation, and that they had
preferred to give another opera on the king's birthday, postponing *Rienzi* till the
end of the month.

as Beethoven, have greatly aided the development of Wagner's genius; but let us exaggerate nothing especially in regard to the first named, and not go so far as to say that Richard Wagner has imagined nothing which Gluck has not done or indicated before him. It would be impossible to make a claim of this kind after seeing the scores of these two composers side by side, for they are as different as night is from day. Gluck has not modified in any way the general form of the opera; the air exists as the essential element, and the airs, duets, trios, choruses and *divertissements* follow each other in the simplest possible manner; moreover he often had in view the pure vocal effect, when he would repeat words without constraint, and troubled himself so little about the unity of conception between the poetry and the music, that he very often reset old Italian airs to French words, without the slightest scruple; indeed, it was only by the power and vigor of his declamation that Gluck has acted upon Wagner.

As to Weber, Wagner himself has explained, with the respect which he had for his chosen master, in what particulars they differed from each other. "There is no denying it, the discouraging effect proceeding from a knowledge of the true character of the opera-going public, is of paramount importance, and with an artist of a feeble nature always ends by becoming the principal consideration. They tell me that Weber himself, this pure, this noble, this profound spirit, fell back affrighted time and time again, before the consequences of his method so full of originality; he conferred upon his wife the right of "the gallery" as he expresses it; he undertook to make through her, in the sense of "this gallery," all the possible objections to his ideas, and they often resulted in his making expedient concessions, in spite of the requirements of the style. These concessions which my first model, my venerated master Weber, believed himself obliged to make to the opera public, I flatter myself you will never encounter in

my *Tannhäuser*, and that which is peculiar to the form of this
work, that which distinguishes it perhaps more than anything
else from those of my predecessors, consists precisely in that."

In drawing upon this German legend for the subject of his
drama, Wagner had remained faithful to his preferences for
the myth, since the heart of his naïve and pious legend expresses the struggle of the sensual love personified by Venus,
and the ideal love represented by the chaste Elizabeth. A
knight of Thuringen, Tannhäuser, has allowed himself to
wander into the subterranean empire of the pagan divinity,
the Court of Venus. The goddess intoxicates him with pleasures and employs a thousand seductions for detaining him;
but Tannhäuser has felt awaken in him the memory of his
youth; remorse has seized him. He resists the further
supplications of Venus, who predicts that he will sooner or
later return to her and disappears. Tannhäuser finds himself transported to the earth, in a pleasant valley; one hears
in the distance the song of the pilgrims, who are on their way
to Rome to implore of the Holy Father pardon for their faults.
Some huntsmen arrive on the scene, who recognize Tannhäuser; these are his friends, the chevalier-poets, with the
landgrave of Thuringen. They question him, they demand of
him why he has quitted his brothers, and whence he has come;
Tannhäuser vaguely responds that he has committed a great
fault, and that he must expiate it by fleeing from all whom he
loves. "Forgettest thou, then Elizabeth," his friend Wolfram
murmurs in his ear, "Elizabeth, the niece of the landgrave,
who since thy departure has lost all the graces, all the spright-
liness of youth?" At this cherished name, which recalls to
him a happy past, Tannhäuser yields, and returns with his
friends to the court of the landgrave. — Behold the great hall
of Wartburg. Tannhäuser conducted by Wolfram, there meets
Elizabeth, who at the approach of the new festival, calls to
mind the tourneys of the past, from which Tannhäuser always

went forth conqueror; recognition and reconciliation quickly enter the hearts of the two lovers. Then commences the fête of the singers. In the presence of the high lords and grand ladies of Thuringen the landgrave opens the *concours*, and announces that Elizabeth will reward the poet who shall the best " penetrate the mystery of pure love." Wolfram of Eschenbach enters first on the list, and sings of ideal love. But Tannhäuser, who is still under the domination of Venus, challenges these sentiments, and celebrates a passion less mystic. Walther arises and replies to Tannhäuser; then the latter, enflamed by the recollection of Venusberg, again takes up his song with increased enthusiasm. The assembly rise up indignant, the women depart, the knights draw their swords and fall upon the audacious singer. Elizabeth alone defends him against them all. She finally obtains assurance that his life shall be spared, and gives herself up to the love of him who is no longer worthy of it. The landgrave drives out the offender, and persuades him to join the pilgrims, whose last faint accents are heard in the valley. "To Rome!" cries Tannhäuser, suddenly shaking off his hallucination and measuring at a glance the abyss of evil into which the power of Venus had thrown him. At the opening of the third act, Elizabeth is seen kneeling at the feet of the Virgin; she fervently implores the salvation of Tannhäuser. The pilgrims return from Rome, and Tannhäuser is not with them; the young girl then slowly retires. Tannhäuser at last arrives, pale, spent with fatigue, and crushed beneath a weight of remorse. He meets Wolfram and describes to him his pilgrimage, in terms of despair; the Pope has not heard his prayer. "Where goest thou?" "To Venusberg." Then appears Venus, who desires to win back the pilgrim; but Wolfram restrains him, and shows him the body of Elizabeth, who has just given herself up to death. Christianity triumphs over paganism, and Tannhäuser expires by the side of the pure victim, crying " Saint Elizabeth, pray for me!"

This drama, in its grand simplicity, offers a number of tableaux favorable to the inspiration of the musician; moreover, being elevating in its nature, superhuman, almost mystic, it exalts the soul, instead of bringing the mind down to the level of purely terrestrial incidents. In regard to the music, is there anything more beautiful than this overture, in which the violent struggle between the two elements of the drama is so vividly depicted, or than the tableau of Venusberg as it was rearranged for Paris? And all that which follows; the sweet song of the shepherd, with the chorus of the departing pilgrims, then the grand septet of the chevaliers; is not this admirable act all that could be desired? The second act is fairly inferior to the other two. The *entrée* of Elizabeth and the first part of her duet with Tannhäuser are indeed remarkable, but the allegro which follows is by far too commonplace. There are some superb passages in the tourney of the poets, such as the chant of the orchestra at the moment when the pages are seating the lords, or the appeal of Elizabeth as she throws herself before the drawn swords, or yet the conclusion, with the chorus of pilgrims in the distance; but the scene of the *concours* in its *ensemble* is monotonous, and the author does not seem to have realized in it that fusion of the music with the words, which was to become in his eyes the essential condition of musical beauty. The spirit of it is powerful but uniform, and therein the character is faulty, since all the interest should proceed from the contrast and the opposition of the different songs of love improvised by the *trouvères*. The third act, on the other hand, is from beginning to end a conception of genius, a creation so superior that the author has never since been able to surpass it.

Just as it stands, and notwithstanding the imperfections of the second act, *Tannhäuser* clearly shows the tendency of the author, and already gives a forecast of the future mould of opera. Although the forms of the *genre* persist there in many places, particularly in the finale of the first act, and in the duet between Elizabeth and Tannhäuser, Wagner could flatter himself that he had produced a work three quarters individual, and that he had made, victorious or not with the public, a great step in advance of his master Weber, of that Weber who himself also had aspired to the drama, at least in *Euryanthe*, and who in his predilection for the old popular legends, had predicted that it would be possible one day to create a distinctively German opera. It has been said with reason, that Wagner in this last opera, commenced just where Weber left off.

RICHARD WAGNER'S HOME AT BAYREUTH.

CHAPTER VI

I' was during a summer holiday that he spent at Marienbad, in 1845,— perhaps two or three months before the appearance of *Tannhäuser* — that Richard Wagner outlined the plan of *Lohengrin*. He was very glad to have finished with *Tannhäuser;* he expected an early success, and for the first time in many months, he gave rein to his natural high spirits, and turned for a time to the study of more cheerful ideas. His friends had been advising him to treat a subject less painful, which would more easily please the public, and as his mind was still full of *Tannhäuser*, it occurred to him that it would be a good idea to make a comic counterpart to that opera, by bringing the corporation of the Meistersingers of Nuremberg before the footlights, and setting off this pedantic *concours* of *bourgeois* against the poetical tourney of the noble *Minnesinger*. And as he was always disposed to identify himself with his heroes he would have taken great satisfaction in becoming incarnate in Hans Sachs, the last representative of popular poetry, or in the chevalier Walther, the inspired poet of love ; whilst those narrow-minded pedants would have represented the musicians whose insipid productions impeded his progress, and the senseless critics who passed upon him from the height of their ignorance. So he made a preliminary sketch of the *Meistersingers*, but

whether the subject were really too gay for his actual state of mind, or whether he had not yet enough irony to cast upon his detractors, he soon abandoned it, and returned to *Lohengrin*.

He had known for a long time the legend of the " Knight of the Swan "; he had read it in Paris, at the same time that he had read *Tannhäuser*, and he had not found it much to his taste; he classed it with the superficial order, — he of the romantico-Christian poems; but when he came to examine it more closely, at the moment of abandoning the *Meistersingers*, he recognized in *Lohengrin* a myth antedating Christianity and the starting-point of which was not in the supernatural, but in woman's heart itself; henceforth he became as much in love with the subject as he had formerly disliked it. As he himself says, the very feeling of his complete isolation before a rebellious public, — since the aid which he had thought to find near an intelligent sovereign had just come to naught — gave him the courage to undertake a new work, in which he should press still further forward, and should depart more and more from the current form of opera. This indicated on his part a very strange turn of mind, but also a rare tenacity, and a particular inclination to reflect in his heroes the impressions of his own heart. When he had composed *The Flying Dutchman*, he was himself longing after the ideal woman, the distant fatherland, sovereign healers of all woes; just as the Hollander tossed upon the boundless deep, longed after the woman who was to deliver him from eternal damnation. In writing *Tannhäuser* he had symbolized the struggle which had just arisen in his own heart, and in which he had set out to conquer, like his hero, by sacrificing the pleasures of the world to the sweet delights of a satisfied conscience and of a pure ideal. In *Lohengrin* he was going to rise still higher into the ethereal regions, towards the radiant summits, always like his heroes,

while the whole world, the public, the press and his friends
were doing their best to make him descend again to their
level. "In truth," says he, "*Lohengrin* is an entirely new
manifestation. It was possible at no other time, and under
no other conditions than in the mind and intuition of an
artist, who, finding himself precisely in my position, had
arrived at the point of development at which I had arrived
when this subject appeared to me as an imperative duty which
was imposed upon me."[1]

In other words he composed *Lohengrin* and arose forth-
with to the absolute masterpiece; absolute, according to the
ideas which he had at the time, because he was irresistibly
driven to it by a mysterious force, in spite of attacks or remonstrances, and he could not do otherwise than obey this inner
impulse.

Wagner arranged the situations and composed the principal musical motives of his drama during the winter of 1845,
immediately after the failure of *Tannhäuser;* so that he was
able to commence the music in the month of September,
1846, while he was *en villegiature* at Grosgraufen, near the
royal residence of Pilnitz. Just as in *The Flying Dutchman*
he had instinctively commenced with the ballad of Senta,
which became the musical pivot of the score, so in *Lohengrin*,
and this time with a deliberate purpose, he began with the
third act, and composed first the recitative of the Holy Grail,
on which he wished to build the entire work. In the meantime *Tannhäuser* was again performed, and as it succeeded
this time a little better, he felt renewed courage to work. He
was so thoroughly absorbed in the composition of *Lohengrin*,
that he meditated isolating himself from the world, in order
to obtain the necessary concentration of thought; so during
the summer of 1847 he managed to gain absolute solitude in

[1] *Richard Wagner d'après lui-même*, by M. Georges Noufflard, p. 215.

the old *palais Marcolini*, with the result that he was able to finish the introduction by the 28th of August; by the end of the following spring, all the instrumentation was completed. Surely, it was something to have finished the score; but he was anxious to have it seen, to have it performed. Now neither the editor Meser, who had published without profit his first three operas, nor the royal intendant who had mounted them, seemed disposed to incur further expense. A story went the rounds that the unfortunate Meser, who lodged on the first floor before the publication of *Rienzi*, and had been obliged to mount an additional flight of stairs after each new opera, had nothing left but to install himself in the garret, if he wished to publish *Lohengrin;* it was also declared that at the approach of the masterpiece, the price of violin strings was considerably increased; harmless pleasantries, which ran their course at Dresden, and even reached so far as the journals of Vienna. After some hesitation the royal intendant consented, but not the publisher, to whom Wagner was already considerably in debt through former transactions; and it was the house of Breitkopf and Härtel, who, for a few hundred thalers, finally acquired the ownership of *Lohengrin*.

Meanwhile Wagner had still other projects in mind; he hesitated between a *Siegfried*, a purely mythical subject, and a *Frederic Barbarossa*,[1] a subject wholly historical; again his mind was disturbed by a conflict between history and legend.

At first he favored Barbarossa, intending to make a prose drama of it, without music, but he soon found that in order to place the grand figure of Barbarossa in his own time, with the proper surroundings, he must bring together so many im-

---

[1] From the historical studies made with a view to *Barbarossa*, there resulted only a curious essay, *Die Wibelungen*, a history of the world according to tradition, originally intended for a drama in prose, and treating upon the points of contact between history and myth; it was written in 1848, and published at Leipsic in 1850.

portant facts, that there would be no room left for the drama, properly speaking ; whereas, if he attempted to treat the subject literally, making use of mythical processes, he would completely destroy the history, and take away the real character of his hero. He concluded then that in order to employ the mythical form in the most perfect manner, he must reject all compromise, and select a veritable myth. Once convinced of the double idea that the ideal drama *ought not to be historical*, and that it *ought to be musical*, he abandoned all thought of Frederic Barbarossa, and in the autumn of 1848, he wrote the poem of *The Death of Siegfried*. He wrote it in alliterative verse, for he had his own ideas upon language, and had constructed for himself quite a system of versification, holding that alliteration is nothing less than the generative force of language, and that music with its aid, attains to an infinite richness and variety ; he claimed also that it would have been his duty to renounce his *Siegfried*, if he had been unable to couch it in other verse than that in common use. He found in alliteration, strongly accenting the rhythm, a very *melody of language* whence sprung directly the equivalent musical melody, etc., and this is what he tried to realize in *The Death of Siegfried ;* but without the desired result, for the same thing is true of the alliteration as of the rhyme, namely, that the verses are much weakened when set to music, as one may be convinced by listening to the *Nibelungen*.

In 1848 Richard Wagner obtained at Dresden a hearing of the finale of *Lohengrin*, at a concert given on September 22, on the occasion of the third centennial of the founding of the chapel royal. At the close of the festival there was the customary banquet, and Wagner made a short speech in which he expressed the sentiment so often repeated since then, that the theatre had a duty to perform : to encourage exclusively the national artistic production ; that it had an object to attain : to assist in the education and enlightenment of the people for and by the German fatherland. Thus all proceeded regularly, and after the public hearing of this important page, *Lohengrin* would have been played at Dresden, like *Rienzi*, *The Flying Dutchman* and *Tannhäuser*, if the author had not taken part in a grand political disturbance. It must be said that Richard Wagner, perhaps under the influence of the subversive theories which he had absorbed in the Universities, but also because of his natural propensities to reform everything, was much carried away with revolutionary notions. Not that he had settled, deeply-rooted convictions, but because he was miserably poor, over head and ears in debt, and hunted by his creditors; therefore he awaited a political change to bring about a sudden amelioration of his own condition, or the immediate realization of his more or less chimerical projects. He had already given many of these projects to the public ; he had written a paper on the reorganization of the theatre at Dresden, and of the Conservatory at Leipsic, which latter he proposed to transport without ceremony to Dresden. The irritation which the people of Leipsic felt at such a proposition as this can be easily imagined. A little later, immediately following the troubles produced in Germany by the reaction from the Revolution of 1848 in France, when a ministry of the opposition had replaced the Koenneritz ministry in Saxony, he had addressed to the new minister of the interior, Martin Oberläuder, with whom he sympathized, a long project for the reorganization of the theatre ; he requested that the budget of the opera should be separated from that of the court, and that the subsidy, which had hitherto been given out of the king's private purse, should be replaced by an annual appropriation made from the public treasury. His aim was to centralize all the institutions of art existing in Saxony, with headquarters at Dresden. He wished to put the theatre in a state to guide the public taste instead of following it, and in order to give it a purely intellectual character, he proposed to transform it into a sort of artistic republic, subject to a representative government; finally to make of this ideal theatre a kind of annex to the church, and to connect it with the ministry of public worship.

But nothing came of all these fine propositions; they were not even examined, and Wagner, irritated at the small amount of attention which his labors excited, turned more than ever towards the revolutionary party. He consorted with several of his leaders, with Semper, director of the school of architecture; with Kichly, the philologist; with Roeckel, director of a new democratic journal; he joined secret societies, and went away to deliver a grand discourse at the *Dresdener Vaterlandsverein*, with the object of giving the projected revolution more of an artistic and less of a political character; for which he was regarded by the leaders of the party as a visionary and shallow-pated artist. For his part, he did not judge them much more favorably, and allowed them to see it; but he had none the less received a reprimand for his conduct from the authorities, who judged that a royal capellmeister had something better to do than to go about haranguing at the clubs. At this moment of his life, isolated in a society which could not understand him, he had conceived the idea of depicting his own voluntary annihilation in a drama of *Jesus of Nazareth*, in which Jesus would not have been a God descended upon earth to die, but a man capable of enjoying life, and whom the unworthiness of this world had so disgusted, that he sought death as a deliverance. He did not carry out this idea for a poem, because, as he says, a drama of that nature would have been forbidden by law, since society would not have submitted to so radical a change.

Notwithstanding his difficult position, notwithstanding the ideas of social and musical reformation, with the theatre for the base, and universal happiness for the goal, which agitated his mind, he probably would not have gone any farther, had

REPRESENTATION OF "LOHENGRIN," AT WEIMAR, IN 1850.
(Act I : Arrival of Lohengrin). — After an engraving of the time.

not the Russian revolutionary Bakounine arrived in the country, which was then in a state of fermentation. The latter immediately gained a great influence over Wagner, and led him up to such a degree of exaltation, that one day the ambitious musician, — I have the fact from a good source — addressed a letter to the King, counselling him to proclaim the Republic himself, and to become thus the first citizen of that free State. Finally, on the 1st of May, 1849, when the King pronounced the dissolution of the Saxon diet, and the Socialist party called the people to arms, Wagner did not hesitate to seize a gun and run to the barricades; again the influence of Bakounine. At first the insurgents had the upper hand; the arsenal was taken and burned, the regular army defeated, and the king left the city; but thirty-six hours later the Prussian troops arrived, who promptly restored order, and Richard Wagner, together with Semper and many others took to flight; Bakounine was arrested.

Once outside of Saxony, Wagner went undisturbed to Weimar, to ask protection from Liszt, with whom, forgetting his first impression at Paris, he had formed a strong friendship when the latter had come to Dresden to give concerts; a marked similarity of tastes and of temperament had brought them together forever. Liszt having retreated to the court of Saxe-Weimar, had testified to his devotion to Wagner by executing first the overture to *Tannhäuser* (Nov. 12, 1848), then the entire opera, on Feb. 16, 1849, for the fête of the reigning grand-duchess; and, as he boasts with good reason, in a letter addressed to the *Journal des Débats*, of Paris, this little capital, always hospitable to good and great things, had made the reputation of this work for all of Germany. The success had been decisive, and Wagner had received confirmation of it at Dresden, in the classic form of a gold snuffbox. Received by Liszt with open arms, the fugitive would willingly have prolonged his stay at Weimar, had he not suddenly learned, on the 19th of May, during a rehearsal of *Tannhäuser*, that orders had gone forth from Dresden to arrest, in any part of the German Confederation an "individual politically dangerous," by the name of Richard Wagner. At the same time the *Wochenblatt* of Frankfort, published his discription : "Wagner, thirty-seven or thirty-eight years of age, of medium height, brown hair, high forehead, brown eyebrows, gray-blue eyes, well proportioned nose and mouth, round chin, wears glasses. Words and gestures rapid. Clothing, redingote of dark green buckskin, black pantaloons, velvet waistcoat, silk cravat, the usual felt hat and boots." There was no time to be lost ; Liszt succeeded in procuring for him a passport and escorted him as far as Eisenach on the way to Paris.

In departing thus, Wagner knew that he left behind him a friend who would watch over his work, and propagate it. "One day," he has related, "when I was sick, miserable and discouraged, my eyes fell upon the score of *Lohengrin* which I had nearly forgotten. I experienced a painful shock in the feeling that these notes would never be heard, would be dead while yet living, and I wrote a few words to Liszt. He replied by assuring me that notwithstanding the limited resources of Weimar, he would make the greatest efforts to have my work performed there." And Liszt kept his word. At that time preparations were being made at Weimar for grand festivals for the inauguration of the statue of Herder on the 25th of August, his birthday, and also on the 28th of August, Goethe's birthday, the centennial of which had been celebrated in the preceding year with a religious respect. When they came to discuss the program for these two days, as it was necessary to select something with grand scenic effects, it was decided to execute on the 25th the *Chained Prometheus* by Herder, of which Liszt would write the music, and on the 28th, to represent for the first time the last opera of Richard Wagner.

Liszt, aided by the leader of the orchestra, Genast, immediately set about preparing the execution of *Lohengrin*,
according to the minute instructions sent him by his friend;
only three days before the representation Wagner sent still
further explanations about the minor details of the play.　It
was a great happiness for him to know that his work was going
to be executed without a single suppression, but how short a
time this happiness was to endure!　The very day after the
first performance, he received the most pressing requests
from Liszt and Genast, to authorize them to cut out certain
portions of the work.　Wagner replied by a letter to Genast,
in which, notwithstanding the pleasure which so devoted a
collaboration gave him, he showed a sorrowful resignation,
and remained convinced that they would not be able to
add to the public interest by making these mutilations;
however he left his friends to act according to their discretion,
only insisting, that if a similar case should arise in the future,
they should not consult him about it.　And twenty years
later *apropos* of the representation of the *Meistersingers* at
Berlin, he uttered the same sentiments in these words.　"This
time I am quite powerless, as usual, but if this wrong is to be
done, I desire to know nothing of it."　Liszt and Genast
made use of the permission with moderation, but they did
make use of it, and thence arose all the injury which is
deplored by the intimate friends of the master; the tradition
of these rejected portions is preserved, and even in the heart
of Germany to-day, *Lohengrin* is still executed with certain
suppressions tolerated, if not actually consented to, by the
author.

This musical festival at which Liszt presided, had attracted
a large number of people to Weimar; the foreign press
eagerly responded to the invitation of the celebrated artist,
and exhibited a strong desire to judge the work which he
patronized so warmly.　The first representation was given on

the day appointed, the 28th of August, 1850; if not a triumph, at least the work so remarkably sustained by Mmes. Agthe and Faiztlinger (Elsa and Ortrude), by MM. Beck, Milde and Hoefer (Lohengrin, Frederick and the King), was very favorably received. Among the journalists present at Weimar, was a French writer of note, who had received an invitation probably by reason of his having made the first French translation of Goethe's *Faust;* it was Gérard de Nerval. In describing these ceremonies in *La Presse*, Gérard was obliged to say at least a few words about *Lohengrin*, and this brief judgment, cautious, and feebly sanctioned though it was, has its importance, for it was probably the first echo which resounded in France of the success of Richard Wagner. "They also gave on that day, for the first time, *Lohengrin* by Wagner. The music of this opera is very remarkable, and the more it is heard, the more it will be appreciated. It is a bold and original talent which has revealed itself to Germany, and which has as yet said only its first words. M. Wagner has been reproached for having given too much importance to the instruments, and having, as Grétry said, put the pedestal on the stage and the statue in the orchestra; but he has undoubtedly kept to the character of his poem, which stamps the work with the form of a lyric drama, rather than that of an opera. The artists have valiantly executed this difficult score, which, to give a summary idea of it, seems to resemble the musical tradition of Gluck and Spontini. After *Rienzi*, and before *Lohengrin*, Wagner had already given *Tannhäuser*, which obtained a marked success at Dresden and afterwards at Weimar. The last opera has appeared a less happy attempt, from the idea which it pursues of an intimate alliance between the poetry and the music."

And all this time Wagner, detained at Zurich, anxiously awaited tidings of *Lohengrin*. One of his pupils, Carl Ritter — for he had undertaken to give lessons in composition — had

gone to Weimar in order to report to him the most precise
information upon the effect produced, and Wagner did not
weary of questioning him, in order to try to figure to himself
what his work had become in taking form upon the stage.
In any case, this single opera, played in the little town of Weimar in his absence, had done more 'for him than all his preceding operas, given in the great city of Dresden; it was the
dawning of his celebrity.   Even those who had not understood
very much of *Lohengrin*, could not speak of it calmly and dis-
passionately; it was the subject of much discussion.   But
the disturbance excited by his preceding works, and which
another opera sufficed to revive, had not yet extended beyond
the German states.   " The musicians," said he himself at that
time, " have no objection to my dabbling in poetry, and the
poets are not reluctant to admit my musical talent; frequently
I have been able to stir the public ; as for criticism, it has
always disparaged me."   All over the rest of Europe he was
absolutely unknown,[1] while *Lohengrin* was making a tour of
Germany, and ten long years were passing, during which the
author was not permitted the happiness of hearing the work;
"You will see," said he to his friends, "that I will soon be the
only German who has not heard *Lohengrin*."

Although clearly issued from the same stock as *Tannhäuser*, and coming only two years after it, *Lohengrin* is a work
more ripe and complete than the preceding one.[2]   It is the

[1] On the 24th of November, 1850, perhaps reflecting the Weimar festivals,
Seghers inaugurated at Paris his famous Saint Cecilia concerts, giving the overture
of *Tannhäuser*, which passed quite unnoticed, so completely ignorant were they of the
author.

[2] Wagner felt that with *Lohengrin* he had made a long step in advance of
Tannhäuser, and that he was departing still more from the taste of the times, for
it was Donizetti above all others, who reigned at Dresden at the time of the composition of *Lohengrin* ; but he did not exaggerate his merit, and modestly said in
a letter written in 1847 : " I am disposed rather to doubt my talents than to over-
rate them, and to consider my present enterprise (*Lohengrin*) as a substantial

RICHARD WAGNER, IN 1853.
After a Portrait, by Clementine Strocker-Escher.
Lithographed by Fr. Hanfstœngl.

highest, fullest and best expression of what one might
call the second style of Wagner. Whereas *Tannhäuser* is
still allied to *The Flying Dutchman*, and, by occasional passages, to the tradition of the school, to the French opera
imitated by Wagner in *Rienzi*, *Lohengrin* is a decided
departure from these, while at the same time it affords a
glimpse of the powerful evolution of ideas which was to cul-
minate in *Tristan and Isolde*. The poem of *Lohengrin* is
pure legend, with no suggestion of history, and the mystic
fancies which guide the characters, the motives which they
obey, would be quite insufficient for the building of an opera
libretto after the fashion of *La Muette* or of *Robert*; but they
introduce tender or dramatic episodes, than which a composer
could not desire anything more beautiful. It has been said,
and Wagner himself admits it, that there exist some striking
analogies between the two poems of *Euryanthe* and *Lohengrin*, which borrow from different legends, characters and
situations somewhat similar. The Count of Telramund and
Ortrude, are they not actuated by the same passions as
Lysiart and Eglantine? Elsa and Lohengrin, do they not find
themselves placed in the same poetic and chivalrous situations
as Euryanthe and Adolar? and finally, the German King
Heinrich of Brabant, and the unnamed King of France, do
they not both play the role of judge and mediator? It is from
the famous epic poem of *Parsifal and Titurel*, the author of
which is Wolfram of Eschenbach, one of the most celebrated
Minnesingers of the latter part of the XII. Century, that the
legend of *Lohengrin* is taken; and it was at one of these
tourneys of singers given at the Wartburg, like that of *Tannhäuser*, that Wolfram sung for the first time the poem of
Lohengrin, at the request of the landgrave of Thuringen, of

response to the question, Is the Opera possible?" and the most curious thing about
it is that he spoke truly, since a short time after, he cherished the idea of writing a
Barbarossa without music; strange illusion of a universal mind.

the ladies present, and even of his enemy, the magician Klingsor, " who was endeavoring to win him over to the evil one, by exciting his envy and pride through a science superior to his." But Wolfram, sustained by the Virgin, whom he faithfully served, went forth conqueror from this struggle with the evil spirit.

Lohengrin, Knight of the Swan, is the son of Parsifal, to whom has been confided the keeping of the Holy Grail, upon Mount Salvat: now, the pious knights, charged with this holy office, are permitted to remain upon the earth only so long as they shall suffer nothing to force them to reveal their divine mission and the origin of their invincible power. It is thus that Lohengrin descends from regions unapproachable, in order to defend Elsa, accused by the ambitious Frederick of Telramund, and his malicious wife, Ortrude, of having killed her young brother, heir of Brabant; but before drawing his sword for Elsa, Lohengrin makes her swear that she will never seek to know who he is. Elsa consenting to this condition, Lohengrin crosses swords with Frederick, and throws him down, but spares him his life. All the lords of Brabant then salute him for their chief in the expedition which the emperor of Germany is preparing against the Hungarians. Frederick, dishonored, dispossessed of his estates, feels the cause to be lost, but Ortrude introduces herself as a suppliant to the generous Elsa; she insinuates herself into her confidence, and throws into that candid heart the first germs of doubt and of curiosity on the subject of her mysterious lover. Elsa resists all her suggestions, but at the very moment of her triumphal entry into the church, Frederick calls upon his conqueror to make himself known before the whole court, and Elsa already endures with increasing impatience the disdainful silence of her defender. Scarcely are they left alone in the nuptial chamber, than she presses Lohengrin with questions in order to wrest from him this secret which she is burning to know;

in vain does he recall to her, her solemn vow; Elsa, whose
mind works itself up at each new refusal, believes that her
husband is about to escape her, that the white swan is returning to take her beloved away from her.   At the moment when
this trouble of mind attains its paroxysm, Frederick, who is
concealed by Elsa in an adjoining room, advances to attack
Lohengrin, but the latter turns upon his adversary and kills
him; then, seeing that his happiness has vanished forever, he
directs that Elsa be clothed in white, and conducted to the
tribunal of the king.   There, before the whole court assembled, he discloses his origin and his mission; he explains
the sovereign order which obliges him to depart, but before
returning to Mount Salvat, he gives back the young Godfrey
to his sister Elsa, for the white swan who had brought Lohengrin was no other than the young prince transformed into a
swan by the sorcery of Ortrude.   Lohengrin disappears forever, and Elsa falls lifeless upon the shore.

Reading only the principal lines of this poem, known to-day
throughout the entire world, is one not struck with the great
number of situations of a rare dramatic power which it contains, and does one not recognize that it is, indeed, the antique
fable of Psyche, transported to the middle ages, and engrafted
upon the religious legends of an epoch of fervor and of faith?
That which impresses one at once in reading the score of
Lohengrin, but which is much more striking in the representation, is the absolutely new form in which it is conceived, and
which is in every particular consistent with the strictest truth.
Each act forms in itself a grand symphonic whole, of which the
delineations by the orchestra vary infinitely, according to the
expression of the scenes, or the sentiment of the personages,
but without a break anywhere.   Above this orchestral woof,
in this sonorous atmosphere which doubles the power of the
voice, and the melodious expression of the phrases sung, each
personage declaims exactly that which he ought to say, never

more or less, in a recitative very melodious and elevated, but
without repeating himself and very rarely singing with another ;
for it is equally contrary to truth that two people should talk
at once, as Grimm and Rousseau have long since remarked,
or that an individual should repeat the same refrain many
times, as in a vocal exercise. Besides, Wagner substituted in
a remarkable manner for these inexplicable and inexpressive
repetitions, characteristic phrases which determined not only
a personage, but a situation, an entire scene, even the state of
the mind at a given moment, and which he made reappear or
combined together with an incredible facility. This entirely
new musical form must cause an intense surprise to even the
best prepared hearer, and one would hardly know how to
express the effect produced, taking our ordinary operas as a
point of comparison ; but for all that it seems impossible that
any unprejudiced mind should not be struck with admiration
before a work in which elements so different are handled with
such force of will, such a power of inspiration. To many
people, slower to comprehend, or to be moved, the admiration
will be longer in coming, but it will surely come, and will be
all the more profound and enduring.

"It is impossible" said Liszt in a pamphlet written a short
time after the representation of *Lohengrin*, " to justly appreciate
this work, if one attempts to search through it for the ancient
composition of opera, the customary division of the singing
parts, the accepted distribution of the airs, romances, *soli*
and *tutti*, in a word the whole economy adopted for the
purpose of making the most of the singers and the melodies,
in a proportion often arbitrary in favor of the first. Wagner
solemnly abjured everything adopted out of consideration for
the habitual exigencies of *prima donna assoluta*, or of *basso
cantante*. In his eyes there are no singers, there are only
rôles ; so that he finds it perfectly simple to preserve complete
silence on the part of a *prima donna* throughout an entire act,

when her presence, actually necessary to the probability of the scene, must be indicated by mere dumb show, certainly as despised as it is inexecutable by any Italian *diva*.[1]"

Ortrude indeed, has nothing to say throughout the whole of the first act of *Lohengrin*; she sings a little in the finale only, and yet, if the actress charged with this rôle possess a true dramatic instinct, she will know how to produce the most beautiful effects from these silent scenes.

If it is difficult to explain the technical form, the intrinsic merit and the radiant power of this music to one who has never heard it, it is quite as difficult to cite one *piece* as separate and distinct from the rest; for, properly speaking, there are no pieces, and one would not know how to detach any portion whatever from the complete and concise unit which these operas form, as far removed by their style from the hackneyed recitative, as from the measured periods of our grand arias. The author has wished to produce an effect upon his hearers not by such and such a phrase or page, but by the entire work, and in this he has quite succeeded. Thence arises the impossibility of extracting a melody, a fragment complete by itself, unless a whole scene be sung, like that in the third act, which by far exceeds the ordinary proportions of a duet; thence it comes also that the separate pieces which are played at concerts, the prelude, the religious march, the wedding march, have their full power only when in their natural place in the drama, preceded and followed by the parts with which they are connected.

Each act is equally admirable, considered in its *ensemble*, and he would indeed do well, who could say to which of the three should be given the preference; to the first, with those magnificent recitatives of the king, the poetical entrance and chaste prayer of Elsa, the descent of Lohengrin, the cries of the wondering crowd, the farewell of the knight to his swan, and

---

[1] *Lohengrin and Tannhäuser* (Brockhaus, Leipsic, 1851).

the grand finale of the duel; — to the second, with the scene where Ortrude arouses the pride of Frederick, with the revery of Elsa and the hypocritical supplications of Ortrude, the brilliant trumpet-calls at the break of day, the magnificent religious march and the startling intervention of Frederick; — or to the third, with the wedding march and the betrothal chorus, the incomparable love duet; finally the reunion of all the feudatory lords on the Field of May, and the recitatives, by turns resigned and triumphant, of the knight who returns to guard the Holy Grail.

The success obtained at Weimar through the efforts of Liszt was widely re-echoed, and rapidly spread over all Germany; for thirty years and more, this work, which French writers, hostile yesterday, to-day declare a masterpiece, has been victoriously established upon the lyric stages of the entire world.[1]

Not only is it the opera which obtains every year the greatest number of representations at Vienna and Berlin, but it is considered a classic in Russia, where a whole school, which has produced very remarkable works, look with less favor upon Wagner's later productions; it is accepted in Spain and Italy, applauded in the New World. It has not been long since it was played simultaneously at two London theatres, and gave rise to a friendly rivalry between Nilsson and Albani in the rôle of Elsa; finally it appears regularly on the play-bills at Brussels, where the French language is spoken, and this constant return of the work, always well received and assured of success, seems as natural in Belgium as would that of *William Tell* and the *Huguenots* in Paris.

Moreover, wherever *Lohengrin* is played at present, those

---

[1] *Lohengrin* was represented at Wiesbaden in 1853; at Leipsic, Schwerin, Frankfort, Darmstadt, Breslau and Stettin in 1854; at Cologne, Hamburg, Riga and Prague in 1855; at Munich and Vienna in 1858; in Berlin and Dresden in 1859, etc., etc. — *Lohengrin*, in French, translated by M. Ch. Nuitter, was played for the first time at the *théâtre de la Monnaie* at Brussels, on March 22, 1870.

hearers who are unprejudiced, with minds free to receive new impressions, are always struck, delighted, overpowered by this symphony accompanying and commenting on the drama. They are taken captive by the pure Wagnerian idea, that is to say, by the return, the contact and the fusion of divers characteristic phrases, reappearing under the most different aspects, contradicting each other, or combining, according to the taste, not of the composer, but of the drama, and forming thus an incomparable symphonic whole. Those who, not understanding Wagner, wish to depreciate him, declare that he has only imitated Weber, and so many other composers who have also made conspicuous certain melodies, and repeated them in different situations. But there is a whole world between the manner in which Weber sometimes repeats once or twice certain principal phrases, always with their full development, and the fashion in which Wagner, once these type-motives fixed, takes them up again, couples them, and combines them into a symphonic tissue of a single piece, such as no composer before him has ever conceived.

Now it is to the honor of the first partisans, not to have laughed at such a stroke of genius, as Berlioz has done, and to have comprehended what new horizons such initiative was opening to musical art.

RICHARD WAGNER AS ORCHESTRAL LEADER.
German caricature by Gust. Paul, 1863.

CHAPTER VII

ICHARD WAGNER, exiled from Germany, arrived at Paris in the middle of the month of May, 1849. In counselling him to go to France, Liszt hoped that Wagner would be able to establish himself there, and Wagner had allowed this hope to enter his own heart. But from the first step in Paris, discouragement took possession of him. He tried to make himself known by publishing in a French journal a series of articles setting forth his views upon Art and the Revolution; but that came to nothing, and the director of the *Débats*, to whom Liszt had introduced him, told him frankly that Paris was more disposed to amuse herself than to discuss seriously the theories of a German musician upon the relations between his art and politics. Having once ascertained the sad condition of music in France, and the aversion of all the directors to risk upon the stage a tragic grand opera, Wagner resolved to leave Paris, and the month of June found him in Zurich, where several of his political friends from Dresden had taken refuge. Here he settled down, and in the month of October he became a citizen of that town, whither his wife had come to join him. These years of exile were, on the whole, sweet to him, for he says: " It would be impossible to describe my joy, after I had passed through the first unpleasant impressions, and felt myself free at last from the world of torturing and ever unsatisfied wishes, free from the annoying surroundings which gave birth to those wishes." A wonderful transformation was accomplished in Richard Wagner during that period. He devoted himself to writing, in order to explain and to defend his ideas, and these first years of exile are marked by a long series of theoretical and critical writings. " My mental state," said he, in speaking of these books and essays " resembled a contest; I endeavored to express theoretically that which I was unable to express by a direct creation, by reason of the entire lack of harmony between my artistic aspirations and the tendencies of the public, particularly on the subject of opera."

The first of these papers is *Art and the Revolution*, in which political and social prejudices dominate, culminating in the conclusion that nothing short of a complete revolution can put people in a condition to enjoy pure and true art. Wagner goes back to the theatre of Eschylus and of Sophocles, in which he finds perfect art, the superb manifestation of a race in which men develop themselves with all freedom, knowing and worshiping only the forces of nature, which are personified in their gods. Why has this art declined? For the same reasons that apply to the social state itself: because, first, antique Rome by its pride of domination, then Christianity by its contempt for the world, and finally modern industry by its thirst for luxury and gain, which conquers even artists, have equally stifled art, and turned the human mind from the contemplation of the pleasures of the forces of nature. Let us then have a revolution, which shall overturn the whole social structure, sweep away all the prejudices which blind and degrade man, and bring him back to the natural state, in which he will be able to comprehend art, and make it his aim."[1]

This pamphlet, which gave only an indication of his theories, was soon followed by a long work which occupied Wagner for several months, and which he entitled *Art Work*

[1] *Richard Wagner*, by L. Bernardini.

of the Future, in order to indicate that his ideal would not be realized immediately; he dedicated this work to Feuerbach, expressing his gratitude for the good which the latter's philosophical works had done him. Unfortunately Wagner has allowed himself to adopt the phraseology of Feuerbach, and has applied it to his own theories to such an extent that the result is very puzzling to the reader, and the work, of an animated style and a real value, is in every respect painful to read. He takes up the ideas outlined in the preceding short treatise, and develops them after his own fashion.

"Poetry, mimetics and music were united in the drama of the Greeks; the drama disappeared with the downfall of the Athenian state; the union of the arts was dissolved, each had an existence of its own, and at times sank to the level of a mere pastime. Attempts made during the renaissance and since, to reunite the arts, were more or less abortive, though the technique and width of range of most of the arts increased. In our day each separate branch of art has reached its limits of growth, and cannot overstep them without incurring the risk of becoming incomprehensible, fantastic, absurd. At this point each art demands to be joined to a sister art—poetry to music, mimetics to both ; each will be ready to forego egotistical pretensions, for the sake of an artistic whole, and the musical drama may become for future generations what the drama of Greece was to the Greeks." [1]

In 1850 the *New Musical Gazette* of Leipsic published, without warning, an article entitled *Judaism in Music*, signed by the pseudonym of K. Freigedank (free thoughts). [2]

---

[1] Grove's Musical Dictionary, *Wagner*, p. 367.

[2] When an enlarged edition appeared in pamphlet form (Leipsic, 1869), Wagner signed his own name to it, and a storm of articles and pamphlets poured in from all sides. If he desired a commotion his wish was gratified, for instantly this pamphlet and other works of his, unknown until then, found hosts of purchasers. His friends sought to exonerate him; Meyerbeer, said they, when he patronized

As this journal, then edited by Brendel, had only a few hundred readers, his violent attack against the Jewish race, and particularly against Jewish composers, did not make so much noise at first as Wagner had expected. The only immediate effect was a vindictive feeling in musical circles against the editor, in default of the real author, who was suspected, but who remained concealed. As Brendel was teaching history of music at the Conservatory of Leipsic, eleven of the professors called upon him to abandon his chair or to unmask the writer; but Brendel refused to submit to this alternative; he kept his place and guarded his secret.

Meanwhile the true name of the author was on every tongue, so recognizable was his style, and already many of the journalists were becoming openly hostile to him, for he had attacked the most powerful and the most applauded of German musicians, Mendelssohn and Meyerbeer. He delivers himself of the opinion that Jews, in whatever language they may express themselves, have always the air of foreigners speaking an acquired language, not their natural tongue; and he concludes therefore that they are incompetent to interpret ideas or sentiments through the medium of song, — that they then become insupportable and repugnant. The civilized Jew, when he attempts to manifest himself in art, is inspired by only the most ordinary and trivial things, for his pretended

---

Wagner in the beginning of his career, did so for his own interest, and in order to make sure of an ally which he could not secure among the foremost musicians. Such masters as Spohr and Marschner, Mendelssohn and Schumann appreciated only the commercial talents of Meyerbeer, and regarded his music as an ingeniously constructed farce, etc. It is possible that Meyerbeer had had a vague idea of enlisting Wagner in his cause, which was mainly sustained by literary adherents and newspaper men; but it is none the less true that he had protected Wagner in a very efficacious manner, and that a letter from him had decided the acceptation of *Rienzi* at Dresden; it is none the less true that on several occasions he had solicited the intervention of Meyerbeer and these considerations should have prevented him from writing as he did.

artistic instinct is but his natural instinct for gain, and leads
him to sacrifice pure art for such or such a form, fashionable,
and consequently lucrative; "Small matter what he creates,
provided he forces attention; he has but one anxiety, that for
form." After all sorts of amenities of this nature addressed to
the Jewish race in general, he attacks openly and individually
his two enemies, a mistake which a more prudent person would
not have committed.

In regard to Mendelssohn, he declares that no other
Jewish composer excites his sympathy to an equal degree, and
that it is a sad sight to see him struggle against the original
impotence to which he is condemned by his birth; "The
result at which we have arrived by an examination of the
reasons for our antipathy to the Jewish element, all of which is
contradictory to itself and to us; its inability to put itself *en
rapport* with us; its unsuccessful attempts to develop fruits
germinated in our soil, from which it is excluded; all this is
shown to the highest degree, and as a truly tragic conflict, in
the nature, in the life, in the artistic productions of Mendelssohn, who died so young. In this man we recognize the fact
that a Jew may be gifted with the grandest, the most beautiful
talent; that he may have received the most careful, the most
extensive education; that he may have the highest, noblest
ambition, without once succeeding, notwithstanding all these
advantages, in producing upon our minds and our hearts, that
profound impression which we expect from music, which we
know it to be capable of, having proved it so many times
when the heroes of our art have permitted us to listen to their
accents."

For Meyerbeer there are fewer circumlocutions: "The
faculty for deceiving is so great on the part of this artist, that
he deceives even himself, and perhaps intentionally, as much
for his own sake as for the sake of the public. We believe as
a matter of fact, that he would like very much to create works

of art, and that he knows his inability to do so; in order to avoid this painful conflict between his will and his faculty, he composes operas for Paris, and has them executed in other countries, — which is in our day the surest method of acquiring the glory of an artist without being one. When we see him thus borne down by the trouble which he takes to deceive himself, he appears to us almost in the light of a tragic character; but there was so much self-interest at work with him that he could not prevent himself from dabbling with the *comique;* moreover, Judaism which reigns in the arts, and which the composer represents in his music, is distinguished particularly by its inability to move us, and by the element of ridicule which is inherent in it."

Between the followers of the first, who had a profound horror of the second, and those of the second who were jealous above all of the position of serious composer acquired by Mendelssohn, Wagner denounced a third party; those of the Jews, who continued to compose, and who sought to prevent all scandal between the two factions in order to ward off an attack upon themselves, and to be able to pursue their work in peace. "These people," said he, "consider the fruitful success of Meyerbeer's operas; the very moment a thing succeeds they think that it must have merit although they may not wholly approve of it, or judge it solidly founded."

He concludes as follows: "We have yet to speak of another Jew who is appearing among us as an author. He has renounced his faith, and has united with us, in order to deliver himself; he has not succeeded, and has been forced to the consciousness that he cannot succeed, *except by seeking with us the common deliverance which is to make true men of us all.* But, to become one with us, it is necessary first of all for the Jews to cease to be Jews. Boerne has ceased to be one, and he is just the man who understands that this deliverance cannot be obtained through inertia, through a cold and calm indifference, but that it is for the Jews as for us, a struggle fraught with difficulty, suffering and unhappiness. Let the Jews frankly take part in this struggle, which is to destroy our present nature, and we will be united and inseparable. Let them bear in mind at the same time, that the deliverance from the malediction which weighs upon them, may be nothing less

RICHARD WAGNER IN 1855.
From an engraving on wood.

than that of Ahasuerus, — Annihiliation." All hail to Schopenhauer!

Wagner published about the same time, other articles, which made less commotion, — theoretical papers and personal souvenirs, which he sent to the right and to the left in Germany. During the first two years which he passed at Zurich, besides writing numerous critical works, he conducted grand orchestral concerts, and directed the execution of his works at the Stadttheatre, assisted already by his young dis-

ciples, Carl Ritter and Hans von Bülow; he called together
conferences on the musical drama, at which he read *The Death
of Siegfried* by way of an example; finally, upon the advice of
his friends, who always dreamed of a decisive success for him
at Paris, he joined forces with a French librettist, and mapped
out a drama on the Scandinavian legend of *Wieland le for-
geron*, in which he embodied himself and recounted his own
misfortunes.

He hoped that this poem, once finished and translated into
French verse, would find a ready welcome, and in order to
hasten the affair, he went himself to Paris in February, 1850;
the German journals went so far as to inform their readers that
he lived part of the time in Paris, and part in Brussels, and
that he employed his leisure in translating into German *The
Mysteries of Paris* by Eugene Sue. He did nothing of all
this, and whatever step he might have attempted he would have
run against *The Prophet*, which had just been played during
the preceding year, and which, being helped along by Meyerbeer, occupied then the whole attention of the musical world.
The despair which took possession of him, added to the poor
state of his health, brought on a nervous trouble; he was
obliged to spend some time at Bordeaux and at Villeneuve,
on Lake Geneva, in order to recuperate, and in the month of
July he was on his way back to Zurich. He completely abandoned his *Wieland*, in order to set to music *The Death of
Siegfried*, but more than all, he devoted himself to his critical
writings, and during the year 1851 he published at about the
same time the famous *Communication to My Friends,* — so
often quoted under the form of preface to the three poems of
The Flying Dutchman, Tannhäuser, and *Lohengrin*, united
in one volume, — and his most important theoretical work
entitled *Opera and Drama*.

This work, which contains neither politics nor pseudo-phi-
losophy, is divided into three parts: first, *Opera and the Essence*

of Music; second, *The Theatre and the Essence of Dramatic Poetry;* third, *Poetry and Music in the Drama of the Future;* and all three tend to demonstrate that in the opera, music as a means of expression has been taken as the only object and aim, whereas the true aim, the drama, has been made subordinate to the musical forms. The respective situation then of the two arts has been completely reversed, and the efforts of the author are directed towards re-establishing it.

Whence comes this evil? From the Italian dramatic cantata, embryo of the opera, in which the scenery and action were only an excuse for the airs, in which the task of the composer was limited to writing pieces according to the type adopted by such or such a subject, or singer. When the ballet was added, the musician was obliged to reproduce popular dance forms, as he reproduced popular songs for the voice, with elaborate variations; the songs were connected by means of conventional recitatives; as for the dance airs, they simply followed one another.

We see in Gluck the first reformer, who made strenuous efforts to better adapt his music to dramatic action. He modified melody, in following the inflections, the accents of the spoken language; he put a stop to the display of pure virtuosity, and forced the singers to become the interpreters of his dramatic designs; but as to the form itself, — and this is the main point — he left the opera as he had found it. The whole work remains a collection of recitatives, airs, choruses and ballets as before, and Gluck's librettists furnished for his airs, words in which the action, without being absolutely neglected, was made a secondary consideration.

The great successors of Gluck,—Mehul, Cherubini, Spontini, developed the musical and dramatic *ensemble*, and thus freed themselves from the uninterrupted monologue formed by the airs of the ancient opera. This was a long step forward, and the opera acquired at that time its full development, at least in all essentials; for although Mozart has produced pure music which is richer and more beautiful than that of Gluck, it is not questioned that the elements of the opera are precisely the same in the case of both of these masters. After them, in the works of Weber and of Spohr, of Rossini, Bellini, Auber, Meyerbeer, etc., the history of the opera is nothing more than the history of " operatic melody."

In the second part, Wagner occupies himself with form in the spoken drama. In that which bears upon this subject he indicates two distinct factors; first, the mediæval romance and its offspring the modern novel; then the Greek drama, or rather the essential form of that drama, such as is given in the Poetics of Aristotle. The greater part of Shakespeare's dramas are, for him, only dramatized histories, whereas those of Racine are constructed according to the theories of Aristotle.

Continuing this study, he examines the works of Goethe and of Schiller, and arrives at this conclusion: that historical subjects offer great difficulties to dramatic treatment, and that the modern theatre takes a wrong step in pursuing the representation of contingent reality, instead of provoking the exercise of our imaginative faculties. Schiller, for example, was crushed beneath the mass of historical facts contained in his *Wallenstein*, while Shakespeare, by way of exciting his spectator's imagination, would have given him the vision of the whole of the thirty years war, in the same time occupied by the trilogy of the German poet.

He goes on to establish an ingenious comparison between the tragedy of Racine and the opera of Gluck. Racine, says he, gives less heed to action, properly speaking, than to the motives which determine it, and the effects which result from it; now, Gluck's instincts impelled him to translate the *tirade* of Racine into the *aria*. In view of the difficulties experienced by Goethe and Schiller in their efforts to fuse dramatic matter

RICHARD WAGNER, ABOUT 1857.
After a lithograph.

and poetic form, Wagner asserts that mythical subjects are best for an ideal drama, and that music is the ideal language in which such subjects are best presented. In the third part he shows that it is only the wonderfully rich development of music in our time, totally unknown to earlier centuries, which could have brought about the possibility of a musical drama such as he has in view. The conclusions arrived at in *The Opera and Drama* are again discussed in his lecture *On the Destiny of the Opera* where particular stress is laid on the fact that music is the informing element of the new drama.

After having written so much, Wagner was seized with an intense longing to hear some of his music, and since he could not go to Germany, he desired that Germany should come to him. He undertook to organize at Zurich a musical week, consecrated exclusively to the execution of his works, as had been done at Weimar; and he addressed a pressing appeal to the musical societies of Germany and Switzerland, all of which, save that of Munich, responded to his request. He assembled thus an orchestra of seventy-two musicians, and a chorus in proportion. He had the theatre of Zurich arranged as a concert hall according to his own ideas; then, to enable the public to enter more easily into his thoughts, he wrote explanatory programs for the overture of *The Flying Dutchman* and the prelude of *Lohengrin*. The first concert, which comprised fragments of his four published operas, took place on the 18th of May 1853; when the master appeared at the desk, he was cheered by the whole assembly, and the orchestra saluted him with a thrice repeated *fanfare* of trumpets. At the third concert, which fell on the 22d of May, his birthday, enthusiasm knew no bounds; they covered him with wreaths of flowers, and with compliments in verse, after which one of the ladies in the chorus stepped from the ranks and presented him with a magnificent gold vase in the name of his comrades.

During the summer of 1853, he visited a place near Saint

Maurice, and from there he undertook a trip into the north of Italy. While travelling through Turin he heard an execution of Rossini's *Barber*, complete and correct to a degree which he had never heard in Germany; afterwards he went to Genoa, and it was during a sleepless night at Spezzia that the first ideas of the *Rheingold* music passed through his mind. He brought his journey to an end, and hastened to regain his tranquil home at Zurich, that he might not commence such a work on Italian soil. He put his whole heart into the work and at the close of the autumn he went to hunt up Liszt at Bâle, where he laid before him the entire poem of the Nibelungen; and Liszt reciprocated the courtesy by executing for him alone, as he would have done for a sovereign, some of Beethoven's last sonatas. Once reunited, they went together to Paris, where their presence was announced about the middle of October, but they remained there but a short time. The German journals openly attributed this visit, so closely following the preceding one, to the ever increasing desire on Wagner's part to hear one of his operas performed at Paris, and they even designated the theatre and the work: the Theatre Lyrique and *Tannhäuser;* but it is very improbable that Jules Sévest, then director of the Lyrique, where they were giving the *Bijou Perdu*, and where they were going to represent *La Promise*, had ever dreamed of *Tannhäuser*. Be that as it may, Wagner retreated to Zurich in the month of November, and plunged himself into *The Nibelungen*.

This was the great work of his exile. But how had he come to make four works out of a simple opera like *The Death of Siegfried*. "When I attempted," says he, "to dramatize the most important moment of the myth of the Nibelungen in *The Death of Siegfried*, I found it necessary to indicate a great number of antecedent facts, in a manner which would give the essential episodes their true coloring. But I could only re-count these preparatory facts, whereas I felt the necessity of making them enter into the dramatic action itself; this is how I came to write *Siegfried*. But here a new embarrassment presented itself; I did not come anywhere near finding the means of incorporating all that was necessary in order to make the dramatic action explain itself." And it was thus that in tracing the legend back, he came to write *The Walküre* and the general prologue to his trilogy, *The Rheingold*. The poem, as before mentioned, had been published in 1853, only for the friends of the author. Having once commenced to write the music, after his precipitate return from Italy, things proceeded rapidly. In May, 1854, the score of *The Rheingold* was completed. In June he commenced *The Walküre*, which he finished the following year, and as for *Siegfried*, the first outlines of which date from 1854, he had finished the first two acts of it by the spring of 1857.

This elaborate work was interrupted for short periods, once by the rehearsals and representations of *Tannhäuser* at Zurich, in February, 1855, once by a violent attack of erysipelas which he had in the spring of 1856, later by a prolonged visit from Liszt, during which Wagner conducted at Saint Gall the *Heroic Symphony*, and Liszt his *Symphonic Poems*, *Orpheus* and *The Preludes;* but he was obliged to totally abandon his work when he arranged to go to London to direct the eight concerts of the *Philharmonic* Society. In the month of January, 1855, one of the directors, Mr. Anderson, had come to Zurich to see him, and to lay before him the embarrassment of the Society, which, since the death of Mendelssohn, had experienced the greatest difficulty in finding each year an orchestral leader of renown; it was tired of Lindpaintner; Spohr could not come, and Berlioz had been engaged for the season which was about to open, by the rival society, the *New Philharmonic*. After having heard *Tannhäuser* at Zurich, Mr. Anderson departed, carrying with him the desired promise from Wagner.

The latter, announced by numerous editorial puffs, arrived at London on the last of February; but before beginning his duties he saw that the journalists, particularly Mr. Dawson of the *Times* and the *Musical World*, and Mr. Chorley of the *Athenæum*, who led the campaign, were violently opposed to him. It was still worse when they learned that the unworthy successor of the celebrated Michael Costa was acting contrary to the so-called traditions of Mendelssohn; that he demanded of the orchestra more energy and life; that he was not willing for them to play everything with a colorless uniformity, nor to precipitate the movements inordinately, etc. Then all the inhospitable diatribes were summed up in the general cry "that he was going to treat Mozart, Cherubini, Beethoven, as if they also had written *music of the future*."

The eight concerts of the season commenced on the 12th of March and closed on the 25th of June; outside of the classic repertoire, Wagner directed only two pieces of his own; the overture to *Tannhäuser* and a selection from *Lohengrin* (prelude, wedding march, march and chorus of the betrothal). The overture to *Tannhäuser* was such a success that Prince Albert demanded a repetition of it for the seventh concert, at which the entire royal family was present; this was a new triumph, and the queen, in course of the evening, had the author summoned to her box in order to congratulate him.

Among other complaints against Wagner, he was criticised severely for his habit of directing Beethoven's symphonies from memory, which was called mere affectation of contempt; and this judgment was made known to him; labor lost, for at the last rehearsal of the *Heroic*, there was no sign of a score. This was too much, and Wagner was made to promise that he would direct at the concert with the symphony before his eyes. He kept his word, and the execution proceeded in a masterly fashion; then his critics pressed about him to congratulate him. "Were we not right? This is a very different

matter from yesterday! How well you have caught the movement of the *scherzo!* Bravely done!" And while they were
all talking, one of them seized the score lying open upon the
desk. Horrors! It was *The Barber of Seville*, and a piano
arrangement at that! The farce is unique, and is like Wagner. Rossini, later on, so it is said, attempted to decipher
Tannhäuser upside down; "It will not go any other way,"
said he. This story very likely sprung from the other one,
— a Roland for an Oliver.

Meanwhile Wagner, openly sustained by the Prince Con-
sort, had finished by gaining the good will of the British public as well as of his orchestra, and the eighth and last concert
attained for him a reparative ovation. Immediately he turned
his back upon London, and some years after, peremptorily
refused to return there; it was a long time before he went
again, this time to try to repair the deficit of the *Nibelungen*.

" Magnificent orchestra, so far as the principal artists were
concerned " — wrote he in reviewing this three months' campaign — " superb sound, the leading musicians provided with
incomparable instruments; solid *esprit de corps*, but no particular style. The fact is that the gentlemen of the Phithar-
monic Society, orchestra and audience, consume more music
than they are able to digest. As a rule, one hour of music
requires several hours of rehearsing. How can it be expected
that a director with the small amount of time at his disposal,
can properly prepare the enormous programs which the directors put before him. Two symphonies, two overtures, a
concerto and two or three songs at each concert. The directors continually remind me of what they are pleased to call the
traditions of Mendelssohn; but I suspect that Mendelssohn
was simply subject to the traditions of the Society. One
morning when we commenced to rehearse the overture to
Leonore I was astonished. All was cloudy, characterless, in-
distinct, as if the musicians were worn out, and had not slept

for a week. Was such a thing to be tolerated on the part of the famous philharmonic orchestra? I stopped them and addressed them in French; ' I know very well, said I to them, what you are capable of doing, and I expect nothing less from you.' Some of them understood me, and translated; they were all astounded, but they felt that I was right and they took it good-naturedly. They commenced the overture again, and the rehearsal proceeded admirably. I have every reason to believe that the majority of the artists had come to appreciate me before I was obliged to leave them."

He was right. And yet when he departed, the *Musical World*, stubborn in its hostility, launched after him the following: " Mr. Richard Wagner has left London, the very next day after the last concert of the Philharmonic Society, delighted no doubt to depart in all haste from a city so wrapt in impenetrable darkness, and so deaf to the prophetic voice of the future."

At London Wagner had encountered Berlioz, who had come to direct the rival orchestra ; but notwithstanding this unexpected competition, and in spite of their contrary ideas upon art, they had renewed their pleasant relations. After his return to Zurich, Wagner invited Berlioz to visit him, but the latter was not able to arrange this " reunion, which would have been for me a veritable treat," writes he in his very cordial response ; he asks Wagner to send him *Tannhäuser*, to add to *Lohengrin* which he already possesses ; he promises him in return his *Te Deum*, *l'Enfance du Christ* and *Lélio* which is about to appear, and he goes on to say " So you are in a fair way to melt the glaciers, while composing your *Nibelungen*. It must be superb to write thus in the presence of grand nature ! A happiness which has so far been denied me ! Beautiful landscapes, lofty summits, the grand aspects of the ocean, completely absorb me, instead of inspiring me with ideas. It is then that I feel, and cannot express. I can depict the moon only when regarding her image in the bottom of a well. It is all one; if we lived a hundred years from now, I think we would be set right by many things and many men. The old Majesty on high must laugh up there in his ancient beard, at the constant success of the farce which he makes of us. But I will not speak ill of him; he is one of your friends and I know you take his part. I am impious, full of respect for the mag-pious. Pardon this frightful pun, with which I close, with friendly greetings." [1]

Wagner hoped, by working without relaxation, to finish the trilogy in 1859; he projected having a provisional theatre erected at Zurich, where he would give himself the treat of seeing it performed; but on reflection, he saw that such an enterprise was impracticable in a town of so few musical resources; that he would have to gather in artists from the four quarters of Germany, and that the opening representation of this four-day festival would require enormous sums of money, which he did not know where to find. All these reasons, and the fear also that it would not soon be finished, joined to the ardent desire which he had to hear one of his works, conforming absolutely to his definite ideas upon the musical drama, led him to write an opera of ordinary length, and of a moderately easy *mise en scène*. A trifling incident sufficed to decide him upon this course. A certain individual claiming to be sent from the Emperor of Brazil, came to ask him if he would be willing to compose a work for the Italian troupe who were playing at Rio Janeiro, under what conditions he would do so, and if he would agree to come and personally direct the execution of it. [2]

The composer, much surprised at the proposition, hesitated

---

[1] Berlioz's letter to Wagner, Sept. 10, 1855.

[2] This offer from Rio Janeiro seems to have had a serious foundation, for the emperor of Brazil was, later on, one of the patrons of the Bayreuth theatre, and was present at the first execution of the *Nibelungen*.

about giving a formal reply, but in order to be ready at all events, he laid aside the trilogy, and devoted himself to the shorter poem. This was in the summer of 1857, and the poem was that of *Tristan and Isolde*, which had shortly before presented itself to his mind, at the same time as *Parsifal;*[1] he had traced the first outline of it in 1854 or 1855, soon after having published the first sketch of *The Ring of the Nibelungen*, and when he had just been initiated into the philosophy of Schopenhauer. It was indeed in 1851 that the appearance of the *Parerga und Paralipomena* had so greatly surprised intellectual Germany, and stirred up such a general reprobation against the official representatives of the philosophy in the universities, who had kept quiet about the preceding works by the same author. The little colony of refugees at Zurich did not allow itself to be forestalled in saluting in Schopenhauer a mighty moralist, and Wagner in particular, accepting with closed eyes his metaphysical doctrine, adhered to his teaching, of which he pretended, later, to develop some of the most debatable points. In 1854, he sent to him at Frankfort a copy of the *Ring of the Nibelungen*, in testimony " of gratitude and veneration." Schopenhauer, although he played the flute, like Frederick the Great, surely did not expect so much from a simple musician.

Wagner, having again taken up the reading of *Tristan*, finished it very quickly, in the beginning of 1857, and during the winter of that year, he gave the first act to the publishers, Breitkopf and Härtel. Towards the month of January, 1858,

---

[1] He had already written, in 1856, the outline of a Buddhist drama, which lent itself better than the Celtic legend of *Tristan and Isolde* to the expansion of the theories of Schopenhauer, and the plan of which was found, dated at Zurich, May 16, 1856, among his posthumous papers; this is as far as he ever got with this drama. Finally, the outline of *Parsifal* was sketched by him in the spring of 1857. One may see that all these subjects germinated almost simultaneously in his mind, and that there would be no improbability of discovering traces of the influence of Schopenhauer even in *Parsifal*.

he was again in Paris, always, its appears, with the intention of having one of his operas heard there, and Arban signified his intention of having the overture to *Tannhäuser* executed in honor of the foreign musician. But Wagner could not stay long in Paris; he left very quickly, and pursued the composition of *Tristan and Isolde*, of which the second act was written at Venice, where the Austrian authorities had permitted him to reside, and dated at that city, March 2, 1859; finally the third act was finished at Lucerne, in the month of August of the same year. He saw that nothing was coming from the direction of Brazil, and so immediately took steps to have one of his operas performed in Germany; he concluded arrangements with the theatre of Carlsruhe.

He was hoping that the grand duke of Baden, after having authorized him to come and direct *Tristan and Isolde* in his capital, would consent to transform this temporary sojourn into a permanent residence, and during the summer of 1859, he made this request of him. It was refused; furthermore, he learned a short time afterwards that the representation of *Tristan* was declared impossible, and that the artists declined to play it. The same thing happened at Strasburg. Then all his hopes turned afresh towards Paris, since Germany was closed against him, and he formed the wild project of engaging German singers of the first rank, to organize at Paris, at the *Italiens*, during the following winter, a model representation of *Tristan and Isolde*, to which he would invite all the German directors; in this way he hoped to obtain the same result which he would have obtained at Carlsruhe. Henceforth this trip to Paris, which he had been planning for some time by way of diversion, in order to taste the pleasure of hearing the incomparable Conservatoire orchestra, took quite another importance in his eyes, and became an essential factor in his projects for the future. He had two objects in view in leaving Switzerland; he must first educate the French public, by means of concerts, to the point of enjoying his music, and then he must realize his ardent desire to mount, at last, *Tristan and Isolde.*

JUDAISM IN MUSIC AS IT PLEASES RICHARD WAGNER.

This is only when it pays twenty-five florins for a seat.
Kikeriki, of Vienna, May 12, 1872.

CHAPTER VIII

T was in the month of September, 1859, that Wagner went to install himself at Paris. He was known very little more than when he had left there seventeen years before, and the discussions raised by his dramatic works, as well as by his writings, had been but feebly echoed in France. People had not taken any notice of him, for the few lines of Gérard de Nerval about *Lohengrin* counted for nothing, and when Théophile Gautier, having heard *Tannhäuser* at the grand-ducal theatre of Wiesbaden in September, 1857, had communicated his impressions to the subscribers of the *Moniteur Universel*, the latter were much surprised that they should be addressed on the subject of this foreign musician. The more so, as Gautier, a great musical scholar, was not in the least wrought up at this hearing. He had figured to himself beforehand "a Wagner voluntarily devoid of melody, of rhythm and of breadth, a bold innovator, shaking off the established rules, inventing strange combinations, striving after unusual effects; a *paroxyste*, going to extremes in everything, overdoing violence, unloosing, apropos of nothing, the hurricane from the orchestra, and passing like a musical waterspout upon the astounded parterre; a genius complicated and furious, chaotic and fulgurating, a medley of vapors, darkness and lightning flashes, yielding to the ca-

prices of a wild inspiration, etc., etc."; and in place of all that he had only discovered a musician "going back into the past towards the sources of music, instead of surpassing Weber and Meyerbeer."

Therefore, what was the use of speaking so at length of a work in which "the orchestration is full of fugues, of flowery counterpoint, of canons executed with great science, where there is no uncertainty, the apparent disorder being due to the

WAGNER OPENING HIS EASTER EGG.
CHAM, *Charivari*, March, 31, 1851.

absence of accented rhythm, which the master avoids as a matter of course, the same as he abstains from modulating." Another case of the mountain bringing forth a mouse.

Notwithstanding all, Wagner's name began to be spread abroad, and the *Gazette Musicale* had also felt called upon to give an account of this festival. "All that I can say," wrote its correspondent, "is that M. Richard Wagner appears to me very far from being an abundant and easy *mélodiste;* cantilenas are very rare in his score." He recognizes, however, the charm of the song to the Evening Star, accompanied in the

Italian fashion, with a boldness of harmony absolutely German; he praises even the duet of Tannhäuser and Elizabeth, inferior as he deems it to that of Valentine and of Raoul; he applauds the march, built upon a theme full of grandeur and of freedom; finally he accords some praise to the overture, which might be compared to those of *Freischütz* and *Oberon;* then he concludes as follows: "It cannot be denied that Wagner resembles Weber in some respects. He manages the orchestra with remarkable ability. His instrumentation is clear, varied, brilliant, richly colored. He uses modulation too freely. He seeks unusual combinations. He is partial to harmonic effects. But from time to time he makes happy discoveries. . . M. Richard Wagner has undoubted talent, but he is heavy, stiff, formal. Socrates would certainly have counselled him to offer up sacrifices to the Graces. I would not be surprised if it were just this absence of grace which is to distinthe music of the future from that of the past. If this be so may I be condemned for all time to Weber and to Mozart." [1]

Meanwhile there was one man in Paris — perhaps the only one, — who was well acquainted with these operas and admired them profoundly: a modest employé of the Customs, Edmond Roche; and by a providential chance, this admirer was the very first Frenchman whom Wagner encountered when he was painfully wrestling with the formalities of the custom-house; an employé interposed, attracted by the noise of a dispute in which one of the parties made sad havoc with the French language; the traveller gave his name, and the employé saluted him immediately, assuring him that he was too happy to have served so great an artist. Would it not seem as if this episode, which savored of romance, were a good omen to the new-comer?

[1] At this representation at Wiesbaden, the role of Elsa was held by Mlle. Franziska Storck, those of Tannhäuser and Wolfram by Tichatschek and Simon; the orchestra was directed by Hagen, capellmeister of the duke of Nassau.

Wagner, who during his first sojourn at Paris, had seen scarcely any musicians, and had allied himself principally with painters and *littérateurs*, renewed his old relations and

M. WAGNER UNDERTAKING TO HAVE HIS MUSIC OF THE FUTURE
PERFORMED BY MUSICIANS, LIKEWISE OF THE FUTURE.
CHAM, *Charivari*, February, 27, 1860.

formed new ones, so that he was soon able to hold at his house, receptions to his intimate friends, where were gathered many men who were to make their mark in letters and in the arts. He had at first taken temporary lodgings at No. 4 *rue de Matignon;* then had rented in *rue Newton,* near *l'Arc de Triomphe,* a pretty little house, since demolished, where he lived alone with his wife, at a convenient distance from neighbors and pianos.

It was there, in a quarter then almost suburban, that he received his friends every Wednesday; one saw there Emile Ollivier, who had married at Florence, in 1857, the eldest daughter of Liszt and Mme. d'Agoult: a charming and deeply

AT A REHEARSAL OF TANNHÄUSER.
Sapristi, Monsieur Wagner, your music makes too much racket!
Ah, but it has got to be heard from here to Germany!
CHAM, *Charivari,* March, 1861.

artistic young woman[1]; Frédéric Villot, keeper of the imperial museums, to whom Wagner has dedicated the French translations of his four operatic poems; naturally, Edmond Roche, in recognition of his welcome at the Customs; Hector Berlioz, in remembrance of their relations in Germany and at London; Emile Perrin, a director then unoccupied, having left the

---

[1] She died at Saint Tropez in 1862. Her first name, Blandine, was given to her niece, the eldest daughter of Mme. Wagner, now Countess Gravina.

Opera-Comique, and not yet taken the Grand Opera ; Carvalho, director of the Theatre-Lyrique, and strongly attracted by new works ; Gustave Doré, in the meridian of his glory, and Jules Ferry, brought there by Emile Ollivier ; then the writers : Ch. Baudelaire, Champfleury, Charles de Lorbac, Léon Leroy, Gasperini, who added enormously to the reputation of their host, in forcing the attention of the public by their cries of war, and their inflammatory articles. A little later, when Wagner had moved to No. 3 *rue d'Aumale*, one sometimes saw there a person who was to hold in course of time, the first place in his life and in his heart, the younger sister of Mme. Ollivier, Mlle. Cosima Liszt, married two years before to Hans von Bülow. The latter, at the summons of the master, had made the journey expressly to aid him in his preparations for the concerts.

Wagner was full of confidence. He believed he had found in M. Carvalho his ideal director, and so this worse than mediocre pianist, with an arch-false voice, subjected Carvalho to the punishment of a musical reading, which Gasparini has recounted in a most amusing fashion, and which put the victim to rout. At the same time, he was actively engaged in organizing concerts, which were to dispose the public in his favor. Surrounded on all sides by difficulties, he had given up his plan of representing *Tristan*, and wished simply to give some hearings of the principal fragments from his works, as he had already done at Zurich.

He had made the request, through the intervention of Mocquart, the emperor's private secretary, that the free use of the *Salle de l'Opera* be granted him ; but receiving no response, he had concluded arrangements with Calzado, to rent, at a very high rate, the Ventadour theatre ; scarcely had he signed the engagement when he received notice that the *Salle de l'Opera* was at his disposal ; it was too late, and the concerts were given at the Italiens. While Wagner was practising the orchestra at the *Salle Herz*, von Bülow was rehearsing the choruses at the *Salle Beethoven*, with all the more trouble, since, in order to have a good force of singers at a small expense, they had called upon the amateurs of the German colony at Paris.

The three concerts took place on the 25th of January, the 1st and 8th of February, 1860. The program was identically the same for the three evenings; 1st, Overture to *The Flying Dutchman;* 2d, March with chorus, introduction to the third

" You are playing discords, my child."
" Mamma, it is *Tannhäuser.*"
"Ah! that is different!"
(CHAM, *Charivari*, March 31, 1861.)

act, chorus of the pilgrims and overture, from *Tannhäuser;* 3d, Prelude to *Tristan and Isolde;* 4th, Prelude, betrothal march with chorus (from the second act), nuptial feast (introduction to the third act) and nuptial song from *Lohengrin.*[1]

The execution, notwithstanding so many united efforts, was very defective, and Wagner, feverish and nervous, only made

---

[1] At the second concert they added the Song to the Evening Star, from *Tannhäuser*, sung by M. Jules Lefort.

MANUSCRIPT MUSIC OF RICHARD WAGNER.
Preserved at the Music of the Paris Opera.
Part for two violins, from the danse in 'Tannhäuser.'

a bad matter worse. At the very opening of the concert he
had given proof of his irascible and violent character — which
had impressed everybody present — by spitefully throwing
his gloves to the ground. The announcement of these concerts had produced some commotion in the musical world, but
not outside of it; moreover, if there was a good deal of curiosity, it must be said also that there was no preconceived
hostility.

To sum the matter up, the result of the concerts was very
honorable for the artist, who had brought together those portions of his works which were the most clear and accessible to
the public; and quite disastrous for the manager, who sustained a deficit of about six thousand francs; fortunately he
was able to cover this sum by drawing upon the copyright
which Messrs. Schott paid him for the *Ring of the Nibelungen*.
Therefore he did not profit by the offer of Marshall Magnan,
who proposed the *Salle de l'Opera* for a fourth concert, and
he accepted an invitation to go to Brussels; he gave two
concerts there in March, at the Grand Théâtre, and the pecuniary result was no more satisfactory than at Paris.

From Brussels he came straight back to Paris. The French
press and the French public were surprised and disconcerted;
what they had heard had appeared to them neither so tran-
scendent as the master's admirers had proclaimed, nor so barbarous and painful as had been declared by his enemies.
One remained as undecided as ever; as to the journals, just
as, in desiring at any cost to appear informed about this musician who started up unexpectedly in the midst of Paris, they
had confined themselves to fables; so, in attempting to pass
immediate and final judgment upon him, they only talked nonsense. In fact the example had been set by a well-known
theatrical critic, who, before Wagner's arrival, had given the
battle cry. " Here comes a man long since renowned for the
boldness of his attacks, and the dazzling fervor of his criticism.

REPRESENTATION OF "TANNHÄUSER" AT THE PARIS OPERA IN 1861.
Final scene of the first act.   After an engraving of the time.

Here comes a man who must be defied! He is the Marat of music, of which Berlioz is the Robespierre! His style is a thing undefined, his phrase a macaroni, a sticky melopæa. He has written some operas of which I do not even know the names, but for all that, I repeat it, defy him!"

And meanwhile, notwithstanding these cries of alarm, people waited. In the general embarrassment of the press and of the public, all eyes turned toward Berlioz, who was considered the leader of the advanced musical school in France; on the judgment which he was going to pass upon his former collaborator on the *Gazette Musicale*, and his former assistant at Dresden, depended to a great extent the final reception which Paris would accord to Richard Wagner. Finally it appeared, this article, and it was the open declaration of war which has so often been repeated, and upon which Wagner's latest enemies still lean for support. In writing this criticism, Berlioz yielded undoubtedly to an instinctive feeling of jealousy, and did not perceive, poor man, that in sinking his rival he would sink himself also; he did not suspect that the public made no distinction between them, and that the ruin of the one would entail the ruin of the other; later, after *Les Troyens*, he was forced to see that the public placed them, Wagner and himself, in the same category, when there appeared a caricature by Cham, which represented *Tannhäuser* demanding to see his little brother, *Les Troyens*. Until then he had been so blind in his opposition as to flatter himself that he had profited by thus overturning Wagner after his concerts, and in assisting by a studied contempt, without writing anything, in the ruin of *Tannhäuser*. The worst of it was that Wagner responded, and responded with some spirit, at least in the first part of the letter, while affecting a friendly style; " My dear Berlioz, the article in the *Journal des Débats* which you have been pleased to devote to my concerts, not only contains things very flattering to me and for which I thank you; it also furnishes

me the opportunity, which I seize with eagerness, to give you
some summary explanations upon what you call *the music of
the future*, and upon which you have believed yourself bound

TANNHAUSER DEMANDING TO SEE HIS LITTLE BROTHER

(CHAM, *Charivari*, Nov. 25, 1863.)

to enlighten your readers.   You also, you believe then that
this title really covers a school of which I would be the leader ;
that I presumed one fine day to establish certain principles,

certain theses, which you divide into two categories; the first, fully adopted by you and containing only truths long since recognized by everybody; the second, which excites your reprobation, and which comprises only a web of absurdities? To attribute to me the foolish vanity of wishing to make old axioms pass for new, or the mad pretension of imposing as incontestible principles what are known in every tongue as stupidities, would be at once to misunderstand my character, and to do an injury to the little intelligence which heaven has bestowed upon me. Your explanations on this subject, permit me to say to you, seem to me a little uncertain, and as your good will is perfectly known to me, you only require, certainly, that I relieve you of your doubt, if not your error."

This letter, much developed, then carried the discussion into a field quite philosophic, where nobody, neither Berlioz nor the other readers, followed Wagner; but the beginning of it sufficed to unite everybody in league against a musician who did not accept his lessons silently, and who presumed to teach his judges. After that, the feeling of opposition was universal, and there was no end of jokes about the new-comer, and his wild conception of the music of the future; caricatures appeared on every hand which excited general applause, because they responded so exactly to public sentiment; from that day Richard Wagner's cause at Paris was irrevocably lost.

He had not much hope, moreover, of having *Tannhäuser* represented at the Opera. It was rather in the direction of the Theatre-Lyrique and of M. Carvalho that he was looking for an opportunity, when Mme. von Metternich obtained word from the Emperor, ordering immediate preparations for the work to be made at the Academy of Music. It was her desire to raise again in the eyes of the musical world, a German composer, cruelly turned to ridicule, and this unexpected news came to Wagner just at the moment when, confronted by all sorts of obstacles, he was turning anew his anxious glance towards Germany. He was quite wild with joy, without shutting his eyes, however, to the many difficulties to be surmounted before arriving at a complete realization of his ideal.

To begin with, everybody received him with sympathy; there is nothing like the acknowledged favor of a man to calm hostilities, and change indifference into zealous interest; Richard Wagner, in a few days had become all the fashion. He reigned, so to speak, at the Opera, which at that time depended on the emperor's household, and where everything was done to satisfy him. At only one point was he thwarted; he wanted the new baritone Faure to create the rôle of Wolfram, but as the latter demanded eight thousand francs a month, he was obliged to content himself with Morelli, whom he engaged at three thousand francs. There were also some difficulties to be settled as to the number of supplementary instruments, but an understanding was finally reached by means of concessions here and there. One artist only was capable, in Wagner's eyes, of personifying Tannhäuser, a tenor very young and well pleased with himself, who sung the master's operas in Germany, and contributed greatly to their success; young Niemann was engaged at six thousand francs a month, with the express condition that *under no pretext whatever* should he sing in any other opera than *Tannhäuser.*

This tenor was given all sorts of masters, in order to prepare him for the French stage, and the author on his side exerted himself to train the interpreters whom he had chosen, and imbue them with his methods; he took particular pains with Mme. Tedesco (Venus), whose unfitness, notwithstanding her beautiful voice, was soon apparent to him, and whom he treated so badly at the rehearsals, that one day, in an excess of Italian rage, she almost flew at his face; also with the

FIRST DRAUGHT OF AN AUTOGRAPH LETTER FROM RICHARD WAGNER TO THE
(Rough draught not dated.)

baritone Morelli, from whom he obtained sacrifices quite surprising on the part of a singer from beyond the mountains;
and finally Mme. Marie Sax, who had at that time only an
incomparable voice, but who learned under Wagner's harsh
teaching to play almost with warmth and conviction.[1]

As to the stage settings and decorations, to which he at-
tached so much importance, he found in them unalloyed
satisfaction, and could not conceal his delight; never had he
dared to hope for such miracles, such perfection in all the
details. His confidence returned, his enthusiasm overflowed

"Papa, I would like to learn music."
"Impossible, my child. One does not know how it might turn
out. You might become a Wagner! Mercy!"
(CHAM, *Charivari*, March 31, 1861.)

at seeing the progress of the choruses, of the orchestra, of the
soloists, and all these gigantic preparations for one of his
operas, when for more than ten years such a pleasure had
been denied him. One day he exclaimed before Gasperini,
"This is the ideal representation after which I have yearned
so long. Royer is converted, he has understood me, I have

---

[1] The other roles were sung by Cazaux (the landgrave), Coulon (Biterolf),
Rinies, König, Fréret and Mlle. Réboux. Mlles. Rousseau, Troisvallets, and Stoikofl
represented the three Graces in the tableau of Venusberg.

him fast! At last people will be able to judge of this much-attacked *Tannhäuser*, and it is to France that I will owe this glory!"

For a translation of his work he appealed to Edmond Roche, a poet of some talent; he hurried him, worried him, worked him like a galley slave, binding him to the task at seven o'clock in the morning, never releasing him until night-fall and only permitting him to swallow a mouthful when Roche, worn out, let his pen fall, and appeared on the point of fainting. It was a desperate chase with the musician-poet and his translator, after the syllable indispensable, unique, undiscoverable, which ought to strike upon such or such a note in order to render at the same time the accent of the music and the sense of the poem. Roche, who did not understand German, had engaged to assist him, with Wagner's knowledge and approval, one of his friends of German origin, named Richard Lindau, who boasted of being both poet and musician, and who gave Roche the literal sense of the poem. The translation thus brought to an end, not without difficulty, and through the desperate impatience of Wagner who was always urging his collaborators to go faster, had been submitted to the director of the Opera during the month of June; but the latter had immediately declared that the unrhymed verse of the German recitatives ought to be translated into rhymed French verse, and not into blank verse, as Roche and Lindau had done. For reviewing their translation, very defective in many respects, he had recommended to Wagner M. Charles Nuitter, who was accustomed to work of that sort, having already translated *Romeo and Juliet* for the Opera, and *Oberon* for the Theatre-Lyrique.

Nuitter went over the work again with Edmond Roche and Richard Wagner; but M. Lindau, much vexed at being dismissed, brought action against the musician in order to determine his rights as collaborator, and to demand that his

name appear on the play-bills and libretti. The affair was
called March 6th, 1861, seven days previous to the first representation of *Tannhäuser*, before the first chamber of the civil

Still fearing for her Rhine Provinces . . . . Germany sends *Tannhäuser*
to put France to sleep.
(CHAM, *Charivari*, March 25, 1861.)

tribunal, presided over by M. Benoist-Champy. The lawyer
Marie pleaded for the plaintiff, who was recommended as a
translator by Berlioz, as a singer and composer of romances,
by Gounod; Ollivier appeared for Richard Wagner, and the

two advocates vied with each other in quoting passages from Wagner which seemed to them the most likely to aid the opinion of the judges. The latter non-suited M. Lindau, limiting his rights to a pecuniary indemnity, and the direct result of the suit was that Wagner's name figured alone on play-bill and libretto. Roche, who worked from pure devotion, trusted to his friend for remuneration in case of success; he had no desire to be associated with Lindau's claim, and the latest comer in the collaboration, M. Nuitter, followed Roche's example in keeping in the background, and giving all credit to Richard Wagner, the only true author of the poem and of the score.[1]

So much for the translation of *Tannhäuser* into verse; but Wagner, in his desire to be fully understood by the Parisians, had gone still farther. He had had a translation made of his four great poems, in prose, because of the pressure of time, and of the difficulty in rendering the literal sense into verse; then he had united them into one volume, with a preface in which he undertook to give a summary sketch of his life, and to explain clearly his artistic theories to people who cared very little about them. This *Letter on Music* was a mistake on the part of Richard Wagner, who had, moreover, a mania for autobiography, and who began several, always with the object of making himself known to new hearers, French, American, or others, to whom he submitted his music. In principle, the intention was a good one; in fact, it was without usefulness but not without danger.

He could not have had much knowledge of the French,

---

[1] Edmond Roche died at thirty-four, on Dec. 16, 1861, from the reaction of the failure of *Tannhäuser*, upon which he had placed his last hope of renown and prosperity. His poems were united in a volume with a preface by M. V. Sardou, who relates with his usual animation the extraordinary *séances* of labor between Roche and Wagner, and deplores the death of a talented friend. As for the collection of Roche's poems, it was with that as with the poet himself, — quite unknown.

amateurs, critics or musicians, to imagine that they would read this preface before going to see *Tannhäuser*, and even if they had read it, they would have been more perplexed than enlightened by it. As Wagner in 1860 had already written *Tristan and Isolde*, and as that poem figured in his book, he instinctively carried the history of his life and of the development of his ideas beyond the point of *Tristan*, without reflecting that he was thereby exceeding his aim, it being simply a question of preparing people to hear *Tannhäuser*. In drawing up this *Letter on Music*, he lost sight of the immediate object of the preface; he wrote less for the unenlightened than for himself, and thereby a very natural misunderstanding arose between the public and the writer. His profession of faith misled everybody; they thought they saw in it a definition of the style of *Tannhäuser*, and they were frightened off; whereas the author had always had in mind while writing it, not *Tannhäuser*, nor even *Lohengrin*, but *Tristan and Isolde*, and *the Ring of the Nibelungen*.

He has said somewhere: "To consider the explanations which I give you as a preparation to the representation of *Tannhäuser*, would be to conceive an expectation very erroneous in some respects." But then why give them? Explanations which explain nothing only have the effect of confusing the mind; and that is what happened in this case, the more so as the article was skimmed over in a very superficial manner. The public did not read it at all, and the journalists who criticised it were struck only by one or two terms which were new to them, such as *infinite melody* and *table music*, in speaking of the Italian opera, and the explanation of which they did not attempt to seek in the context. They even invented an explanation for the term *melody of the forest*, as they had already done for *music of the future*, and upon these few expressions they built the most absurd and fantastic theories, full of jest and satire.

REPRESENTATION OF "TANNHÄUSER," AT THE PARIS OPERA IN 1861.
Final scene of the second act. Original drawing by Alphonse de Neuville.

Followed attentively, it will be seen that this *resumé* of his life and ideas is made with a great deal of care, by an author who, naturally, saw no fault in himself; but it is confused, like all the writings of Richard Wagner, the essential idea being always overloaded with parasitical developments, with comparisons more confusing than the object which he sets out to explain. Far enough from being clear in itself, it seems very obscure to people who know nothing of the subjects discussed, and who hold as worthless any artist presumptuous enough to attack the best established reputations, and to wish to reform dramatic music. And yet in his *Letter on Music* he naïvely remarked : "The work of which I am speaking, and of which the greater part of the musical composition has long since been completed, is entitled *The Ring of the Nibelungen*. If the attempt which I am now making to lay before you my other operatic poems does not discourage you, perhaps I might be disposed to do the same for my Trilogy also ! "[1]

Difficulties arose apropos of a ballet. The administrator Alphonse Royer, in his first conversations with Wagner, had not concealed the fact that this was an important element of success, and that the ballet, in his opinion indispensable,

[1] In his *Letter on Music* Wagner twice protests against the foolish interpretation put upon the term *music of the future*. After having explained that each art, according to his ideas, having reached the limit of its power, requires to be united to a companion art, and that perfect art work would result from the fusion of all the individual arts, he recognizes that in the existing state of things, this ideal could not attain a complete realization, and he designates it under the name of *Art Work of the Future*. " Under this title also I published a more detailed essay in which I described more closely the ideas which I had just indicated ; and it is to this title, by the bye, that we are entitled to the invention of the spectre of a ' Music of the Future,' which plays its pranks in such a popular fashion even in French publications, and from which it can now be easily understood from what misunderstanding it arose, and with what object it was invented." (*Letter on Music*, to M. F. Villot, translated by M. Challemel-Lacour, at the head of the Four Operatic Poems, translated into French prose. One volume, 18mo, *Librarie Nouvelle*, 1860.)

ought to come in the middle of the second act, for it was not till then that those subscribers to whom the ballet principally belonged entered their boxes. Wagner obstinately refused to interpolate a ballet into the second act, where it would have no meaning; on the contrary he cherished the idea of introducing dances in the Venusberg, and developing this scene in accordance with his new ideas on the drama. This, of course, must only serve to disconcert the singers who already knew the first act, and could in no way benefit the subscribers, since the new scene appeared at the first rising of the curtain. But Wagner adhered strictly to his convictions.

He gave some magnificent developments to the tableau of the Venusburg, for which the interpreters complained bitterly, particularly Mme. Tedesco, forced to learn a new role of Venus; and at which the listeners laughed immoderately, because this portion, differing in character from the rest of the work was written in a style too unfamiliar for the public to accept, even though it had applauded all the rest of the opera; but it is to Wagner's honor to have acted according to his convictions, and not to have heeded the advice of his friends, who tried to dissuade him from making this change, for fear of compromising the success. From every point of view he acted wisely; however, this refusal to put a grand ballet in the accustomed place was sufficient to rouse the fury of the *beaux messieurs* of the clubs, and to decide them to come and hiss *Tannhäuser;* for they were far too much interested in the *corps de ballet* to allow such a matter to pass unheeded.

As the rehearsals proceeded they became more and more stormy.[1] During these long studies Wagner had found on

---

[1] There were not less than one hundred and sixty-four of them; the general expenses of stage settings, etc., amounted to one hundred thousand francs, plus eight hundred and sixty francs extra outlay for each performance. These figures are taken from the carefully prepared article published by M. Ch. Nuitter in the

the part of the *chefs du chant*, Vauthrot and Croharé, the most intelligent and devoted co-operation ; but it was quite otherwise with the leader of the orchestra, who was no other than Dietsch, the same who had set to music with so little success, *The Phantom Ship*, sold by Richard Wagner to Léon Pillet. At the close of the rehearsals, the relations between the author and Dietsch had become most difficult. Wagner much dissatisfied, claimed the privilege of directing the general rehearsal and the first three perform-ances. " I decidedly can-not consent," he wrote to the director, Alphonse Royer, " to have the effect of the unprecedented zeal of so many artists, left to the mercy of an orchestral leader who is incapable, so far as my works are con-cerned, of directing the final execution." It did not rest with the admin-istrator to decide this ques-tion, and Wagner was obliged to address his

AT A GENERAL REHEARSAL OF TANNHÄUSER.
" Say! Isn't it allowable to be tired to death at your opera?"
" No, Sir! to die would be to applaud ; and I don't want any applause at my performances."
(CHAM, *Charivari*, March 10, 1861.)

request to the Minister, who responded by a formal refusal, justified by the customs of the past, and approved, it must be

Bayreuther Festblätter (1884) and which may be depended upon with all confi-dence, in regard to *Tannhäuser*. On the contrary, it is necessary to make allow-ance in reading a very amusing but clever article by M. Paul Lindau, in which, under pretense of being very friendly to Wagner, he tries to demonstrate that he was at fault in everything, and that there existed not even a shadow of cabal. M. Paul Lindau was the brother of Richard Lindau, who had just lost a suit against Wag-ner, and even though it were not already known, the fashion in which he rallies M. Nuitter's verses, would suffice to show that he was closely related to the discharged translator.

confessed, by all the musicians of the orchestra and of the choruses, who saw an opportunity to avenge themselves for the demands and bad compliments of Wagner, by praising to the skies a leader whom they secretly decried.

However that may be, there is in the response of the Minister of State, Count Walewski, a phrase to be preserved as a model of administrative style : " Never in France, be it a question of the works of our own composers or of those of foreign masters, like Rossini or Meyerbeer, has a director of the orchestra been disinherited of his right to remain at the head of his phalanx of performers. *Furthermore, with our French ideas and habits, the leader of an orchestra who would yield up his place at these solemn and decisive moments, would be considered as deserting his duties, and would lose for the future all the prestige of his authority.*" And the rehearsals went on from bad to worse, the leader of the orchestra at his desk, beating time, and the composer seated on the stage a few steps away, beating his own time, with hand and foot, and furiously striking the floor of the theatre, enveloped in a cloud of dust.

It was under these unfavorable conditions that the first performance was given, on Wednesday, March 13, 1861. In a few months Wagner had alienated from himself everybody at the Opera; director, leader, orchestra and *corps de ballet*, even the salaried *claqueurs*, whom his artistic honesty impelled him to banish, but who had been forced upon him in spite of himself; to say nothing of the showers of jokes and caricatures which this unheard-of resolution brought down upon him. "Meanwhile," writes M. Nuitter, who has left us the best account of this performance, "notwithstanding all the rumors of the systematic opposition of a part of the spectators, no one could conjecture how the affair would turn out. The first tableau, although it was written quite in Wagner's latest style, passed without opposition, but when after the change of

scene, the strains of the little shepherd were heard, playing
upon his pipe, the first murmur of discontent arose.   Wagner,
who sat in the director's box, as yet quite innocent of the
meaning of this demonstration, leaned forward in order to
command a better view of the audience-room, and remarked
to his collaborator who sat beside him: " It is the arrival of

RICHARD WAGNER IN 1861.
After a lithograph by Desmaisons.

the emperor." Alas no! It was the first sign of rebellion
from the leaders of the opposition.

In the *entr'acte* a bright idea for amusing themselves
crossed the minds of these individuals ; most of the subscribers,
members of the Jockey-Club or of the *Cercle Impérial*, went
out and bought up all the hunting-whistles they could find in

a certain gunsmith's shop in the *passage de l'Opera*, and the disturbance recommenced with the second act, increasing to the very end of the performance, save during the march with the chorus, when the whistlers had to subside. It must be said that in this uproar, the chevaliers of the *corps de ballet* had been sustained by the personal enemies of the master — he always excelled in creating them — while the impartial spectators, indignant at such pre-conceived hostility, and at such a scandalous outrage, joined their bravos, often very warm ones, to those of Wagner's friends.

For an instant it seemed as if the victory would remain to the defenders ; but the finale to the second act, encumbered with harps and troubadours, brought irrevocable defeat ; of the third, nothing could be distinguished, and the recitative of the pilgrimage to Rome, in particular, the real climax to the whole work, was drowned from beginning to end in furious yells. The interpreters, however, did not give way before these hostile demonstrations, and at least two distinguished people in the room bravely defended the author : Mme. von Metternich, who seemed to wish to be revenged on Solferino ; and the emperor, who on several occasions gave the signal for applause.

Wagner, moreover, seems to have clearly seen through the whole affair, and in an account of the battle, which he gives to his friends in Germany, on March 26, he indicates an appreciative recognition of the Parisian public taken *en masse*. " It seems to me that you have thus far been misinformed with regard to the nature of this reception ; certainly you would be greatly mistaken if you were to derive from it an opinion of the French public, which, though it might be flattering to the German public, would be really very unjust. I persist, on the contrary, in attributing to the Parisian public very agreeable characteristics, especially a very lively receptiveness, and a really magnanimous sense of justice. To see an audience

(I speak of the audience taken in its *ensemble*) to whom I am
personally quite a stranger, who have daily heard the most
absurd things about me through the newspapers and idle
chatterers, and who have been influenced against me with
almost unprecedented efforts, — to see such an audience
declare itself in my favor, and against a clique, by repeated
and earnest demonstrations of applause, for a whole quarter
of an hour at a time — would fill my heart with joy were I
the most indifferent of men."

The second representation, announced for March 15, was
postponed until Monday the 18th, in consequence of an indisposition of M. Niemann, and the director profited by this
delay to demand fresh sacrifices from the author; he had already obtained from him permission to suppress part of the
role of Venus in the first scene, the hunting horns and the
dogs in the final scene of the first act,[1] the *ritornello* of the little
shepherd, the violin passage which terminates the second act,
and the return of Venus in the third; all happy cuts, but insufficient to satisfy the director. "I would have you observe,"
writes he to the minister on March 17, "that it is very difficult
to get a man so convinced of his own merit as is M. Wagner,
to cut out any portion of his work. Those who know him are
amazed at what I have already obtained, although that, I
repeat it, is not sufficient. If it were a question of a recited
piece I would cut it out on my own authority, notwithstanding
the expostulations of the author; but in a score, all curtail-
ment necessitates an agreement of tonalities which I cannot
take the responsibility of making."

The second representation, during which the Emperor

---

[1] These poor dogs, which had roused the sympathy of the sensitive spectators
and served as pretext for the most spirited jests, a short time afterwards contributed
largely to the success of a great drama; — *la jeunesse du roi Henri*, by Lambert
Thiboust and Ponson du Terrail, represented in 1864 at the Châtelet theatre; the
authors had simply made use of Wagner's idea, and had only to congratulate themselves for it.

Monsieur le Directeur,

c'est probablement par un malentendu qu'on n'a pas encore fait droit à ma demande de cent (100) entrées pour la répétition générale de demain. Jusqu'ici si la salle a été trop encombrée aux dernières répétitions, ce n'est point de ma faute. Pour celle d'hier par exemple j'ai même refusé à ma femme la faveur de m'y accompagner pour que la répétition eût le caractère le plus intime. J'ai été fort étonné alors de voir la salle remplie d'individus qui m'étaient parfaitement inconnus. Je crois être dans mon droit en vous demandant, Monsieur, de m'envoyer le plus tôt - préalablement - cent parterre, pour placer mes amis, que jusqu'ici j'ai discrètement renvoyés à cette répétition générale. En outre je vous prie, Monsieur, de satisfaire aux demandes des ministres étrangers pour loges et stalles à cette même répétition de demain soir.
Agréez mes civilités empressées.

Richard Wagner

AUTOGRAPH LETTER FROM WAGNER TO THE DIRECTOR OF THE OPERA.
Dated March 1, 1869. (Opera Archives.)

and Empress joined more than once in the applause of the
partisans, confirmed Wagner's judgment of the public, who
themselves cried "*A bas les Jockeys!*" in order to impose
silence on the disturbers. It was an intrigue so well conceived and carried out by signal, that at this performance the
whole of the first act and half of the second passed without
other interruption than that of warm applause in several
places; then at the close of the scene of the tourney of
singers, as if upon word of command, whistles and pipes were
started up, and the hostile manifestations became even more
violent than on the first evening, so fearful were these leaders
of having left the saving breath of life in the enemy. In view
of the animosity of an all-powerful club, who held the Minister
himself in a state of submission, it was agreed that the third
representation should be given on Sunday, in order to get rid
of the presence of the subscribers; and this took place on the
24th, before a full house, as is proven by the receipts.[1]

But the subscribers, whom they wished to keep out, did
not see the matter in this light, and rather than run the risk
of allowing *Tannhäuser* to make the least headway before an
impartial public, they had come *en masse*, they, whose custom
was never to show themselves at the Opera on Sunday. This
time it was impossible to deal with a cabal so desperate. "Astounded as I was at the unbridled conduct of these gentlemen," says Wagner, "I was still more impressed and touched
by the efforts of the true audience to secure justice to me;
never have I been in the least disposed to doubt the Parisian
public, whenever it is upon an impartial ground." And this,
let us not forget, was written the second day after the third
representation.

It had been rumored, without being officially announced,

[1] Receipts from the three representations of *Tannhäuser*: first, 7,491 francs
(of which 2,790 were subscribed); second, 8,415 francs (subscription 2,758);
third, 10,764 francs (subscription 230 francs). (From article by M. Ch. Nuitter).

that this performance on Sunday would be the last. A strong effort was made to have a fourth given, in order that the Friday subscribers, who alone had not heard *Tannhäuser*, might be entertained in their turn, but Wagner opposed the project so violently, that the Minister consented to the withdrawal of the work.

" Since the members of the Jockey Club are not willing to permit the public of Paris to hear my opera performed on the stage of the Imperial Academy of Music, because they cannot see a ballet danced at the usual hour of their entrance at the theatre, I withdraw my score, and I beg you to communicate to His Excellency the Minister of State my resolution, through which I hope to relieve him of a serious embarrassment."

That was a private note ; the official letter ran thus : "The opposition which is manifested against *Tannhäuser* proves to me how right you were in your observations to me at the outset, in regard to the ballet and other scenic conditions to which the subscribers of the Opera are accustomed. I regret that the nature of my work has prevented me from conforming to these exigencies. Now that the violence of the opposition which is made to me does not even allow those who would like to hear it, to give the attention necessary in order to appreciate it, I have no other honorable resource than to withdraw it. I beg you to make this decision known to His Excellency, M. the Minister of State." This was falling proudly — almost a victor.[1]

This whole affair of *Tannhäuser*, from whatever point of

---

[1] This withdrawal of *Tannhäuser* was a real disappointment for the amateurs and the curious ; in Paris everybody had the *Tannhäuser* mania, and the advance receipts were enormous. Once the piece was withdrawn, people went in crowds wherever a fragment from Wagner was to be heard, — at the Casino, where Arban had the *Tannhäuser* march executed, and the betrothal march from *Lohengrin* ; at the Opera-Comique, where Roger sung in *concert spirituel* the recitative of the pilgrimage to Rome, etc., etc. And adversaries and partisans hissed and applauded, vigorously and blindly.

view it is examined, is very little to our credit. But what is even more sad than this infernal uproar organized by a company of jovial fellows after drinking, and before supper, is the attitude of the press, which was not dependent on the *corps de ballet*, and actually believed itself in the presence of an execrable work and of a second-rate composer. In their ignorance the newspapers vied with each other in scattering abuse and insult, and for many weeks after the composer had left Paris, they attacked the work and derided the man with an unprecedented fury.

" I have sold my score."
" To the music-dealer? "
" No, to the druggist."
" As an opiate; that is quite proper."
(CHAM, *Charivari*, April 7, 1861.)

Probably the blindness of criticism taken *en masse*, and its weakness towards the public, which guided it instead of being guided by it, had never shown up in a more glaring fashion. There were some hundreds of articles in which the artist and his work were abused, simply because it was the fashion, and the worst of it was that all these judges had not the first idea of the thing they were judging; in their eyes the author was a scapegrace, his work rubbish, and the sentence which they rendered must be without appeal.

Many of these have died without seeing their judgments cast aside, in even so short a time; but among those who survive, and who were the most violent at the outset, it is amusing to see how some of them manœuvre to turn with the tide of fashion, and cast the shades of oblivion over their past lucubrations, while others, more courageous, struggle desperately and cry all the louder as they feel the ground sinking beneath them. It would be tiresome to wade through all these articles, of which moreover, Gasperini has detached characteristic passages ; it will suffice to quote one, forgotten in his nomenclature, one of the least violent, and signed by a writer who was at that time classed among the masters of criticism.

" To give without circumlocution our opinion on the opera of Richard Wagner : the overture and the march of the second act excepted, his score is but a musical chaos. The sounds jostle each other, pile themselves up and intermingle like immense clouds in a dull sky. Now it is an opaque and heavy obscurity — what Wagner calls the *infinite melody*, no doubt — which overpowers the strongest attention ; now it is a discordant din which can only be compared to the most violent tumult of tempests. The voices and the orchestra, the winds and the sea, struggle to see which shall make the most noise. If perchance a ray of light pierces the darkness, if the ghost of a melodious idea is outlined against this deep shadow, the musician lets loose his orchestra after the manner of Æolus exciting the winds, and does not rest until the nebulous mass has piled up and quite effaced it. M. Wagner purposely interdicts what the musicians of all times have sought after as the very essense of their art—rhythm, melody, clearness. His music, like that of the Corybantes, who surrounded the caves of the orgiastic Mysteries, seems to have no purpose but to terrify and drive away outsiders. ' He has eaten of the drum and drunk of the cymbal ! ' cried the Hierophantes of these orgies, in order to designate the Initiated who had passed through the terrible ordeal. ' If I know what I eat, I dismiss you,' said an epicure to his cook. In brief, this is like the music of Wagner. In order to reveal his secrets he imposes tortures on the mind which algebra alone should inflict. The unintelligible is his ideal."

Paul de Saint-Victor, the author of this sheer nonsense,

presuming to reproach anybody with being unintelligible!' Is it not droll enough?

" The less said about the causes of this failure, the better," writes Wagner; "but it was a disaster for me. Everybody interested had been paid by me; my part was to consist of the customary honorarium after each representation, and this resource was abruptly cut off. So I quitted Paris with a load of debts, not knowing which way to turn; and yet outside of these unpleasantnesses the recollection of this trying year is not altogether disagreeable to me." He suffered a greater loss at the sudden interruption of *Tannhäuser*, since, in order to remunerate the two translators, he had given up to them half of his rights on the first twenty performances, and it was not until the twenty-first that he was to receive for himself alone the total sum of five hundred francs, fixed at that time to cover all rights of the author at the Opera. These three performances then, brought him only seven hundred and fifty francs, and three hundred and seventy-five francs to each of the two translators.

Berlioz was in a transport of joy. He had preserved silence in the *Débats*, but he made up for it in society. What cries of triumph when he saw his enemy down! "Ah! What a representation! What bursts of laughter! The Parisian showed himself yesterday in quite a new light; he laughed at the wretched musical style; he laughed at the tricks of a fantastic orchestration, he laughed at the *naïvetés* of a hautboy; at last he comprehends that there is a style in music. As for the horrors, he hissed them splendidly." And a week

---

¹ There were few enough critics who defended Richard Wagner, or who were content to criticise him seriously, instead of loading him with ridicule; but among the few should be named Baudelaire of the *Revue Européenne*, Franck-Marie of *La Patrie*, Weber of the *Temps*, and Ortigue of the *Débats*, taking Berlioz's place for a day, and who while rejecting the ideas set forth in the *Letter on Music*, recognized in Wagner an artist with convictions, and combatted him without acrimony.

later, in writing to his son, he says: "The second representation was worse than the first. People no longer laughed, they were furious; they hissed persistently, notwithstanding the presence of the Emperor and Empress, who were in their box. The Emperor is amusing himself. When leaving the theatre, on the stairs, people treat this unfortunate Wagner as a scamp, an imposter, an idiot. If they continue, one of these days the performance cannot be finished, and all will be over. The press is unanimous against it. As for me, I am cruelly revenged!!!" Poor Berlioz!

In the month of June, 1861, Wagner was again in Paris. At that time he left the *rue d'Aumale* to go and lodge with the Minister of Prussia, Count de Pourtalès, but he left France almost immediately, and this time he was able to go in peace to his own country, instead of wandering in exile. Some time before, — about the middle of the year 1860 — the intercession of the grand duke of Baden had obtained from the government permission for Richard Wagner to reside in any of the States of the Confederation except the territory of Saxony, which was still interdicted.[1]

Wagner in speaking of his first sojourn in our midst, has remarked, "Paris has been of the greatest help to me, for Germany." A correct observation, and the accuracy of which is still more striking after the second sojourn, for the infuriated whistlers of Paris did more for his glory and renown, than a success similar to those which came to him in Germany could ever have done. In thinking to bury him they had borne him to the highest pinnacle; thus goes the world sometimes — and all is well.

---

[1] In the month of October, 1851, the King of Saxony had commuted the long imprisonment which Wagner escaped only by flight, to banishment from entire Germany. In 1860, it was only the Saxon kingdom which was closed to him; finally in March 1862, he was even permitted to enter Saxony — after thirteen years of exile.

CHAPTER IX

RICHARD Wagner, in returning to Germany, was possessed always of the same fixed idea : to bring about an execution of *Tristan and Isolde*. He was in such haste to hear this work, into which he had put his whole being, — poet and musician, philosopher and reformer, — that it was a radical impossibility to dissuade him from his wild plan of renting the Ventadour theatre, and mounting his work there at his own risk and peril. But he thought that it ought to walk alone in Germany; a sad mistake ! In fact, the three years which intervened between his return from France and his call to Munich, were perhaps the most trying of his whole life. He had but one thought, and all his efforts to realize it seemed to be struck powerless. His first disappointment was from the Grand Duke of Baden, who did not flatly refuse to have *Tristan and Isolde* played for his anniversary, but who never spoke of it again. At Vienna they had agreed to mount it ; but after fifty-seven rehearsals, the flagrant inadequacy of the tenor Ander forced them to renounce it. At Carlsruhe, at Prague, at Weimar, they did not get so far as to rehearse it ; they refused it on sight.

At this point Wagner was at the end of his resources, and in order to sustain a precarious existence, he was obliged to organize a series of concerts, at which he conducted principally the symphonies of Beethoven, and some fragments from the *Meistersinger* and the *Nibelungen*.[1]

From December 1862 to December 1863, he travelled about directing festivals of this kind at Leipsic, at Vienna, at Prague, at St. Petersburg, at Moscow, at Pesth, at Breslau, and again at Vienna, where he gave several concerts at the theatre *An der Wien*, and where he astonished his audience by an execution, quite in the true spirit, of *Der Freischütz*. He himself has summed up in a few words this Wandering-Jew life of music. "This curious concert," says he, referring to that at Leipsic, where the room was half empty, "was the first of a long series of similar absurd undertakings, to which poverty reduced me. In other cities, at least, people came in good numbers, and I bore away a real artistic success; but it was only in Russia that the pecuniary results were worth talking about." These concerts, on the whole, had done much for his reputation and everywhere people flocked to see him; but he was no nearer the longed-for execution of *Tristan and Isolde*.

---

[1] A few words of explanation in regard to the pecuniary returns will not be out of place here. In Germany, the customary honorarium for the first performance of a work varied from $40 to $240, according to the rank and importance of the theater. For subsequent performances, the author's share consisted of a small sum agreed upon in advance, and a small percentage of the receipts, usually five, sometimes seven, never more than ten per cent. As most of the German towns had a a theatre, an opera successful in its first tour might bring in a considerable sum, but after that the returns quickly diminished; they could not play the same piece very long in a court or town theatre, where the prices are always very low, and where the system of subscriptions tends to reduce the number of performances of a work. "My operas were to be heard right and left, but I could not live on the proceeds. At Dresden *Tannhäuser* and *The Flying Dutchman* had grown into favor, yet I was told that I had no claim with regard to them, since they were produced during my capellmeistership, and a hof-capellmeister in Saxony is bound to furnish an opera once a year! When the Dresden people wanted *Tristan*, I refused to let them have it unless they agreed to pay for *Tannhäuser*. Accordingly they thought they could dispense with *Tristan*. Aferwards when the public insisted on *Die Meistersinger* I got the better of them." (Groves' Dictionary of Music, p. 146.)

After this successful trip through Russia, where the Grand Duchess Helen, a passionate devotee to music, had testified her admiration of this " *Messie du laid*," as Fétis says, with quite a royal magnificence, Wagner took up his abode in Vienna, where he foolishly squandered all the profits of his tour in the North, about thirty-five thousand roubles, which represented at that time more than twenty thousand dollars. He had fancied that he would never come to the end of this fortune, and he had given free course to his love for ostentatious display; they tell of a sofa hung with silk richly embroidered, and for which he paid three thousand florins, more than $1,200. In the front of one of the principal shops of Vienna are shown some magnificent tapestries, which Wagner ordered to be made expressly for his villa in Switzerland; in less than no time the thirty-five thousand roubles were swallowed up. About this time, and when he was practically penniless, some thieves entered his house, and finding very meagre spoils, carried off a rich snuff-box which he had received at the hands of the Grand Duchess, and on which he probably counted on subsisting for some time. This was considered a pretty good joke, and several newspapers in relating the theft added facetiously, " As to the MSS. of *Tristan* and of the *Nibelungen*, the thieves never touched them."

The legend of *Tristan and Isolde*, so famous in the Middle Ages, is of Celtic origin, and consequently French in its essence. We meet it for the first time in literary form, in a romance written in the XII. century, in Norman prose, by *Luc de Gast*. From France it passed rapidly into Germany, where in 1210 Gottfried of Strasburg made of it a chivalric epopee, from which Richard Wagner borrowed the main idea of his drama, subjecting it to the modifications necessary for adaptation to the stage, and above all, introducing the philosophic theories of which his head was full. In the state of unhappy isolation and absolute discouragement in which he found himself during his exile, his mind, naturally prone to philosophic speculation, and especially imbued at that time with the pantheistic doctrines of Hegel and of Schelling, was quite carried away by the theories of Schopenhauer, which are no other than the religious ideas of the Hindoos, of the Nirvana, — distaste for life and a horror of the dazzling day; aspiration for the calm night, kindly death, annihilation.

" Like Schopenhauer," writes Gasperini, in his interesting article, " Wagner thought to find refuge from the agitations of an uncertain and tumultuous world, in this supreme indifference which India extols. It was to this quarter that he now turned ; it was of Buddhism that he demanded the appeasement of his soul; it was in renouncing the fight, in giving himself up entirely to the new faith, that he hoped to keep himself forevermore from terrestial disenchantments, from the violent disappointments which had overthrown him. By a strange contradiction, the causes for which it would take too long to trace, this Buddhism which preaches extinction and annihilation, proclaims and glorifies the unlimited power of the will. With this sentiment at least, Wagner found himself in harmony, and felt himself breathe in the midst of this deep night, this dull torpor which had overpowered him."[1]

That Richard Wagner should have drawn from the most discouraging of philosophic theories, the courage and will necessary to raise himself from the despondency of exile, is sufficiently strange ; but that he should go so far as to make his heroes, two lovers like Isolde and Tristan, the interpreters of the philosophic school then working upon his own mind, and that in the guise of a love-song he should make them launch imprecations at the perverse and deceitful day, at all the falsities of the light, glory, honor, beauty ; that he should make them aspire to darkness, to the eternal repose of death,

---

[1] The *New Musical Germany : Richard Wagner*, by A. de Gasperini, p. 145.

to nothingness; that the supreme burst of love from Tristan should be, "It is I who am the world," as Schopenhauer had said in more abstract terms, "The world is my representation"—this is what shows a mind singularly disturbed by philosophic reveries, and turned aside from the healthy dramatic and musical conception.

Meanwhile, *Tristan and Isolde* had never seen the light, and it had come to be a by-word with everybody. At the close of the year 1863, the management of the Court theatre at Dresden had begun talking about engaging Richard Wagner as orchestral leader. They finally agreed to all his conditions, however exorbitant, — six thousand francs pension for life, an apartment at the grand-ducal castle, box at the theatre, Court equipage at his disposal, etc., etc.; they were about to conclude the bargain, when to all these clauses he added the performance, at a very early day, of *Tristan and Isolde;* this was the last straw, and the conferences dissolved.

SKATING SCENE.
"Look out there! If you carry your head so high you will fall into the hole."
(*Punsch* of Munich, Feb. 19, 1865.)

Tired out and discouraged by so many fruitless efforts, Wagner was about to beat a final retreat into Switzerland, when the death of Maximilian II. of Bavaria, brought to the throne, in March, 1864, a young prince nineteen years of age, visionary and mystic, carried away by the theories on dramatic and national art so often set forth by Richard Wagner, and by the Opera of *Lohengrin*, which he had heard in his sixteenth year; and who, a year before coming to the throne, had thought he had perceived a message from Heaven in the last lines of a supreme appeal of Richard Wagner to his friends.

This article was dated Vienna, April, 1863, and serves as the preface to the final text of the *Ring of the Nibelungen*. In it, Wagner again takes up and enlarges upon the plan outlined in the *Communication to my Friends*, and addresses to them a last appeal for the realization of his art work, for the building of a special theatre with invisible orchestra, formal representations at regular intervals, etc. " I am preparing," said he, " an important event, and one full of consequences, when I seek to procure the means necessary for the first representation of the *grand serious drama* (Bühnenfestspiel). As I possess the experience necessary to insure the success of the artistic part, it only remains now to provide material means. Two ways present themselves to me. An association of rich amateurs of both sexes, to furnish such sums as may be necessary for the production of my work ; but when I reflect how many Germans have little enthusiasm for such appeals for funds, this first mode of procedure does not offer me much hope. On the other hand, it would be very easy for a German prince, without increasing his budget, and by a simple act of transfer, to apply to my enterprises the funds designed for the maintaining of such detestable institutions as the present Opera theatres, which so sadly pervert the German musical taste. And if the theatre-mad amateurs should demand daily performances, the prince of my dreams would leave to their charge the expenses entailed; for in taking them upon himself, it is neither music nor the drama which he is protecting, but the Opera, that is to say, a machine which outrages in the gravest manner both the drama and the German musical sense. If I should succeed in forming the conviction of this prince, the sums set apart each year for the Opera would go to the benefit of the *grand serious drama*, of which representations would take place every year, or at longer intervals, according to the resources. In this way an institution would be founded of infinite importance in the

development of art in Germany, and the formation of a truly
and purely national spirit. This prince will thus assure to his
name an imperishable glory. Will such a prince be found?"

Such a prince will be found, and later on, will form also
the desired association of rich amateurs; for it actually
happened that Wagner, then so hopeless, and who added with
a doleful resignation "I no longer cherish the hope of living
to witness the execution of my work, and long merely to have
strength enough to finish the musical composition," had the
good fortune to see his double aim realized. The first act of
the young king Ludwig II. on mounting to the throne, was to
send his private secretary to Vienna to deliver to Wagner this
simple message "Come here and finish your work." But
Wagner, at his wit's end, had just left Vienna, and was fleeing
from creditors sufficiently wrought up to pursue him. He had
directed his steps towards Zurich, passing through Munich;
then had turned aside at Stuttgart, where his friend Eckert,
leader of the orchestra, offered him a safe refuge. The messenger followed him from one halting place to another, and at
last discovered his retreat; this messenger of fortune was to
Wagner a visitant straight from Heaven; after the interview,
he embraced the faithful Eckert, crying, " I believed everything
to be lost, and see how everything is saved! All my hopes
are realized. The king puts at my disposal everything he
possesses!"

A short time after, Richard Wagner arrived at Munich and
fell into the arms of his protector, who installed him not far
from the royal residence of Starnberg, and assured him a pension of five hundred dollars from his private purse; this was
only a beginning. "My creditors were quieted," wrote Wagner in 1877, " I was able to go on with my work, and the
confidence of that noble young man made me happy. Since
then I have had many annoyances which were not of his
making, nor of mine, but in spite of these annoyances, I am

now free again, thanks to him." At the coming on of winter,
when the king returned to Munich, he placed at his favorite's
disposition a little house opposite the Propylæum, at the end
of the city, and considerably increased his pension.

It was then that Wagner, sovereign master in Bavaria,
and more king than the king himself, wrote by way of
rendering homage to his protector, his *Huldigungs Marsch*,
before resuming the composition of his long-neglected
Nibelungen. At the request of the king he drew up an
essay on *The State and Religion;* he elaborated the stat-
utes of a school of song, similar to that which he had formerly dreamed of establishing at Dresden, and in July 1865
the king closed the old Conservatory, and appointed a
commission for considering the project of establishing a
school on a new plan; but these propositions had no appreciable results, owing to the ill-will of Franz Lachner and
other musicians at Munich, and also for lack of pecuniary
resources.[1]

Moreover Wagner called to Munich, Gottfried Semper,
whom the king wished to consult about building, according to
the instructions of the master, a theatre adapted to the
Nibelungen representations; finally, he engaged, expressly for
the parts of Tristan and Isolde, Ludwig Schnorr von Carols-
feld and his wife, indemnifying their director at Dresden; he
sent for his beloved disciple, Hans von Bülow, upon whom
was conferred the title of pianist to the king of Bavaria, and
under these conditions he consented to have *Tristan and*

[1] The 8th of October 1865, the *Gazette Musicale* of Paris, received and published the following notice from Munich : "The direction of our Conservatory, re-
organized after the plan — considerably modified — of Richard Wagner, has been
confided to M. de Perfall. The classes will reopen in the month of November.
On the 3rd of the same month will be inaugurated the new *People's Theatre*, built
on shares." Apropos of these innovations, a satirical journal of Munich wrote :
"The rumor is abroad that in the new school of song, steam will be employed for
the emission of sound ; the report does not appear to be confirmed."

Isolde put through a course of rehearsals. In the meantime, in order that his royal master should not lose patience, he had *Tannhäuser* played again, and mounted *The Flying Dutch-man* (December 4, 1864) which had not yet been heard at Munich. He recalled, in this connection the judgment of Küstner, who, twenty-four years before had refused this work sent from Paris, on the ground that it was " little suited to the German taste." Finally, he organized concerts, composed exclusively of his own works ; he arranged one for December 11, the object of which was to give his protector a foretaste of his new creations, such as *Tristan and Isolde* and The *Meis-tersinger ;* but the people of Munich, who were beginning to entertain a sentiment of dissatisfaction towards their king, left him to his own enjoyment in the great almost empty theatre, and Wagner's friends and followers, by way of consol-ing themselves for this hostility, went about declaring "that the ground was not yet sufficiently prepared."

Meanwhile the first performance of *Tristan and Isolde* was close at hand, and all the artists, from M. and Mme. Schnorr (Tristan and Isolde)[1] to Mme. Deinet (Brangäne) Mitterwurzer, Gottmayer, and Heinrich (the King Marke, Kurwenal and Melot) vied with each other in penetrating and faithfully interpreting the master's ideas. The announce-ment of this festival had attracted to Munich large numbers of people from all parts of Germany and of Europe; but the author, profiting from his experience with *Tannhäuser*, had

---

[1] In regard to these two exceptional artists, it would seem as if such a complete identification of actors with their characters, was never seen ; in certain places, one almost feared to see them succumb to their almost superhuman emotions. Rich-ard Wagner paid to Schnorr a just tribute of homage and regret, when a malignant fever carried off the artist, soon after the performances of *Tristan and Isolde*, July 21, 1865. The opera was again consigned to oblivion, and was not heard for four years, when M. and Mme. Vogl sung it with great success at Munich, in June 1869. See the chapter entitled : *My Recollections of Ludwig Schnorr von Carols-feld*, in the *Souvenirs of Wagner*, p. 187.

taken precautions to keep out all individuals suspected of opposition. Far from concealing his purpose, he issued a public letter, inviting his friends in all parts of the world to witness these *model* performances, as he himself styled them, which were reserved for adepts alone; it will be seen later if there was occasion to admit the masses to enjoy "what is most elevating, most profound in art."

This *Invitation to my Friends*, to witness the first performance of *Tristan*, published in April 1865 in the *Vienna Messenger*,—a very peculiar letter, and one which nobody else could have written—led off with a burst of grateful recognition of Ludwig II.: "when I was abandoned by all, a noble heart beat only the more warmly for the ideal of *my* art. It was he who cried to the despairing artist, 'What you create, that is my will!' and this time the will was all-powerful, for it was the will of a king." He proceeds to speak of many things apropos of this *action* in three acts —this word he substitutes for that of *opera* — reverts to the time of his sojourn in Paris, and congratulates himself upon the failure of *Tannhäuser;* very different language from that which he afterwards employs in his conversation with Mme. Judith Gautier, and in his letter to M. Monod.'

The first representation, already announced on the bills for May 15, 1865, was carried over to June 10, owing to a bad hoarseness of Mme. Schnorr, and the hostility against Wagner had made such headway, that he was held responsible for this difficulty; he was also reproached for having taken away a whole row of stalls, in order to increase the orchestra,

---

' Later, the German newspapers valued at 80,000 florins the sum expended in mounting *Lohengrin*, and at a still greater figure, the expenses of *Tristan and Isolde*, without including the different presents in money and in kind, which brought the total up to 250,000 florins. The Cologne Journal, in particular, announced one day that the king was going to present to his favorite musician a cane, the head of which was a gold swan, chased and enriched with brilliants worth several thousands of ducats.

and, on the 29th of May, a small popular theatre which had prepared a parody on *Tristan*, got tired of waiting, and actually launched the parody before the appearance of the regular opera. It was under these untoward circumstances that *Tristan* first saw the day; there were in all four performances, all four admirably directed by Hans von Bülow, and all four received with a frenzy of enthusiasm; at the first two, it was the king himself who gave, after each act, the signal for applause.[1]

The echo of these bravos reached even to France, where it created only merriment. The palm for sarcastic comment fell to M. Blaze de Bury, who made a great show of wit, both against the work, and against the "Invitation to my friends," a sort of encyclical letter addressed to the Wagnerian world, which had served as a preface to the performances at Munich. "Happy Bavaria! Bavaria felix! She had painting and statuary, she had Cornelius, Kaulbach and Schwanthaler; but Gluck was still wanting to complete her good fortune; he was given to her. Let us respect the generous illusions, and let us never reproach a sovereign for excess of zeal in such a cause; it is better to take Richard Wagner for a Gluck and for an Æschylus, than to know neither Gluck nor Æschylus, which is sometimes the case with powerful monarchs ... In the main all this idle twaddle of a personality intoxicated with itself, does not concern us much, and yet it is something too droll to be passed over without remark. Speaking of his campaign in France and of one whole *long year* of his existence foolishly *frittered away* on this occasion, Wagner takes up the question of *Tannhäuser* at the Opera, and so far

[1] The Munich Theatre, compared to the Vaudeville of Paris, was rather poorly lighted, and gloomy in its aspect. On the first floor, facing the stage, and flanked by two caryatids, was the royal box lighted by a small chandelier; above the curtain, in the place of the arms or emblems used by us, a clock perfectly indicated the hour; finally, the leader was placed in the middle of his orchestra instead of near the footlights, and directed while standing up.

REPRESENTATION OF "TRISTAN AND ISOLDE," AT MUNICH, IN 1865.
Final scene of the first act.   After an engraving of the time.

from complaining of his misfortune, so far from deploring the catastrophe, he questions, with irony and bitterness on his lips, if it be not better after all, that things happened thus, 'for, said he, if a grand success had been possible, I really *would not have known what to do with it.*' It is the story of the player, who, not winning, preferred to lose. To succeed in Paris, in this capital of the empire of the Iroquois, just reflect, what an embarrassment! If Wagner, this great grumbler, knew not what to do with success, at least those who have read his *Letter to a Friend* know what use can be made of it. 'The performances, three of which are completely guaranteed, will be quite outside all ordinary customs, and will be *model representations.*' Impossible to explain oneself more clearly to the public which one addresses. He admitted, then, that in these three famous performances, all would take place among friends *en famille.* It is not sufficiently borne in mind how much can be done for the glory of a single great man by two hundred friends, duly grouped, and who manœuvre under the indefatigable direction of eight or ten journalists playing on fife and drum. They are scarcely two hundred, and you would think that they were ten thousand. Witness at the Châtelet theatre the magnificent defiles which they obtain with a few supernumeraries passing and repassing, ever the same individuals. It is thus with the success of *Tristan and Isolde.* The room is never empty, and what bravos, what cheering, what stamping! Above all, what recalls! But of all this phantasmagoria, what remains after a few days? That which remains of a sky-rocket after it has been fired. A little stir, exchange of gossip, an uproar, and all is over! *Tristan and Isolde* at Munich or *Tannhäuser* at Paris, two *soirées* which, each after its own kind, may indeed be reckoned as model representations!"[1]

It was no small matter, it must be confessed, even for an

[1] *Revue des Deux-Mondes,* July 1, 1865.

audience prepared, and selected from among the best, like that of Munich, to listen thus to three long acts, during which there is not the slightest opportunity for applause, nor even for taking breath; where everything is so woven together that the ear can not detect a single connecting point in this uninterrupted symphony, above which the characters sing their parts with a superb intensity of expression, and without once repeating themselves, more than would be done in a spoken drama. It need not be thought, however, that this non-repetition of the words is prejudicial to the symphonic development of the musical idea; on the contrary it aids and emphasizes its power. Nevertheless, the author in giving as a key to his entire work, an exquisite and impassioned phrase upon which is built the prelude, establishes beforehand a secret current which stirs his listeners, and acquaints them with the generative idea of the drama. One should witness what enthusiastic bravos greet, among other fine points, the magnificent coronation of the first act, that brilliant conclusion towards which one feels himself borne by the superior force of genius which steadily increases its magnetic power throughout the entire act; there is in this act an unheard-of effect of the accumulation of musical electricity, which cannot be understood except by actually experiencing the shock.

This intimate fusion of poem and music, or to express it better, this simultaneity of conception involving a single creative idea and the double musical and poetic faculty in the same brain, is one of the points to which Wagner clings the closest. "In *Tristan*," says he, "the musical execution no longer offers an empty repetition of words; the poetic tissue has all the expanse intended for the melody; in a word, the melody is already poetically constructed." The musical form being thus preconceived in the poem, and having a particular value given to it, which responds exactly to the poetical aim, it remains to be seen if the invention of the melody will lose nothing of the freedom necessary to its development.

And Wagner, the instant that this question is raised, replies to it with absolute conviction. " On the contrary this treatment of melody and its form admits of an inexhaustible richness of development, and one of which no idea could be formed before having tried it." This statement is fully borne out by facts, for a single hearing of his work fills one with amazement, not only at the genius of the composer, but at the power and lucidity of mind of the man who has conceived this " art work " as he calls it.   After hearing *Tristan*, one is at a loss which to admire most in Wagner, the conception or the execution; in any case it is the wonderful genius, which challenges admiration in whatever form it may appear.

In Richard Wagner's own opinion, *Tristan and Isolde* was the most faithful, the most living expression of his theoretic ideas.   Notwithstanding their great worth, *The Flying Dutchman*, *Tannhäuser* and *Lohengrin* are but admirable creations of a genius, ignorant as yet of the prodigious height which it will be given him to attain. " It will be admitted," said he, " that I have made a greater step from *Tannhäuser* to *Tristan*, than in passing from my first point of view, that of the ordinary opera, to *Tannhäuser*. In *Tristan* at last, his ideal is clearly set forth, and the new art, of which he has made himself the founder and the apostle, being inspired, as he says, by the greatest masters, takes upon itself an authority which suffers no compromise.

Wagner has written somewhere that *Tristan* might be judged after the most rigorous laws which proceed from his theoretic affirmations, but he declares that in composing it he was freed from all speculative fancy, and that he felt, as he proceeded in his work, how much this freedom was doing to make clear his written system.   He adds, with a shadow of regret, " There is no happiness superior to that perfect spontaneity of the artist in the creation, and I have known it in composing my *Tristan*." One may well believe that he felt the same in completing *The Nibelungen Ring*, interrupted for *Tristan*, and in writing the *Meistersinger* and *Parsifal*.

Tristan, the child of Brittany, has come to Cornwall, where reigns King Mark, his uncle. He has delivered his adopted country from the tribute which it paid to Ireland, and killed in combat Morold, nephew of the king of Ireland, and the betrothed of the beautiful Isolde. But in this terrible combat Tristan has received a wound in the head. He is cared for by Isolde herself, who recognizes in him, in spite of the false name of Tantris, the murderer of her *fiancé* Morold; she is about to kill him in revenge, when her eyes meet those of the young hero ; at this glance she feels herself disarmed. When he has recovered she leaves him to return to the Court of Cornwall. But soon after, Tristan is sent back by the old king, his uncle, to demand the hand of the princess Isolde. The latter is given by her father to the victorious sovereign, in pledge of alliance, and the drama opens with a scene on board the vessel which conducts Isolde to Cornwall.

Tristan, faithful to his mission, watches over the young girl, and brings her back pure to King Mark; he feels a mighty passion surging in his breast, but he bravely resists it, and holds himself resolutely aloof from Isolde. She, on her part, feels herself irresistably drawn toward Tristan ; but shrinking from the idea of loving the conqueror of her first love, that proud conqueror who feels only indifference for her, she opens her heart to her friend and attendant Brangäne. She relates to her with suppressed emotion all the preceding drama, and commands her then to go and fetch Tristan, who keeps his place in the ship's stern. The latter, put on his guard by the prudent Kurwenal, his faithful equerry, at first refuses to leave his post; he ends by obeying the princess, and when the latter proposes to him to drink in pledge of friendship and pardon, he insists that she wishes to poison him, to avenge Morold; however, he accepts and drinks. But the distracted Brangäne has prepared for them a love potion in place of the beverage of death; Isolde and Tristan drain the cup, and fall into an unspeakable ecstasy. At that moment the ship draws near the land, and on all sides burst forth cries and cheers saluting king Mark, who is perceived on the shore awaiting his *fiancée*. Scarcely have Isolde and Tristan, roused by this joyous clamor, awakened from their delirium, when Isolde is offered the crown and the royal mantle. An admirable climax, and a fine dramatic effect.

Those who no longer have the courage to deny the musician in Wagner, attack the poet, and find the first act of Tristan, which is passed entirely on ·the vessel, empty and meagre. Less meagre and less empty, surely, than the third act of *l'Africaine*. And after all, is it so empty, and does it not contain all the elements of an interesting drama? Does one not clearly follow there the progress of a passion, at first restrained, then bursting its bounds, leading the two heroes to a forgetfulness of their vows, to an outrage towards the old king, and at last even to death?

In the second act, it is night. One hears the king galloping away, and when all noise has ceased, Isolde, impatient, seizes the torch, which is burning, and extinguishes it, notwithstanding the counsels of the wise Brangäne. At this signal Tristan comes in, and Isolde runs to meet him. During this long scene of love Brangäne has nothing to do but to keep an outlook; she does this badly enough however, for the king, forewarned by the treacherous Melot, returns unexpectedly, and surprises Tristan and Isolde; he sorrowfully reproaches his nephew for his treason. Tristan at first stands

abashed, then he throws himself upon Melot, from whose sword he receives a grievous wound; he falls, and the aged Kurwenal bears him away to Brittany, to the mansion of his ancestors.

There, wounded, sure that death will soon overtake him, he feverishly awaits the arrival of Isolde, who has been summoned by the good Kurwenal. The latter affectionately consoles his master and endeavors to awaken hope within him; but Tristan does not desire to live; he courts death, and only asks to see his loved one before expiring. Suddenly a joyous melody bursts forth; it is a shepherd placed on the lookout, who sights afar off the expected ship. Already Isolde is nearing the shore; at last she has come. Tristan, summoning all his strength, arises and goes to throw himself in her arms; but this supreme effort exhausts him; he looks once more upon Isolde and his soul takes flight. The old king, informed by Brangäne that this wild passion was the effect of a magic philter, comes to pardon and to unite the two lovers; but he finds before him only the dead body of Tristan, and the almost unconscious Isolde. At the voice of Brangäne, she arises as in an ecstasy, and seems on the point of leaving the earth. Unconscious of all around her, she hears and sees only Tristan, far beyond the finite; she aspires to join him, through luminous spheres, and slowly falls, lifeless, upon the body of her beloved.

What is to be said of the score? Each act, taken by itself, forms a gigantic scene of a marvellous intensity of expression, and the entire work is powerfully condensed in this incomparable prelude, which Berlioz failed to understand; in this admirable prelude, built upon that ascendant and infinitely tender phrase in half tones.[1]

---

[1] Why not recall here a certain annotation of Voltaire? He wrote on one occasion: " The chromatic proceeds through several consecutive semitones, which

"It is singular," said Berlioz after having heard it at the
Italiens, "that the author should have had this prelude performed at the same concert with the introduction to *Lohengrin*, for he has followed the same plan in both. It is
another case of a slow movement, beginning *pianissimo*,
rising little by little to a *fortissimo*, and falling back again to
the shade of his point of departure, without any other theme
than a sort of chromatic groan, but full of discordant harmonies, of which long appoggiaturas, replacing the real note
in the harmony, make the torture still greater. I have read
and re-read this strange page with the most profound attention, and with a keen desire to discover the sense of it, but it
must be confessed I have not yet the slightest idea of what
the author has tried to do." On the other hand, he found
the prelude to *Lohengrin* admirable in every point. Is there
any way of reconciling these contradictions?

The heroic loyalty of Tristan, charged with conducting the
princess Isolde to the old King Mark, and who, feeling his
heart torn with an ardent passion, keeps himself as far away
from her as possible, and even refuses to approach her when
she sends for him; — the vexation of Isolde, disturbed by the
irresistible love which drives her towards the knight who has
killed her first love, Morold; irritated to encounter only mute
indifference on the part of this proud conqueror, and resolved
to poison him in order to avenge Morold; — by their side,
the complete, absolute devotion represented by the equerry
Kurwenal and the amiable Brangäne, with their wise counsels,
now ironical, now affectionate; — the obstinate reserve of
Tristan, the increasing passion of Isolde and her thirst for
vengeance; the irresistible power which throws them into

produces effeminate music very appropriate for love." Has not Voltaire, then, who
was as little of a musician as possible, and superlatively antagonistic to music,
anticipated, divined, foreseen *Tristan and Isolde*? This would be droll, and even
humiliating for some.

each other's arms after partaking of the love philtre, served by Brangäne in place of the poison which Isolde believed she was giving Tristan ; their intoxicating bliss, and sorrowful awakening when, as the ship approaches land, the cries of the sailors salute the king awaiting his bride upon the shore; — these are the episodes of the first act, which the author has interpreted with a truth and a variety, of which no idea can be

RICHARD WAGNER ABOUT 1865.
Drawing by M. Renoir, after a photograph.

formed except by hearing it. At the second performance in Munich, this finale reached such joyous transports that the audience rose in a body, applauding and cheering the author with uncontrollable enthusiasm.

The rest of the work is at least equal to the preceding, and the third act, especially, filled entirely with the lamentations and outbursts of Tristan, who is about to die, is a conception so powerful, so rich in traits of genius, in marvellous combinations, that it loses all its monotony and holds one spell-bound. The sorrowful appeals of Tristan; that touching moment of the return of his youth, when he hears the shepherd piping the same plaintive song as on the day that his father died; the rude consolations of Kurwenal; the terrible starts of passion which gives temporary strength to the unhappy one when the vessel which bears Isolde to him is signalled afar; his last cry of love in beholding her, and the transfiguration of Isolde, "disappearing in the great billows of the ocean of delights, in the sonorous harmony of the regions of perfumes, in the infinite breath of the universal soul," from these different elements Wagner has formed a poetic and musical whole, of an incomparable depth of expression and magnetic power.

As for the second act, which opens with a charming scene between Isolde and the gentle Brangäne, where the voices hold their own so well above the *fanfares* of the chase and the night murmurings and rustling of the forest; this second act, which closes so grandly with the paternal reproaches of King Mark to Tristan, contains also that long duet of love — more than a duet, a complete poem and drama — which is certainly the most extraordinary of musical and dramatic conceptions. The sudden awakening of these two lovers to an uncontrollable infatuation, their recollections, their hymn to the night which brings them together, the distant warnings of Brangäne, finally, their supreme abandon, which no human prudence can check; these dramatic episodes, these inner workings of the soul and of the heart, the musician-poet has interpreted and condensed in a page where the characteristic motives are interwoven and superposed in the most marvellous fashion; where incessantly recurring melodies come to bloom at the surface of this symphonic ocean. A masterpiece, beyond all doubt. But has the author created this masterpiece in direct deduction from his theories and from his views upon art? We will proceed to examine.

It is in this piece that he has especially developed Schopenhauer's ideas, and one will admit that the moment of the drama is singularly chosen. Does one ever see two passionate lovers embracing in a purely intellectual transport, and fervently

M. AND MME. VOGL IN "TRISTAN AND ISOLDE,"
at Munich, 1869.

clasping each other in order that they may philosophize better concerning the superiority of night over day, and of death over life? "These so-called lovers," says Gasperini, "are two pupils of Kant, of Schopenhauer, of the Buddhist School. Never, thank heaven, has love spoken this high-flown and barbarous language; never has it thrown itself into mourning

and death with this madness of destruction and submersion."
Take their first cry of love! This outburst of recognition
towards the night which brings them together, this abhor-
rence of the day which separates them, form a happy poetic
antithesis; but the development which follows, is no more than
philosophic dissertation; and behold what Wagner makes them
sing, at the most delicious moment of their ardent embrace!
—"Descend upon us, night of love; give me forgetfulness of
life, receive me to thy bosom, deliver me from the universe.
Already are departing the last rays; that which we have
thought, that which we have believed to happen before our
eyes, the recollections and the images of things, the traces of
illusion, all this is wiped out by the august presentiment of the
holy darkness, in freeing us from the world.... The world
and the paling fascination, the world which the moon illumines
with her deceptive glimmering, the world, fallacious spectre
which the day places before me; it is I who am the world.
Holy life of love, august creation of voluptuousness, delicious
desire of sleep eternal, without manifestation and without
awakening!"

This whole work, I repeat it, is a masterpiece; but it is so
because Wagner, in putting into the mouth of the two lovers
ideas inexpressible by the musical language, is involuntarily
reduced to interpret by his music nothing more than the general idea of love. "I plunged," says he in good faith, "with
an inward confidence into the depths of the soul and its mysteries, and from this innermost centre of the world I saw its
exterior form expand before me." Could there be a greater
illusion! Instead of depicting, with a precision impossible to
obtain by sounds the inner motives which he supposes to be
at work in the soul of his lovers, he has simply rendered their
outward movements, and the transport of love which seizes
them. Would his musical creation have been different if he
had lent to his heroes the philosophic ideas of Pascal or of

Spinosa, of Kant or of Hegel, in place of those of Schopen-hauer? Assuredly not.

Thenceforth, no more philosophy. He has merely inter-preted, with an incomparable genius, a general idea— love; a common enough situation — a nocturnal rendezvous of lovers. Through what cerebral contortions has he been able to believe that he has accomplished more than this in his music, and what aberration has permitted him to fancy that he has here substituted philosophy for love? Mystery. It is fortunate that he has not succeeded, and that in consequence of wishing to push his idea to an extreme, he has run against the impossible. He has not, then, written this truly unique page in direct application of his system, but rather almost contrary to it, since the inner motives by which he claims to be guided escape the musical art, and he arrives, without perceiving it, only at the expression of a well-worn sentiment and a very ordinary situation. He did not think how truly he spoke when he declared " he had forgotten all theory while composing *Tristan and Isolde*, and at that time had thought only of how much his creative flight was doing to break down the barriers to his written system."

There must be no misconception in regard to the nature of this discussion, which is purely musical, and aims to prove nothing except that in order to interpret love through the medium of music it is best to keep to the " commonplaces of lubric morals," which Boileau talks about. Music, of all arts the most vague, can express only generalities when dealing with the inner workings of the heart and soul. It were quite otherwise with a literary composition, where thought acquires the acme of precision; a love-scene be-tween Héloïse and Abélard, for example, might properly admit of school disputations, and philosophic arguments. Each epoch, indeed, repeats after its own fashion the eternal theme of love, and the letters of Héloïse and of Abélard,

prove that this doctor *en robe* and that doctor *en jupons*
entertained Cupid with arguments on the real and the nom-
inal, etc.; it is this that M. de Remusat has rendered ex-
cellently in his beautiful drama of *Abélard*, in which the
spirit of the twelfth century breathes again. But, to repeat,
a literary composition is one thing, a musical work is another, and whether it be a question of *Abélard and Héloïse*,
of *Romeo and Juliet*, or of *Tristan and Isolde*, music is
essentially inappropriate for interpreting anything more than
the "*lieu commun*" of love, without respect of epoch or of
person. Wagner has dreamed of a chimera in believing
that he could stretch indefinitely the sphere of action of
music; and neither he nor anybody else could ever succeed
in doing it.

" It is not without much meditation"— has said an instinctive admirer of Richard Wagner — "not without close study
and an indefatigable estimation of the elements which he employs, that Wagner has been able to radically master the various agents of the lyric drama. To dominate thus the harmonic exigencies, to join these broken rhythms, to blend these
fierce modulations, to fuse, at length, into a single crystal, all
these dissimilar fragments of crystals, requires not only a will
of iron, but also an unprecedented penetration of the resources
inherent in each element of action. It is not enough to be
trained by and obedient to science, it is necessary to be an
artist ; and this dispersion of the central life, of the general
expression, into all the parts of the common structure, is not
accomplished without a deep sentiment of truth and of passion, where the soul bursts forth and sheds abroad its lustre."

Gasperini proceeds to say that Wagner, in *Tristan and
Isolde*, has reacted against that baleful tendency of the Italian
and French schools, which readily sacrificed the whole for the
sake of the various constituent elements, and gave themselves
less concern about making the entire work live, than about

animating the accessory parts. " In doing this," adds he, " Wagner has turned people's minds to the side of an urgent reform, and has shown them the true road to follow. As a thinker, he will have prepared the hitherto rough and untilled ground ; he will have made the path easy for those who would follow him. As an artist, he will have enormously enriched the arsenal whither composers may go to draw their inspiration and their arms."

The prediction is already verified, and how many musicians have striven to appropriate his formulas, his style, in short, the material side of Richard Wagner's art work, who, unhappily, have not his genius, and who, having accomplished nothing with this borrowed plumage, have turned against the innovator, upon seeing him gain ever so little ground in France, and become, if not an immediate menace, at least a danger ahead !

There are but two alternatives in listening to this work, even in the opinion of those who admire it the most; — it is everything or nothing to the hearer. If it takes hold upon you at the outset, you will follow it to the end; if not, it will remain a closed letter. M. Schuré, recalling the indescribable impression experienced at the memorable soirées at Munich in 1865, is the first to confess that such performances are almost as rare as the works of genius which give rise to them. They are possible only through the union of all the performers in a single thought, and through the power of enthusiasm. Of what use, inquire certain critics, are works which call for so many efforts, and which, after all, are comprehended by so few people? To this might be made the reply that all that is great is difficult and rare ; or better still, to say with Berlioz : " It would be truly deplorable if certain works should be admired by certain people ! "

These critics are no longer numerous ; but how entirely they justify this little sling from Berlioz !

END OF VOLUME ONE.